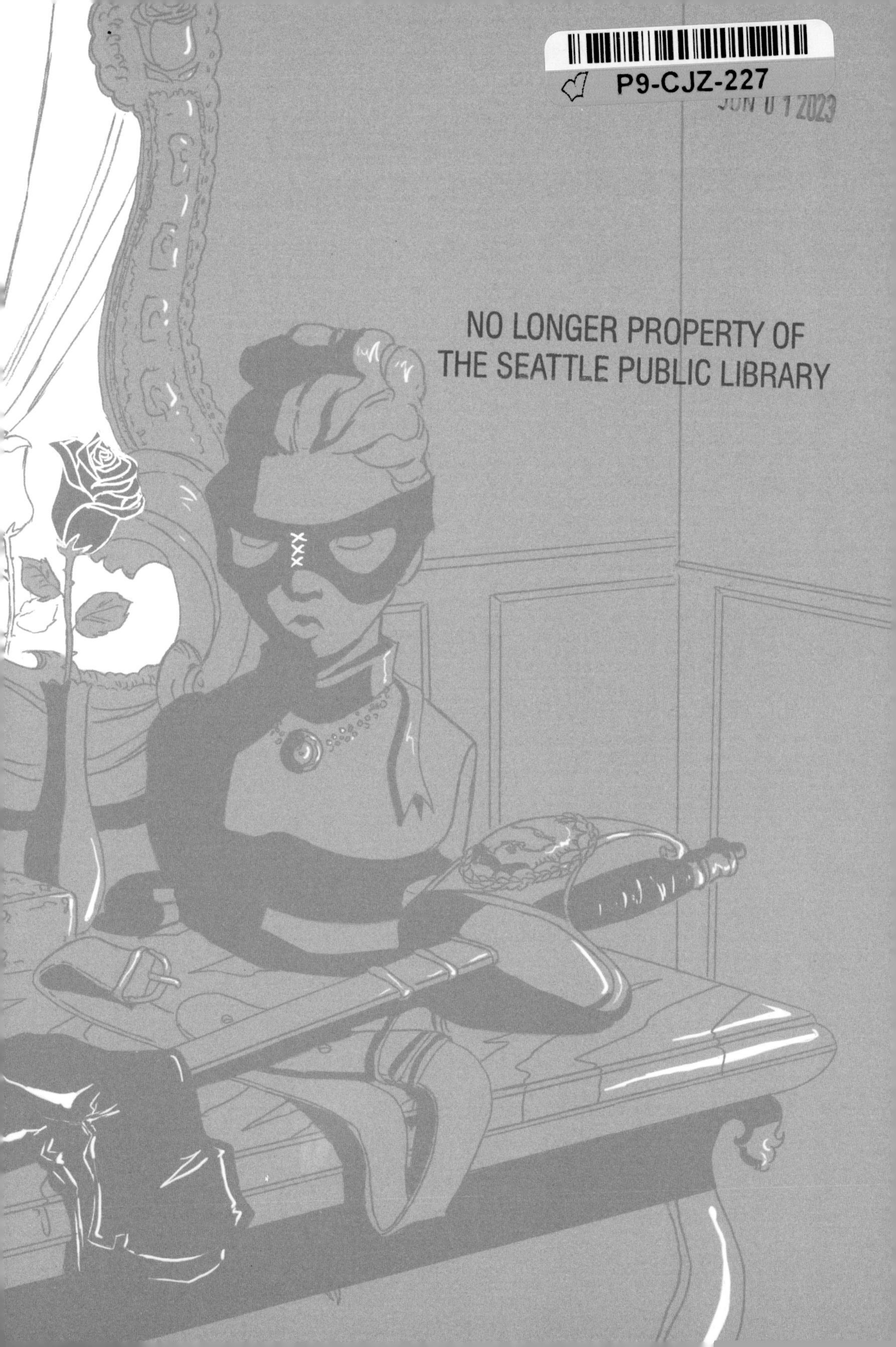

The Scarlet Rose

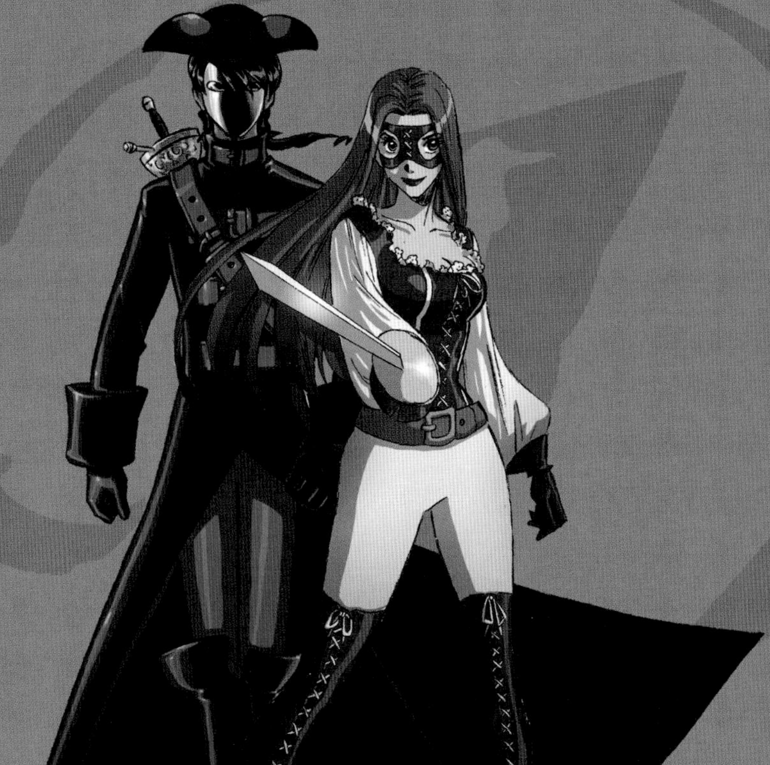

charmz™

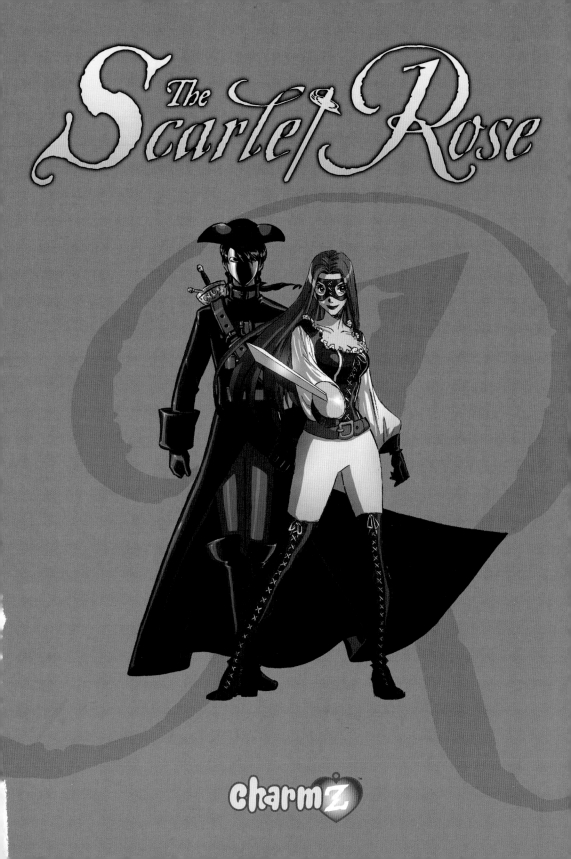

MORE GRAPHIC NOVELS AVAILABLE FROM charmz

**STITCHED #1
"THE FIRST DAY OF THE
REST OF HER LIFE"**

**STITCHED #2
"LOVE IN THE TIME
OF ASSUMPTION"**

**G.F.F.s #1
"MY HEART LIES
IN THE 90s"**

**G.F.F.s #2
"WITCHES GET
THINGS DONE"**

**CHLOE #1
"THE NEW GIRL"**

**CHLOE #2 "THE QUEEN
OF HIGH SCHOOL"**

**CHLOE #3
"FRENEMIES"**

**CHLOE #4
"RAINY DAY"**

**SCARLET ROSE #1
"I KNEW I'D MEET YOU"**

**SCARLET ROSE #2
"I'LL GO WHERE YOU GO"**

**SCARLET ROSE #3
"I THINK I LOVE YOU"**

**SCARLET ROSE #4
"YOU WILL ALWAYS BE MINE"**

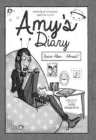

**AMY'S DIARY #1
"SPACE ALIEN...
ALMOST?"**

**SWEETIES #1
"CHERRY SKYE"**

MONICA ADVENTURES #1

**ANA AND THE
COSMIC RACE #1
"THE RACE BEGINS"**

SEE MORE AT PAPERCUTZ.COM

Les Filles au Chocolat [SWEETIES] © Jungle! 2014-2019. The Chocolate Box Girls © 2010-2019 by Cathy Cassidy. Mistinguette [CHLOE] © 2011-2018 Jungle! STITCHED © 2017-2018 Mariah McCourt and Aaron Alexovich. GFFs: Ghost Friends Forever ©2017-2018 by Monica Gallagher and Kata Kane. ANA AND THE COSMIC RACE © 2017 by Amy Chu and Kata Kane. La Rose Écarlate [THE SCARLET ROSE] ©2009-2019 Éditions Delcourt. MONICA ADVENTURES © 2019 Maurcio de Sousa Editora. Le Journal d'Aurélie Laflamme [AMY'S DIARY] ©2015 Jungle!/Michel Lafon.

THE SCARLET ROSE

"You Will Always Be Mine"

STORY & ART BY

PATRICIA LYFOUNG

COLOR BY

FLEUR D. AND PHILIPPE OGAKI

charmz

NEW YORK

For Mina.
For Papa.
For Pépito.
For Capucine, Thomas, Linoa, William, and Adrien.
Thanks to Philippe, for his patience and love.
Thanks to Fleur! You helped me like a boss!
And finally, thanks to all the readers of THE SCARLET ROSE,
as well as the members of Matthieu's discussion group.
-Patricia Lyfoung

PREVIOUSLY IN *The Scarlet Rose* ...
Maud de Laroche and Guilhem de Landrey, known as the vigilantes the Scarlet Rose and the Fox, united to search for the man who murdered Maud's father. Their journey brought them closer together as they trekked all across Europe to find the mysterious killer. Ultimately, Maud's father is avenged. And Maud even discovers a shocking surprise. While reeling from all this, Maud is asked for her hand in marriage by Guilhelm, and the two vigilantes head back to France, engaged...

The Scarlet Rose

by Patricia Lyfoung
La Rose Écarlate, volumes 7 and 8
Lyfoung © Éditions Delcourt-2011/2012
Originally Published in French as
"Tu Seras Toujours À Moi"
and "Où Es-Tu?"

English Translation and all other
editorial material © 2019 Papercutz.
All rights reserved

THE SCARLET ROSE #4
"You Will Always Be Mine"

Story, art, and cover by Patricia Lyfoung
Color by Fleur D. and Philippe Ogaki
Translation by Joe Johnson
Lettering by Bryan Senka

Grant Frederick—Editorial Intern
Jeff Whitman—Managing Editor
Jim Salicrup
Editor-In-Chief

PB ISBN: 978-1-5458-0161-1
HC ISBN: 978-1-5458-0160-4

Charmz is an imprint of Papercutz.

Charmz books may be purchased for business or promotional use.
For information on bulk purchases please contact Macmillan
Corporate and Premium Sales Department at
(800) 221-7945 x5442

Printed in China
July 2019

Distributed by Macmillan
First Charmz Printing

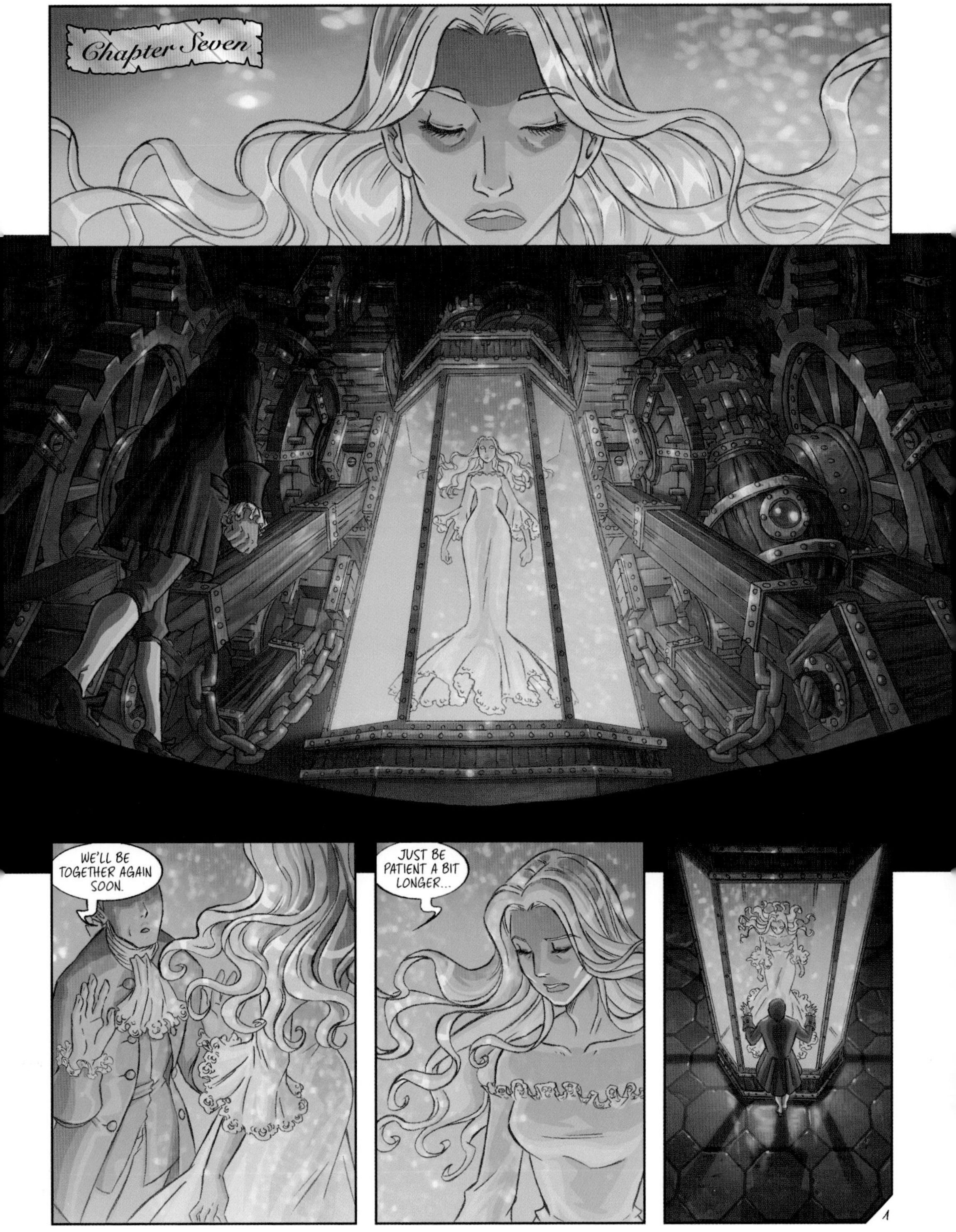
Chapter Seven
WE'LL BE TOGETHER AGAIN SOON.
JUST BE PATIENT A BIT LONGER...
1

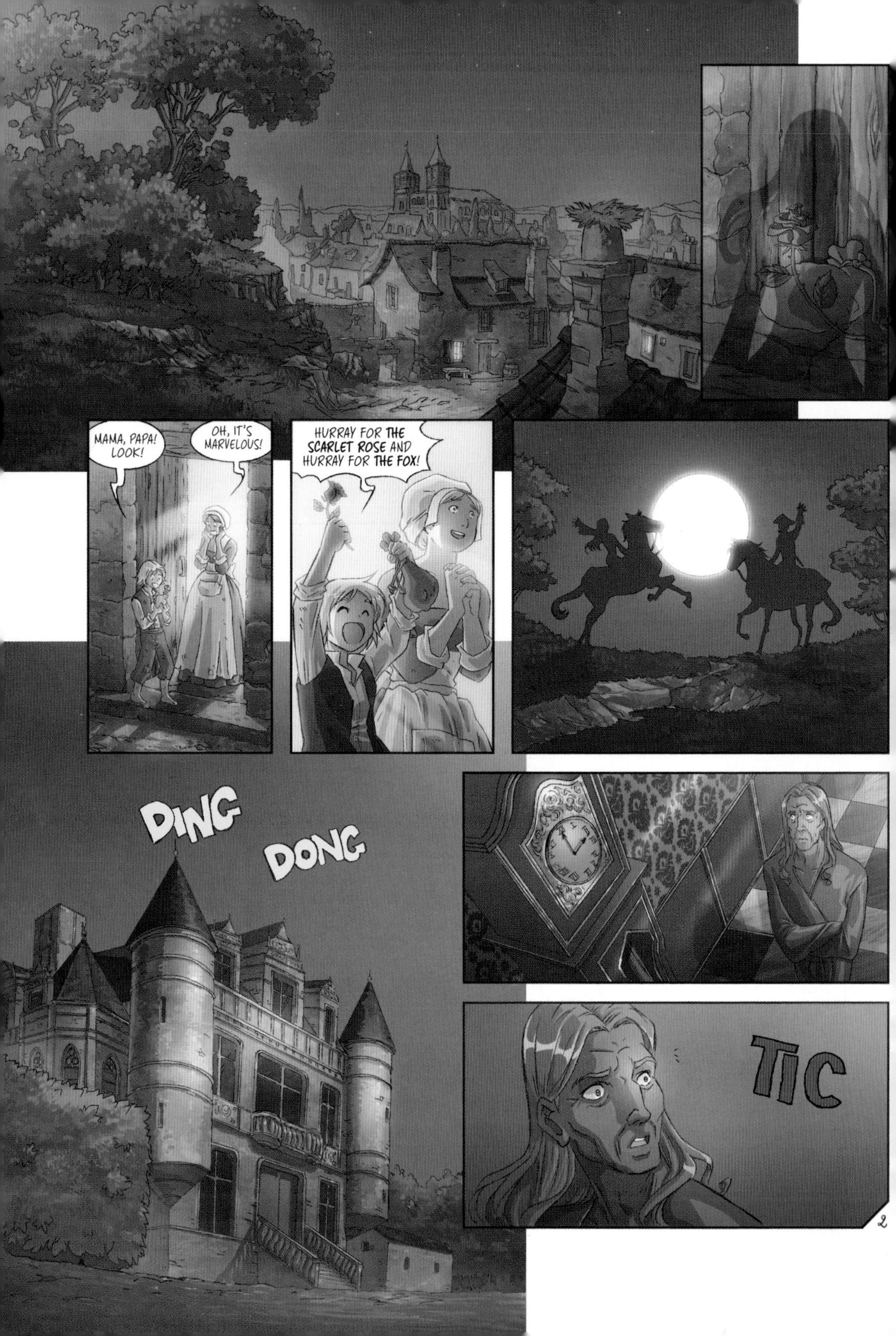

MAMA, PAPA! LOOK!
OH, IT'S MARVELOUS!
HURRAY FOR THE SCARLET ROSE AND HURRAY FOR THE FOX!
DING
DONG
TIC

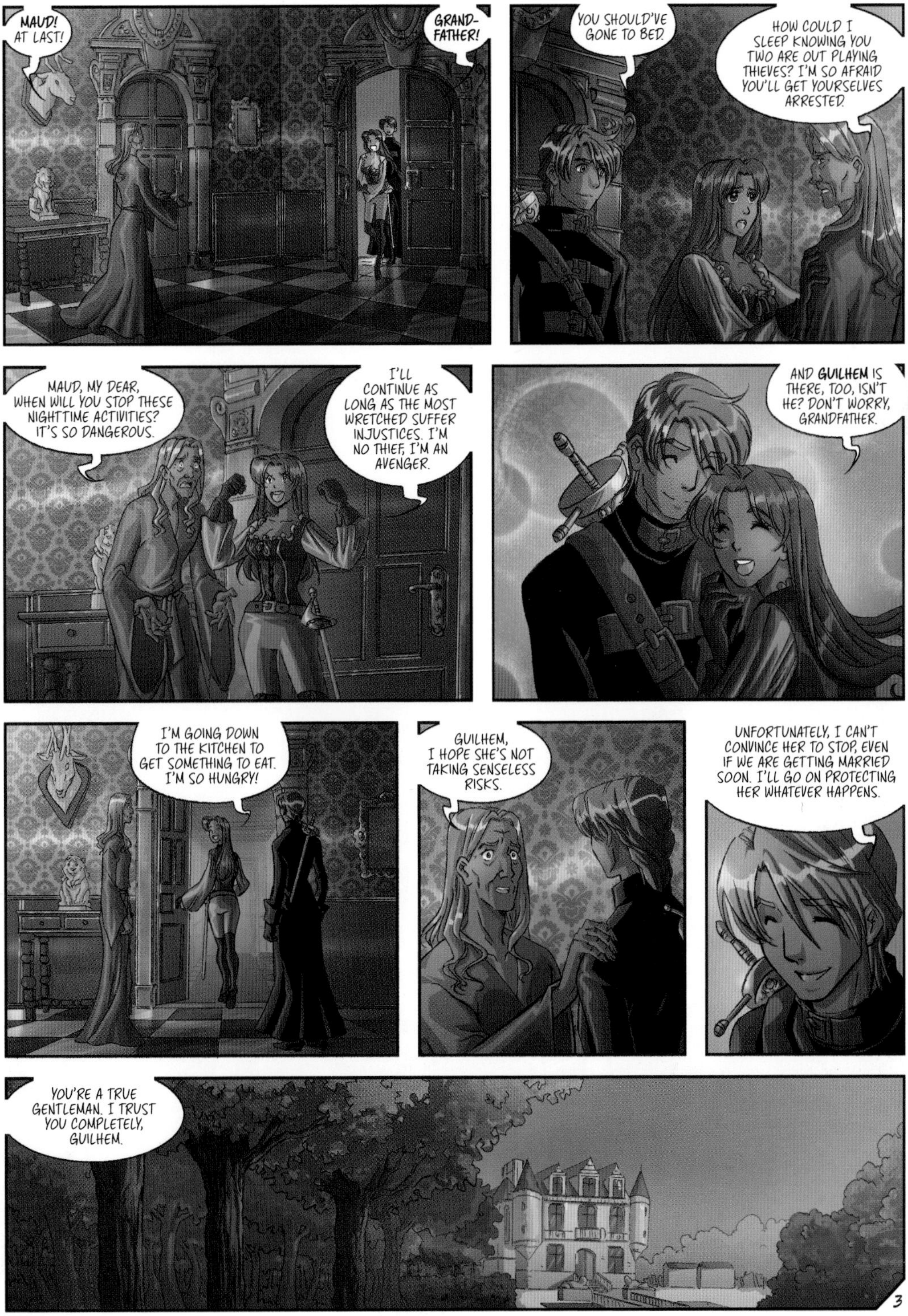

MAUD! AT LAST!
GRAND-FATHER!
YOU SHOULD'VE GONE TO BED.
HOW COULD I SLEEP KNOWING YOU TWO ARE OUT PLAYING THIEVES? I'M SO AFRAID YOU'LL GET YOURSELVES ARRESTED.
MAUD, MY DEAR, WHEN WILL YOU STOP THESE NIGHTTIME ACTIVITIES? IT'S SO DANGEROUS.
I'LL CONTINUE AS LONG AS THE MOST WRETCHED SUFFER INJUSTICES. I'M NO THIEF, I'M AN AVENGER.
AND GUILHEM IS THERE, TOO, ISN'T HE? DON'T WORRY, GRANDFATHER.
I'M GOING DOWN TO THE KITCHEN TO GET SOMETHING TO EAT. I'M SO HUNGRY!
GUILHEM, I HOPE SHE'S NOT TAKING SENSELESS RISKS.
UNFORTUNATELY, I CAN'T CONVINCE HER TO STOP, EVEN IF WE ARE GETTING MARRIED SOON. I'LL GO ON PROTECTING HER WHATEVER HAPPENS.
YOU'RE A TRUE GENTLEMAN. I TRUST YOU COMPLETELY, GUILHEM.
3

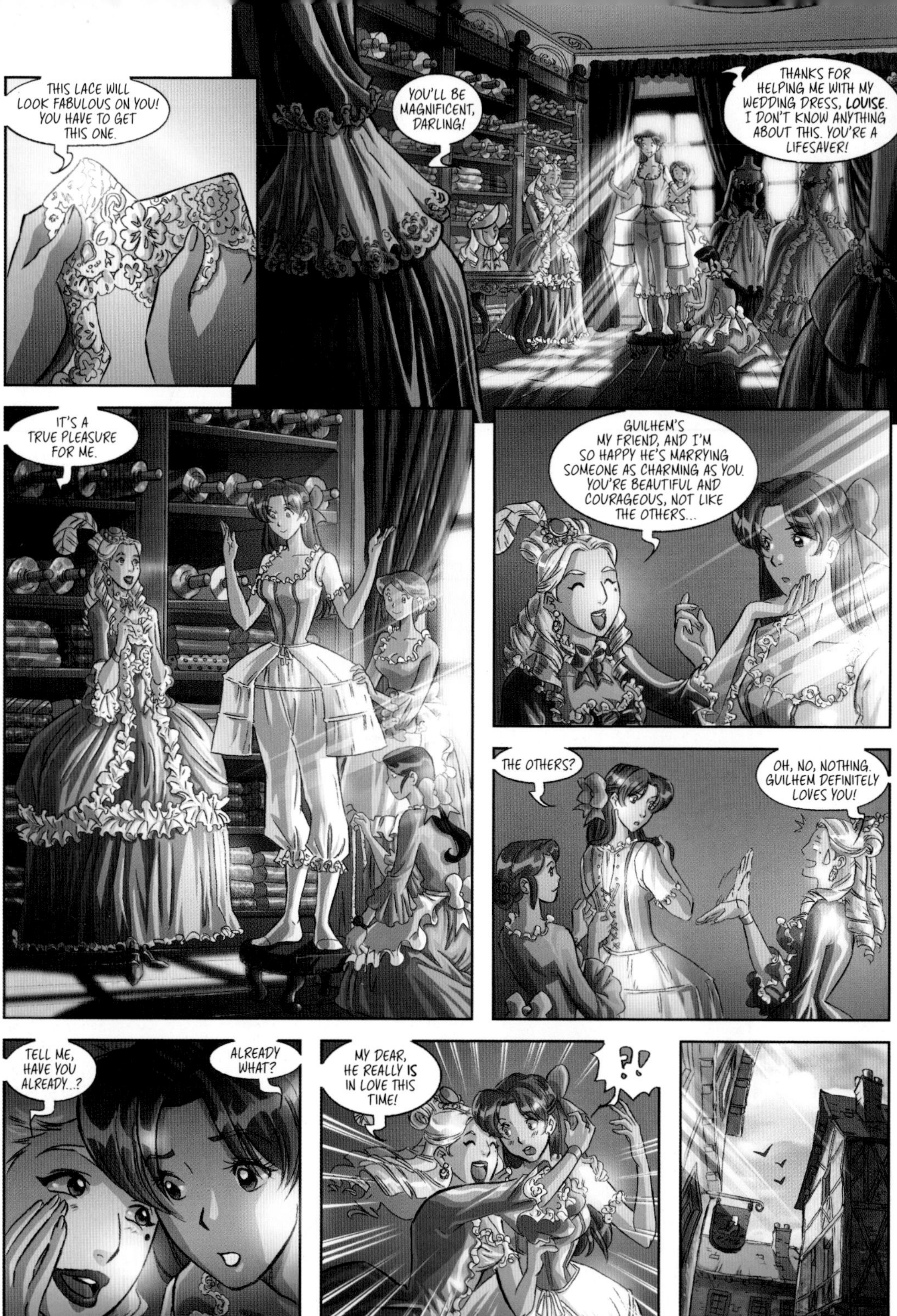
THIS LACE WILL LOOK FABULOUS ON YOU! YOU HAVE TO GET THIS ONE.
YOU'LL BE MAGNIFICENT, DARLING!
THANKS FOR HELPING ME WITH MY WEDDING DRESS, **LOUISE**. I DON'T KNOW ANYTHING ABOUT THIS. YOU'RE A LIFESAVER!
IT'S A TRUE PLEASURE FOR ME.
GUILHEM'S MY FRIEND, AND I'M SO HAPPY HE'S MARRYING SOMEONE AS CHARMING AS YOU. YOU'RE BEAUTIFUL AND COURAGEOUS, NOT LIKE THE OTHERS...
THE OTHERS?
OH, NO, NOTHING. GUILHEM DEFINITELY LOVES YOU!
TELL ME, HAVE YOU ALREADY...?
ALREADY WHAT?
MY DEAR, HE REALLY IS IN LOVE THIS TIME!
?!
4

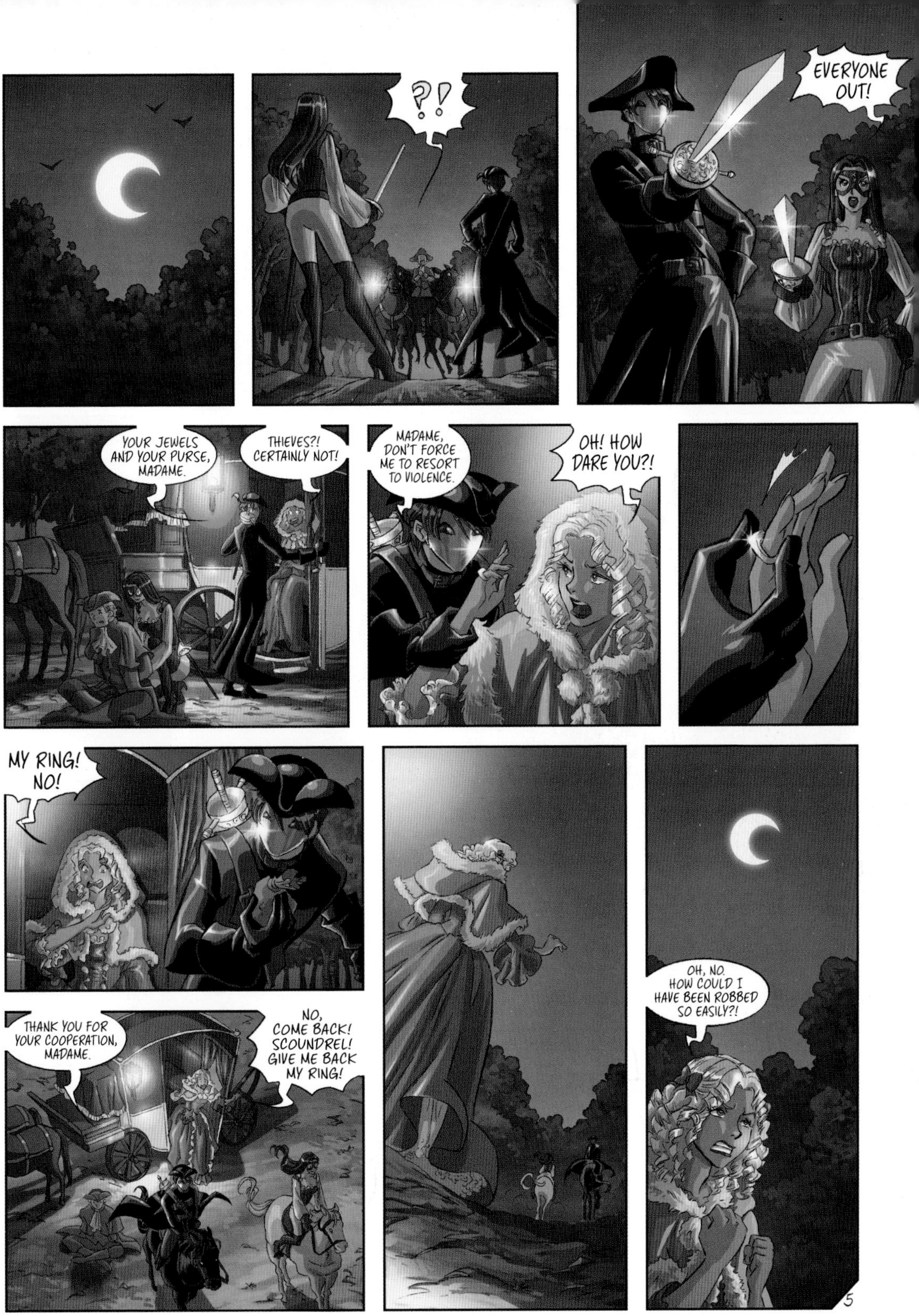
?!
EVERYONE OUT!
YOUR JEWELS AND YOUR PURSE, MADAME.
THIEVES?! CERTAINLY NOT!
MADAME, DON'T FORCE ME TO RESORT TO VIOLENCE.
OH! HOW DARE YOU?!
MY RING! NO!
THANK YOU FOR YOUR COOPERATION, MADAME.
NO, COME BACK! SCOUNDREL! GIVE ME BACK MY RING!
OH, NO. HOW COULD I HAVE BEEN ROBBED SO EASILY?!
5

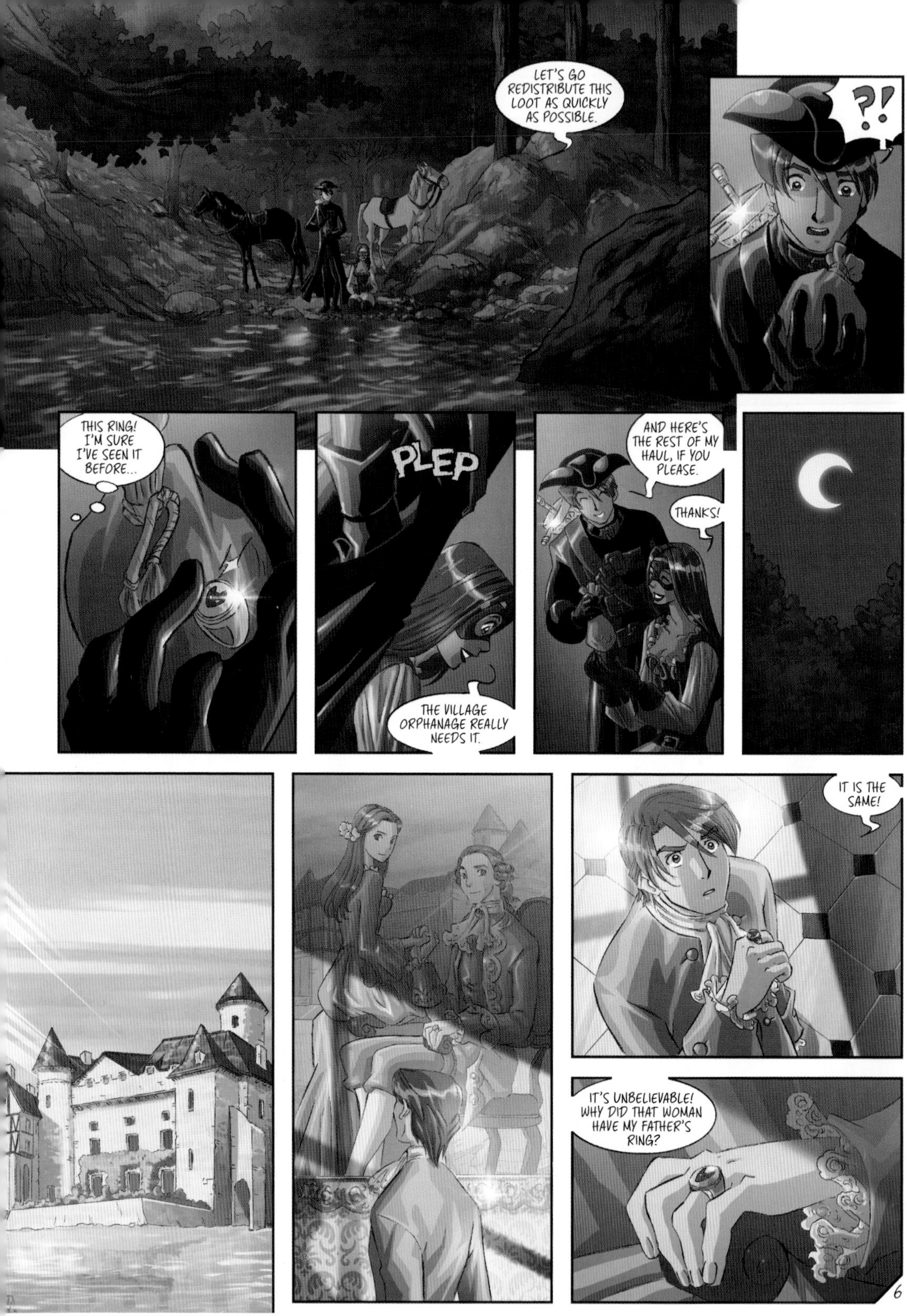
LET'S GO REDISTRIBUTE THIS LOOT AS QUICKLY AS POSSIBLE.
?!
THIS RING! I'M SURE I'VE SEEN IT BEFORE...
PLEP
THE VILLAGE ORPHANAGE REALLY NEEDS IT.
AND HERE'S THE REST OF MY HAUL, IF YOU PLEASE.
THANKS!
IT IS THE SAME!
IT'S UNBELIEVABLE! WHY DID THAT WOMAN HAVE MY FATHER'S RING?
6

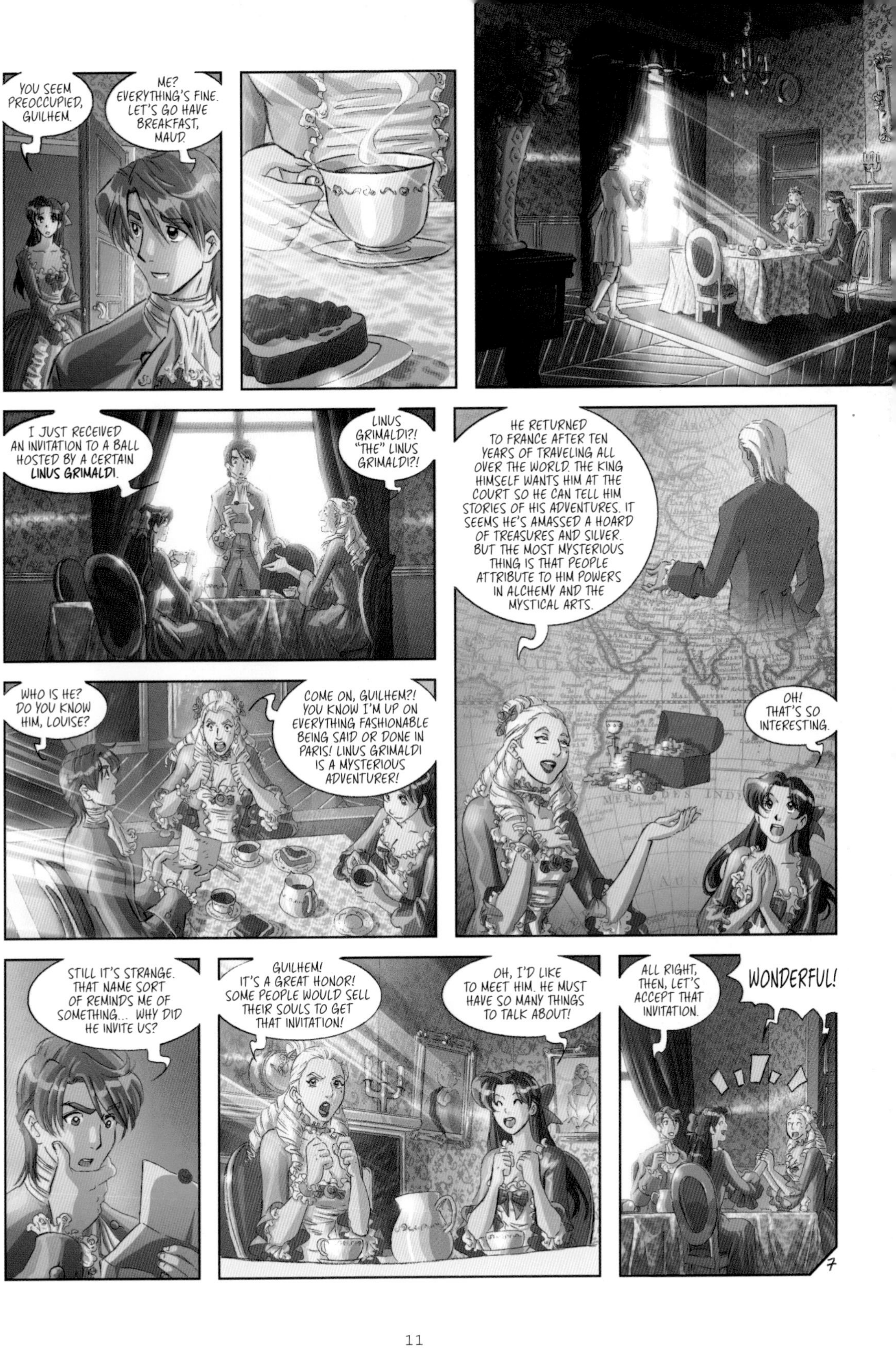
YOU SEEM PREOCCUPIED, GUILHEM.
ME? EVERYTHING'S FINE. LET'S GO HAVE BREAKFAST, MAUD.
I JUST RECEIVED AN INVITATION TO A BALL HOSTED BY A CERTAIN LINUS GRIMALDI.
LINUS GRIMALDI?! "THE" LINUS GRIMALDI?!
HE RETURNED TO FRANCE AFTER TEN YEARS OF TRAVELING ALL OVER THE WORLD. THE KING HIMSELF WANTS HIM AT THE COURT SO HE CAN TELL HIM STORIES OF HIS ADVENTURES. IT SEEMS HE'S AMASSED A HOARD OF TREASURES AND SILVER. BUT THE MOST MYSTERIOUS THING IS THAT PEOPLE ATTRIBUTE TO HIM POWERS IN ALCHEMY AND THE MYSTICAL ARTS.
WHO IS HE? DO YOU KNOW HIM, LOUISE?
COME ON, GUILHEM?! YOU KNOW I'M UP ON EVERYTHING FASHIONABLE BEING SAID OR DONE IN PARIS! LINUS GRIMALDI IS A MYSTERIOUS ADVENTURER!
OH! THAT'S SO INTERESTING.
STILL IT'S STRANGE. THAT NAME SORT OF REMINDS ME OF SOMETHING... WHY DID HE INVITE US?
GUILHEM! IT'S A GREAT HONOR! SOME PEOPLE WOULD SELL THEIR SOULS TO GET THAT INVITATION!
OH, I'D LIKE TO MEET HIM. HE MUST HAVE SO MANY THINGS TO TALK ABOUT!
ALL RIGHT, THEN, LET'S ACCEPT THAT INVITATION.
WONDERFUL!
7

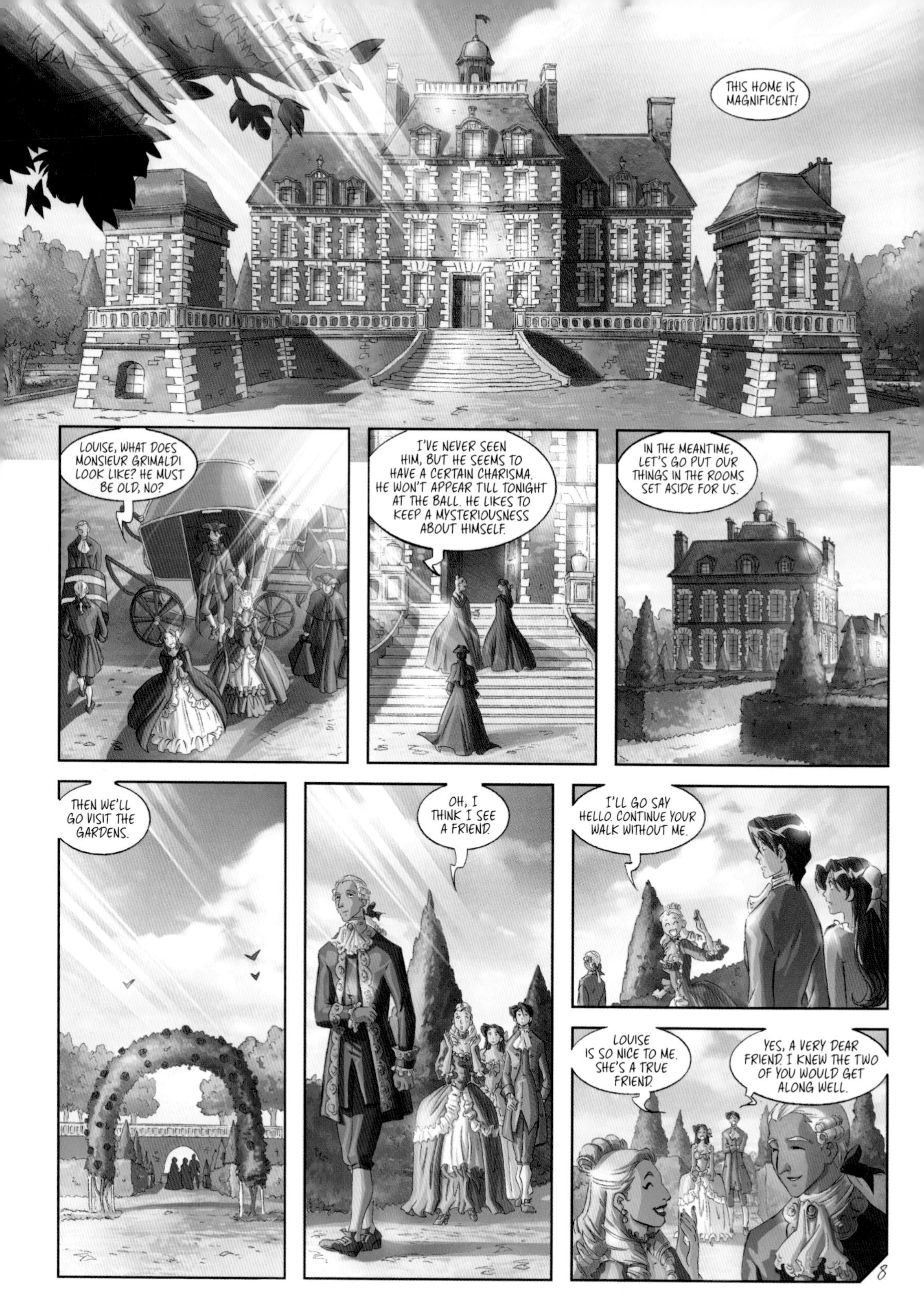
THIS HOME IS MAGNIFICENT!
LOUISE, WHAT DOES MONSIEUR GRIMALDI LOOK LIKE? HE MUST BE OLD, NO?
I'VE NEVER SEEN HIM, BUT HE SEEMS TO HAVE A CERTAIN CHARISMA. HE WON'T APPEAR TILL TONIGHT AT THE BALL. HE LIKES TO KEEP A MYSTERIOUSNESS ABOUT HIMSELF.
IN THE MEANTIME, LET'S GO PUT OUR THINGS IN THE ROOMS SET ASIDE FOR US.
THEN WE'LL GO VISIT THE GARDENS.
OH, I THINK I SEE A FRIEND.
I'LL GO SAY HELLO. CONTINUE YOUR WALK WITHOUT ME.
LOUISE IS SO NICE TO ME. SHE'S A TRUE FRIEND.
YES, A VERY DEAR FRIEND. I KNEW THE TWO OF YOU WOULD GET ALONG WELL.
8

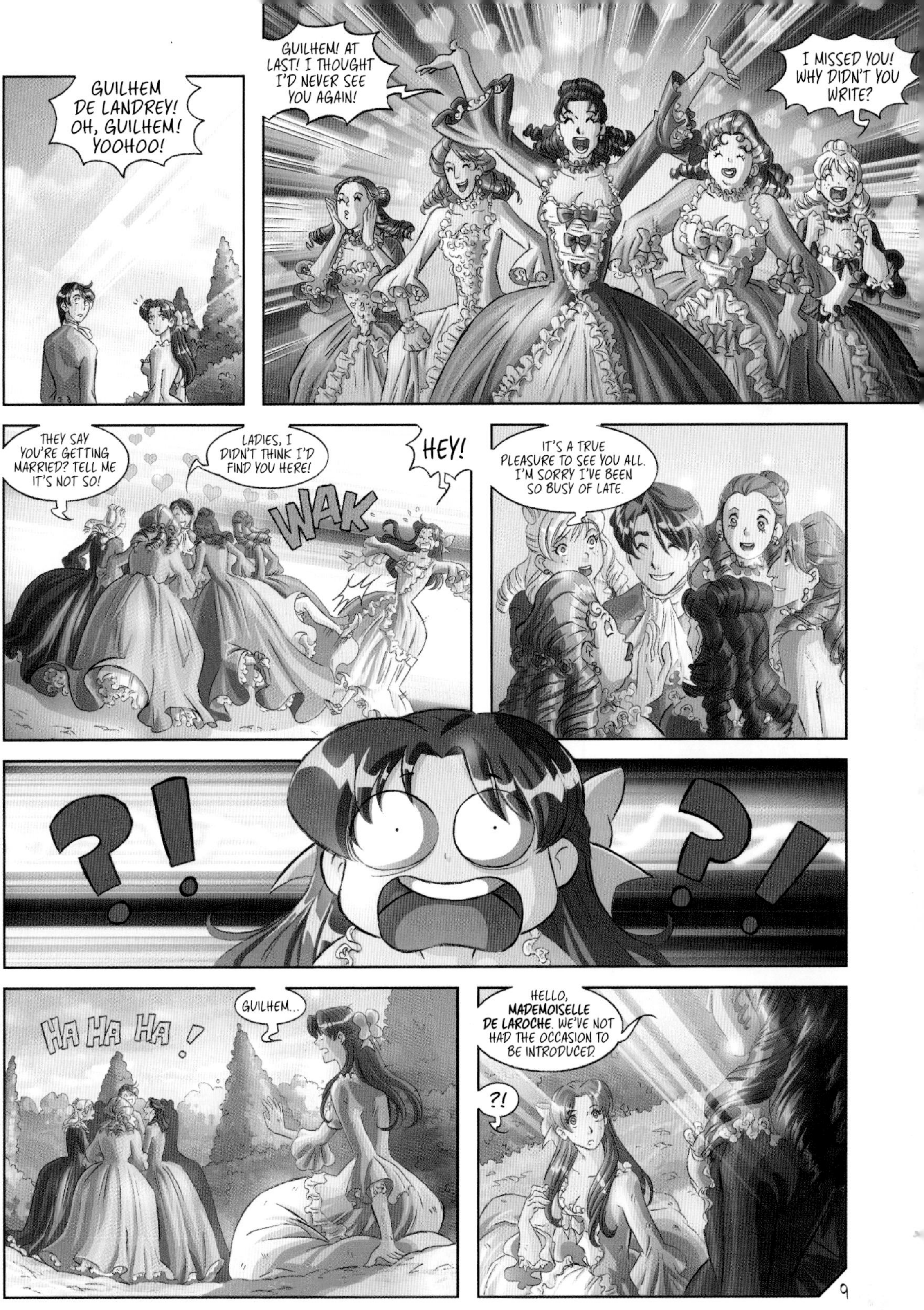

GUILHEM DE LANDREY! OH, GUILHEM! YOOHOO!
GUILHEM! AT LAST! I THOUGHT I'D NEVER SEE YOU AGAIN!
I MISSED YOU! WHY DIDN'T YOU WRITE?
THEY SAY YOU'RE GETTING MARRIED? TELL ME IT'S NOT SO!
LADIES, I DIDN'T THINK I'D FIND YOU HERE!
HEY!
WAK
IT'S A TRUE PLEASURE TO SEE YOU ALL. I'M SORRY I'VE BEEN SO BUSY OF LATE.
?!
?!
HA HA HA!
GUILHEM...
HELLO, MADEMOISELLE DE LAROCHE. WE'VE NOT HAD THE OCCASION TO BE INTRODUCED.
?!
9

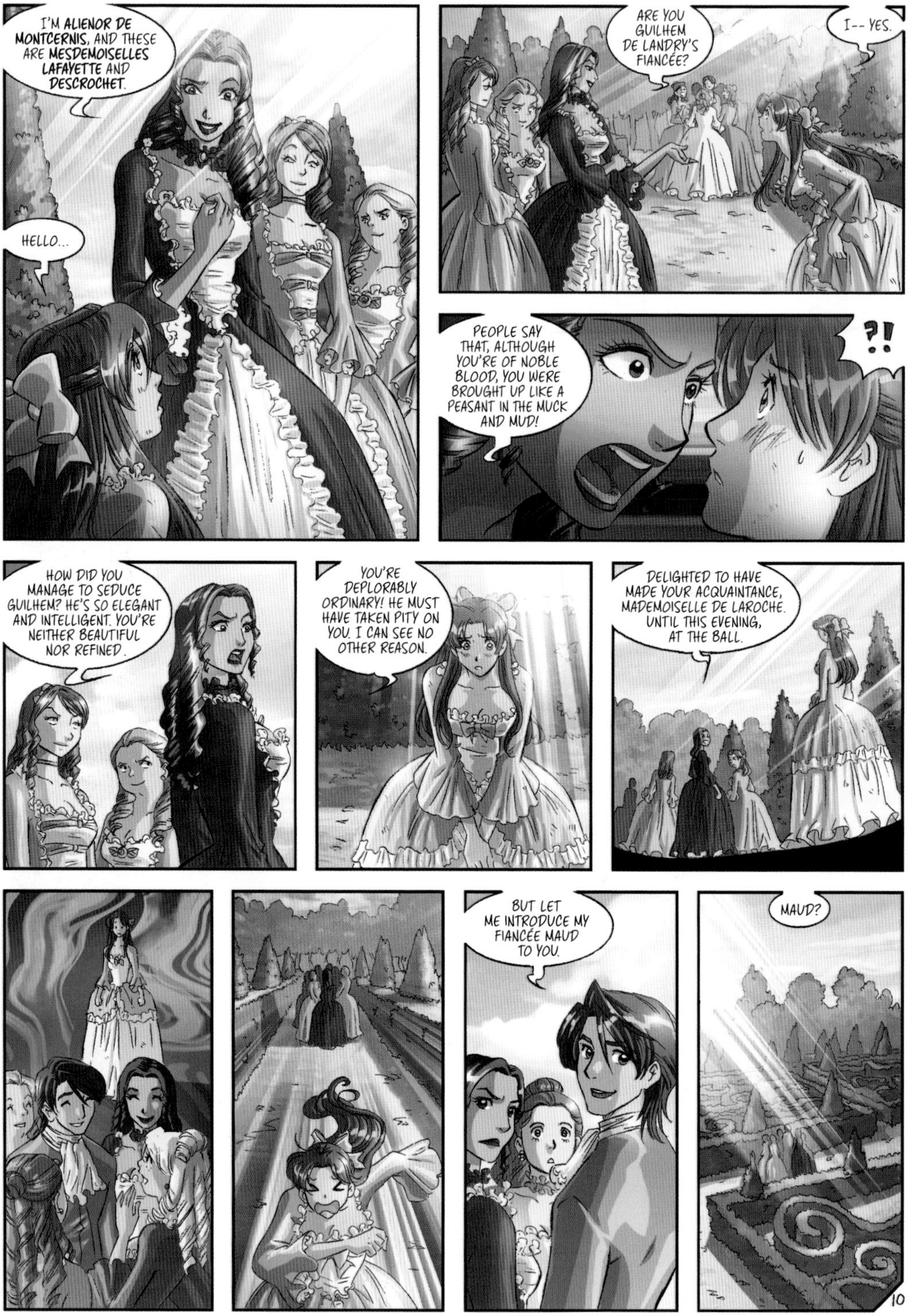
I'M ALIENOR DE MONTCERNIS, AND THESE ARE MESDEMOISELLES LAFAYETTE AND DESCROCHET.
HELLO...
ARE YOU GUILHEM DE LANDRY'S FIANCÉE?
I-- YES.
PEOPLE SAY THAT, ALTHOUGH YOU'RE OF NOBLE BLOOD, YOU WERE BROUGHT UP LIKE A PEASANT IN THE MUCK AND MUD!
?!
HOW DID YOU MANAGE TO SEDUCE GUILHEM? HE'S SO ELEGANT AND INTELLIGENT. YOU'RE NEITHER BEAUTIFUL NOR REFINED.
YOU'RE DEPLORABLY ORDINARY! HE MUST HAVE TAKEN PITY ON YOU. I CAN SEE NO OTHER REASON.
DELIGHTED TO HAVE MADE YOUR ACQUAINTANCE, MADEMOISELLE DE LAROCHE. UNTIL THIS EVENING, AT THE BALL.
BUT LET ME INTRODUCE MY FIANCÉE MAUD TO YOU.
MAUD?
10

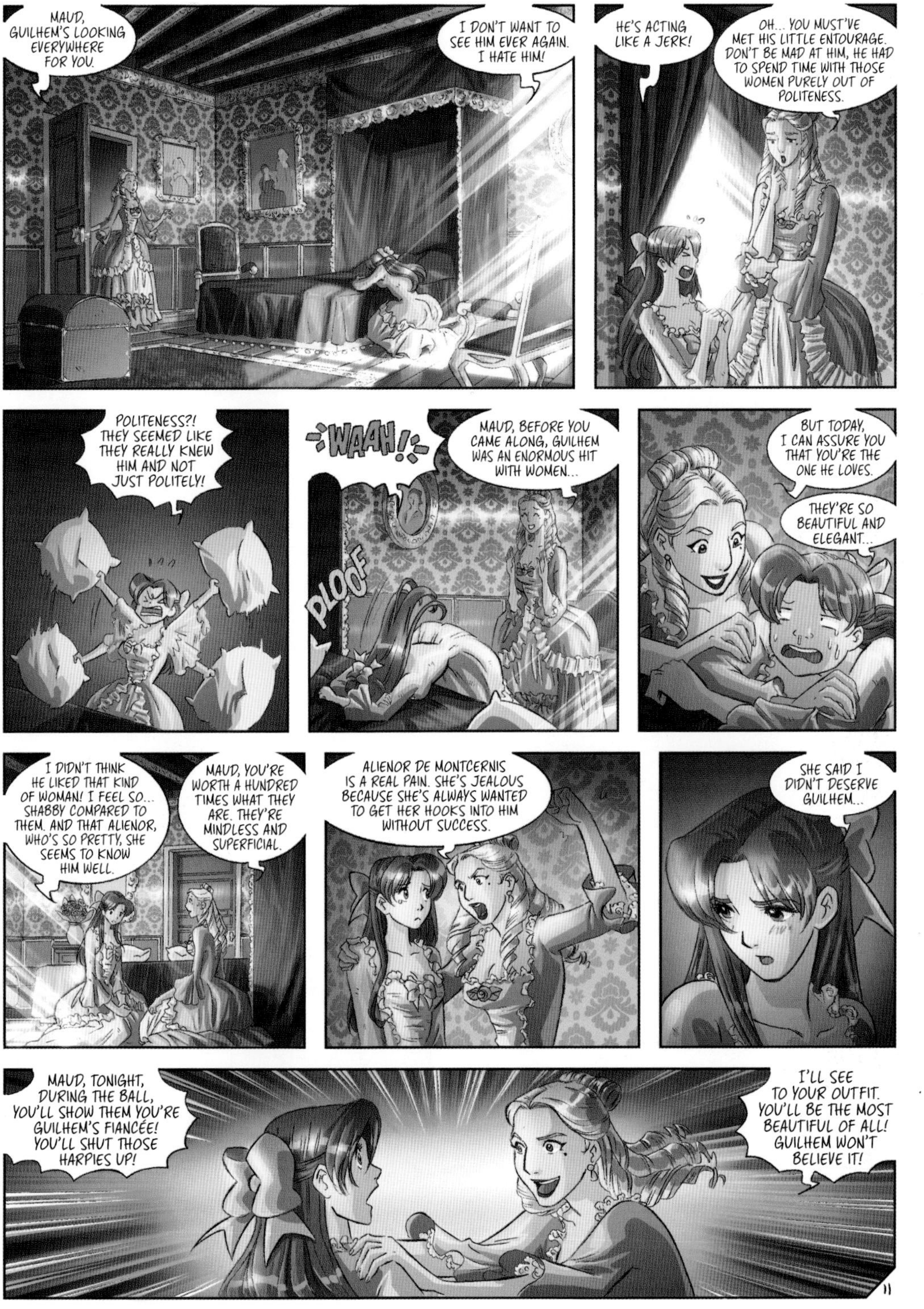
MAUD, GUILHEM'S LOOKING EVERYWHERE FOR YOU.
I DON'T WANT TO SEE HIM EVER AGAIN. I HATE HIM!
HE'S ACTING LIKE A JERK!
OH... YOU MUST'VE MET HIS LITTLE ENTOURAGE. DON'T BE MAD AT HIM, HE HAD TO SPEND TIME WITH THOSE WOMEN PURELY OUT OF POLITENESS.
POLITENESS?! THEY SEEMED LIKE THEY REALLY KNEW HIM AND NOT JUST POLITELY!
WAAH!
PLOOF
MAUD, BEFORE YOU CAME ALONG, GUILHEM WAS AN ENORMOUS HIT WITH WOMEN...
BUT TODAY, I CAN ASSURE YOU THAT YOU'RE THE ONE HE LOVES.
THEY'RE SO BEAUTIFUL AND ELEGANT...
I DIDN'T THINK HE LIKED THAT KIND OF WOMAN! I FEEL SO... SHABBY COMPARED TO THEM. AND THAT ALIENOR, WHO'S SO PRETTY, SHE SEEMS TO KNOW HIM WELL.
MAUD, YOU'RE WORTH A HUNDRED TIMES WHAT THEY ARE. THEY'RE MINDLESS AND SUPERFICIAL.
ALIENOR DE MONTCERNIS IS A REAL PAIN. SHE'S JEALOUS BECAUSE SHE'S ALWAYS WANTED TO GET HER HOOKS INTO HIM WITHOUT SUCCESS.
SHE SAID I DIDN'T DESERVE GUILHEM...
MAUD, TONIGHT, DURING THE BALL, YOU'LL SHOW THEM YOU'RE GUILHEM'S FIANCÉE! YOU'LL SHUT THOSE HARPIES UP!
I'LL SEE TO YOUR OUTFIT. YOU'LL BE THE MOST BEAUTIFUL OF ALL! GUILHEM WON'T BELIEVE IT!
11

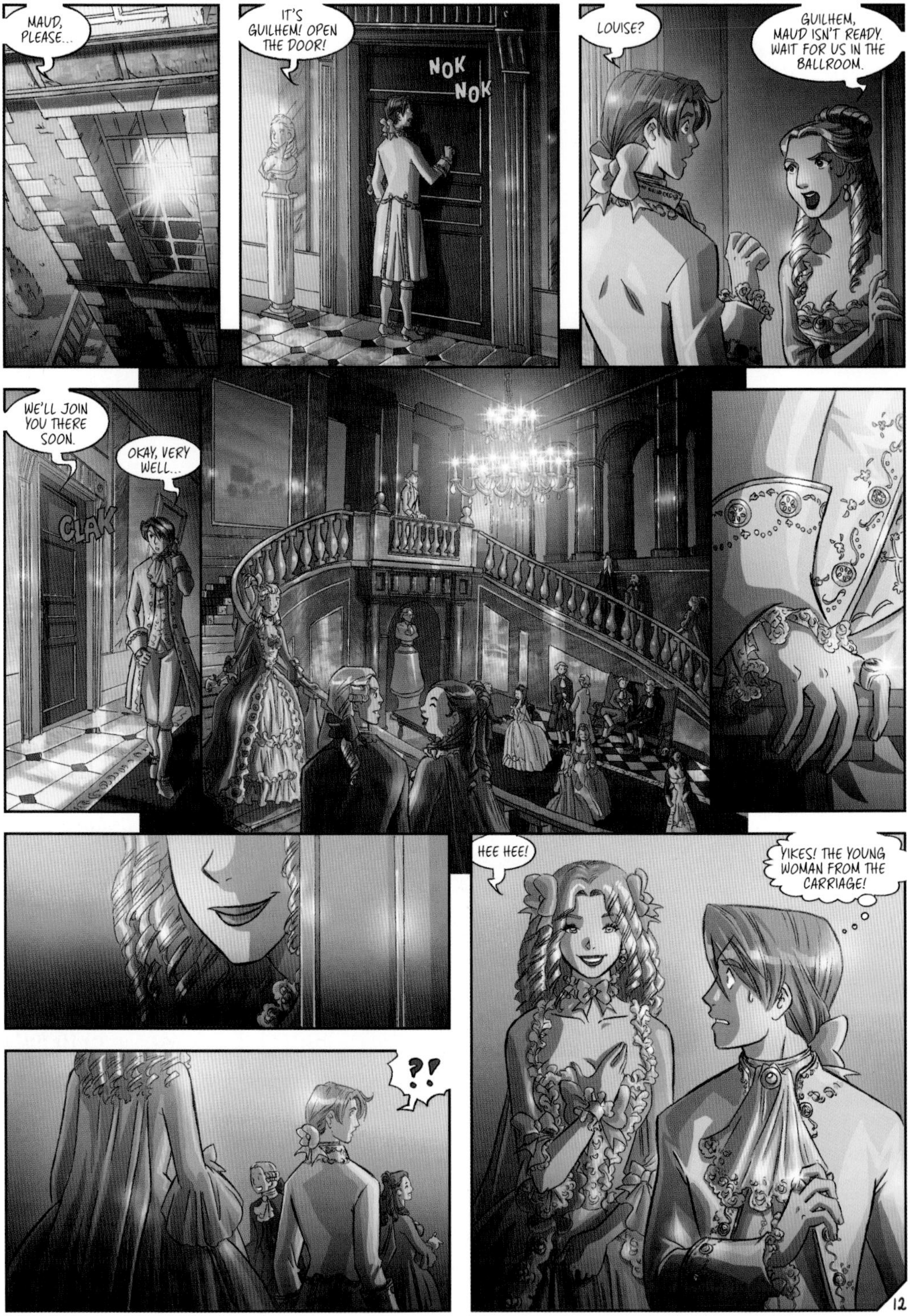
MAUD, PLEASE...
IT'S GUILHEM! OPEN THE DOOR!
NOK NOK
LOUISE?
GUILHEM, MAUD ISN'T READY. WAIT FOR US IN THE BALLROOM.
WE'LL JOIN YOU THERE SOON.
OKAY, VERY WELL...
CLAK
?!
HEE HEE!
YIKES! THE YOUNG WOMAN FROM THE CARRIAGE!
12

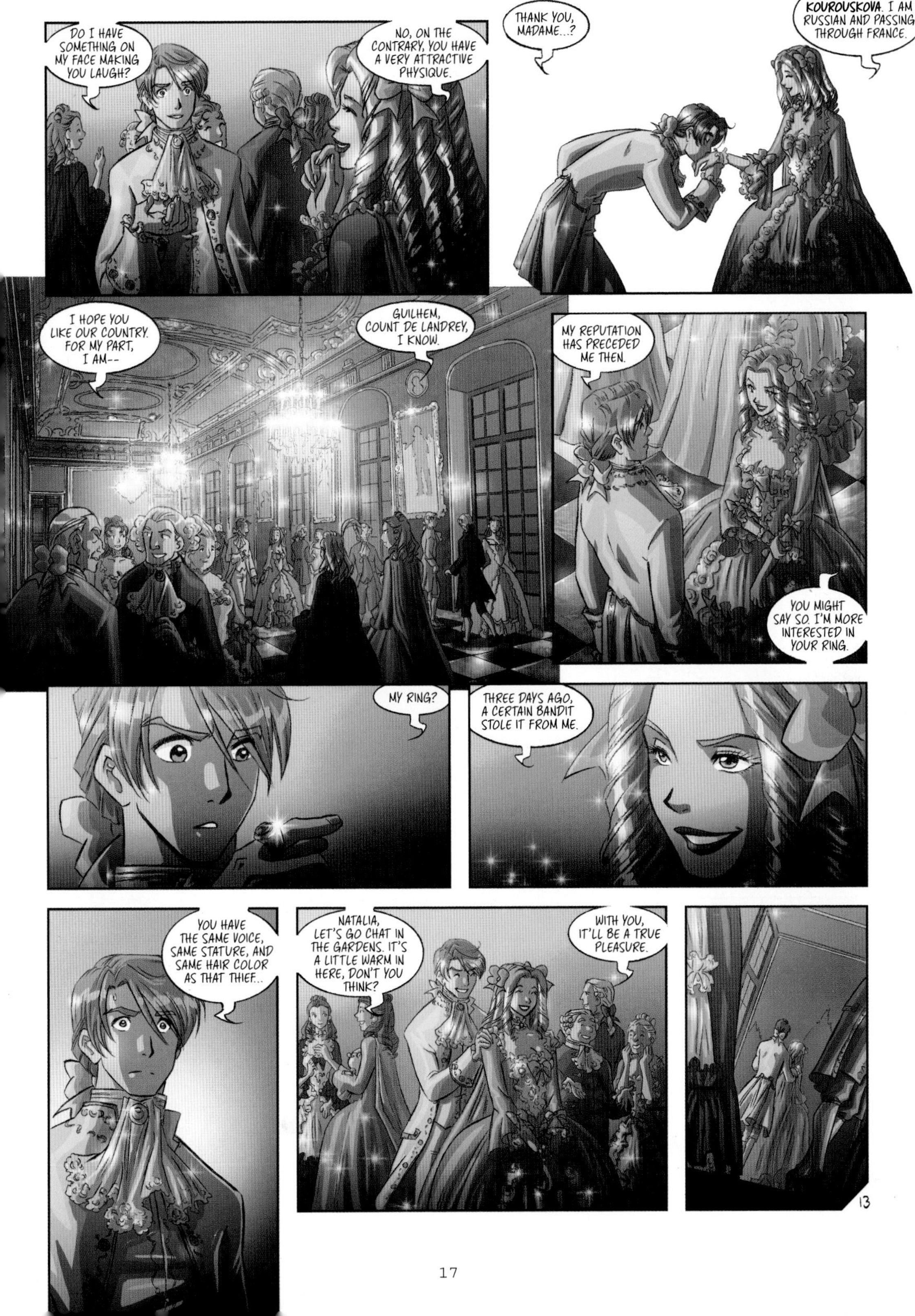
DO I HAVE SOMETHING ON MY FACE MAKING YOU LAUGH?
NO, ON THE CONTRARY, YOU HAVE A VERY ATTRACTIVE PHYSIQUE.
THANK YOU, MADAME...?
NATALIA KOUROUSKOVA. I AM RUSSIAN AND PASSING THROUGH FRANCE.
I HOPE YOU LIKE OUR COUNTRY. FOR MY PART, I AM--
GUILHEM, COUNT DE LANDREY, I KNOW.
MY REPUTATION HAS PRECEDED ME THEN.
YOU MIGHT SAY SO. I'M MORE INTERESTED IN YOUR RING.
MY RING?
THREE DAYS AGO, A CERTAIN BANDIT STOLE IT FROM ME.
YOU HAVE THE SAME VOICE, SAME STATURE, AND SAME HAIR COLOR AS THAT THIEF...
NATALIA, LET'S GO CHAT IN THE GARDENS. IT'S A LITTLE WARM IN HERE, DON'T YOU THINK?
WITH YOU, IT'LL BE A TRUE PLEASURE.
13

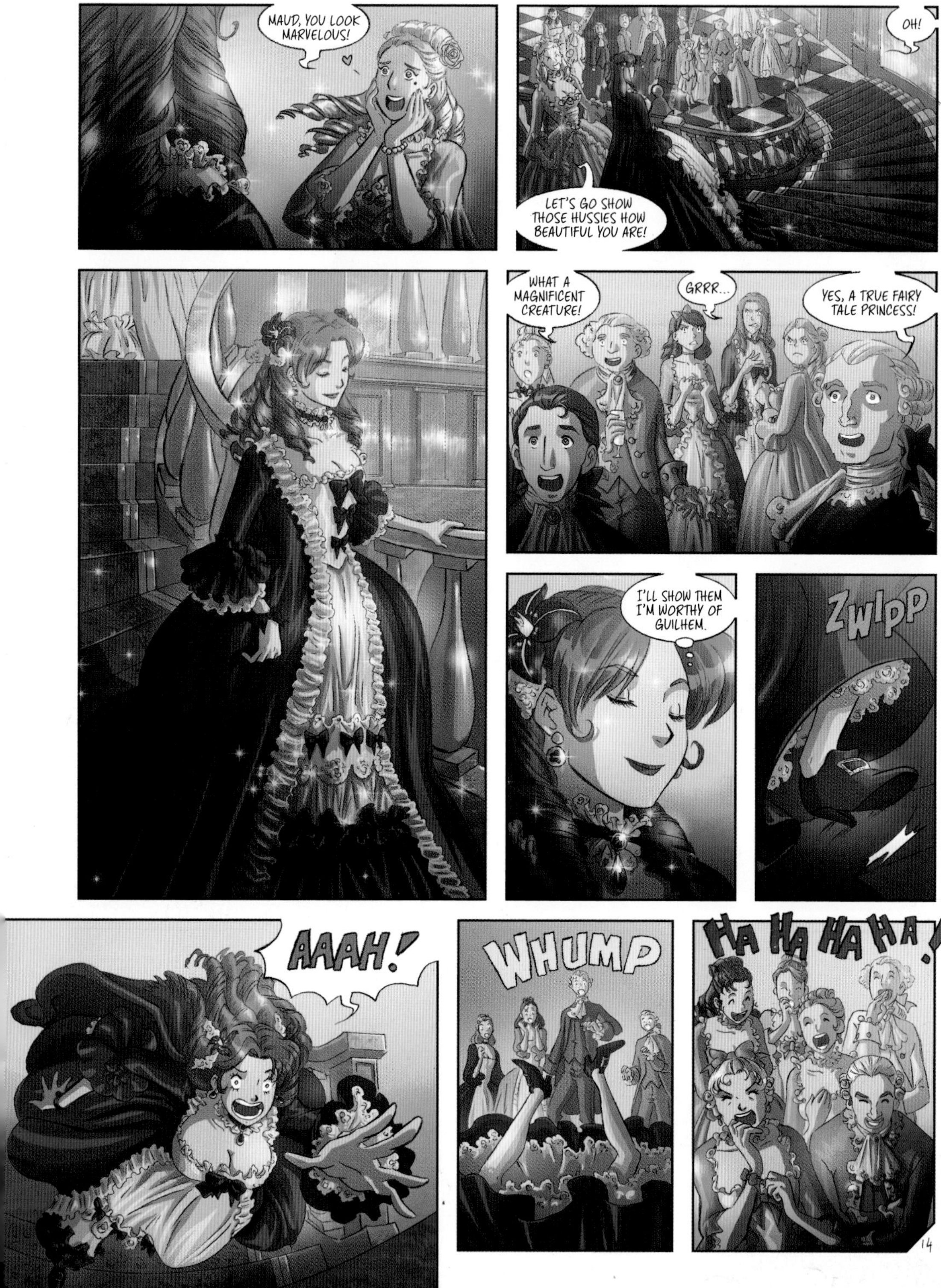
MAUD, YOU LOOK MARVELOUS!
OH!
LET'S GO SHOW THOSE HUSSIES HOW BEAUTIFUL YOU ARE!
WHAT A MAGNIFICENT CREATURE!
GRRR...
YES, A TRUE FAIRY TALE PRINCESS!
I'LL SHOW THEM I'M WORTHY OF GUILHEM.
ZWIPP
AAAH!
WHUMP
HA HA HA HA!
14

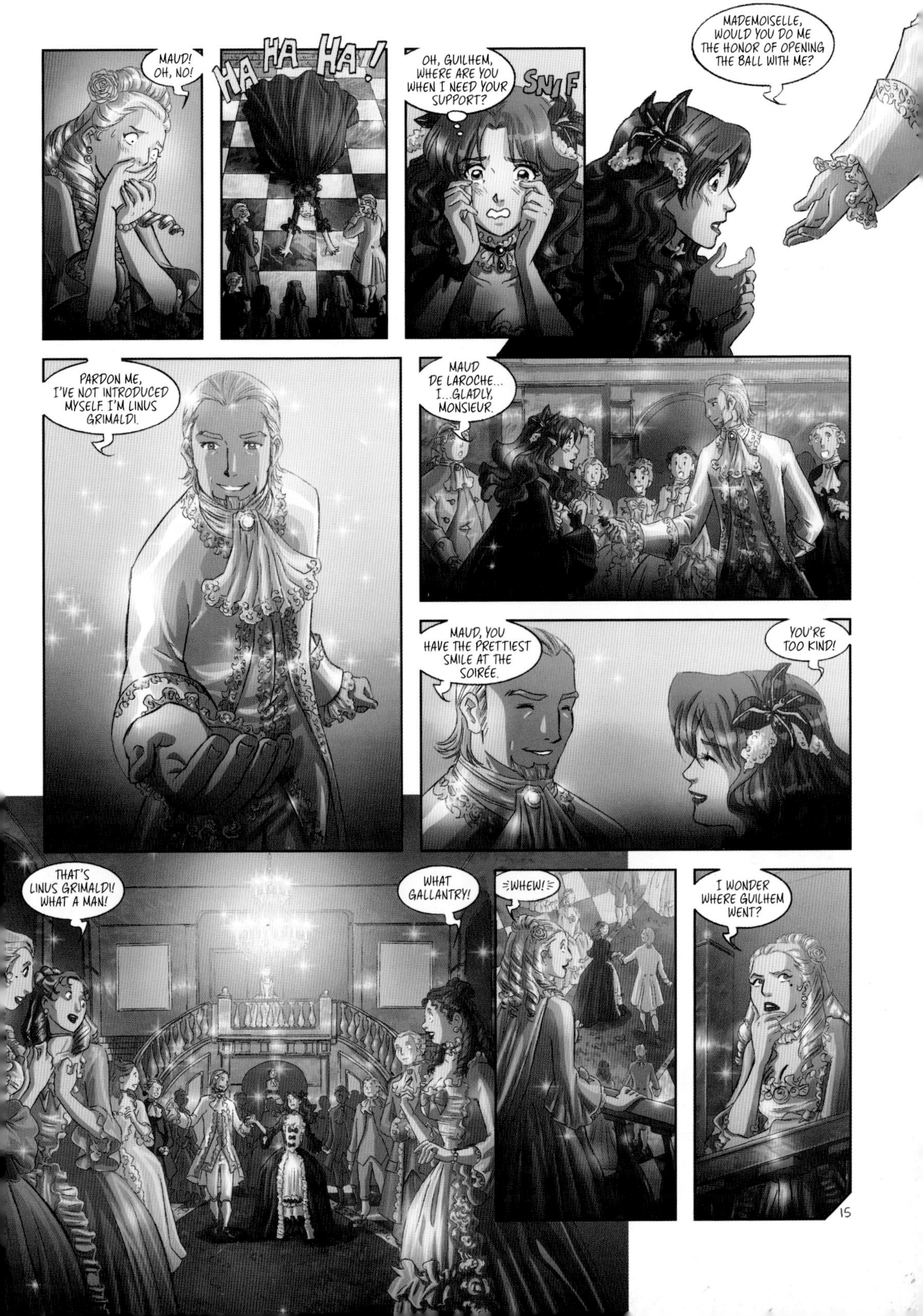
MAUD! OH, NO!
HA HA HA!
OH, GUILHEM, WHERE ARE YOU WHEN I NEED YOUR SUPPORT?
SNIF
MADEMOISELLE, WOULD YOU DO ME THE HONOR OF OPENING THE BALL WITH ME?
PARDON ME, I'VE NOT INTRODUCED MYSELF. I'M LINUS GRIMALDI.
MAUD DE LAROCHE... I...GLADLY, MONSIEUR.
MAUD, YOU HAVE THE PRETTIEST SMILE AT THE SOIRÉE.
YOU'RE TOO KIND!
THAT'S LINUS GRIMALDI! WHAT A MAN!
WHAT GALLANTRY!
WHEW!
I WONDER WHERE GUILHEM WENT?

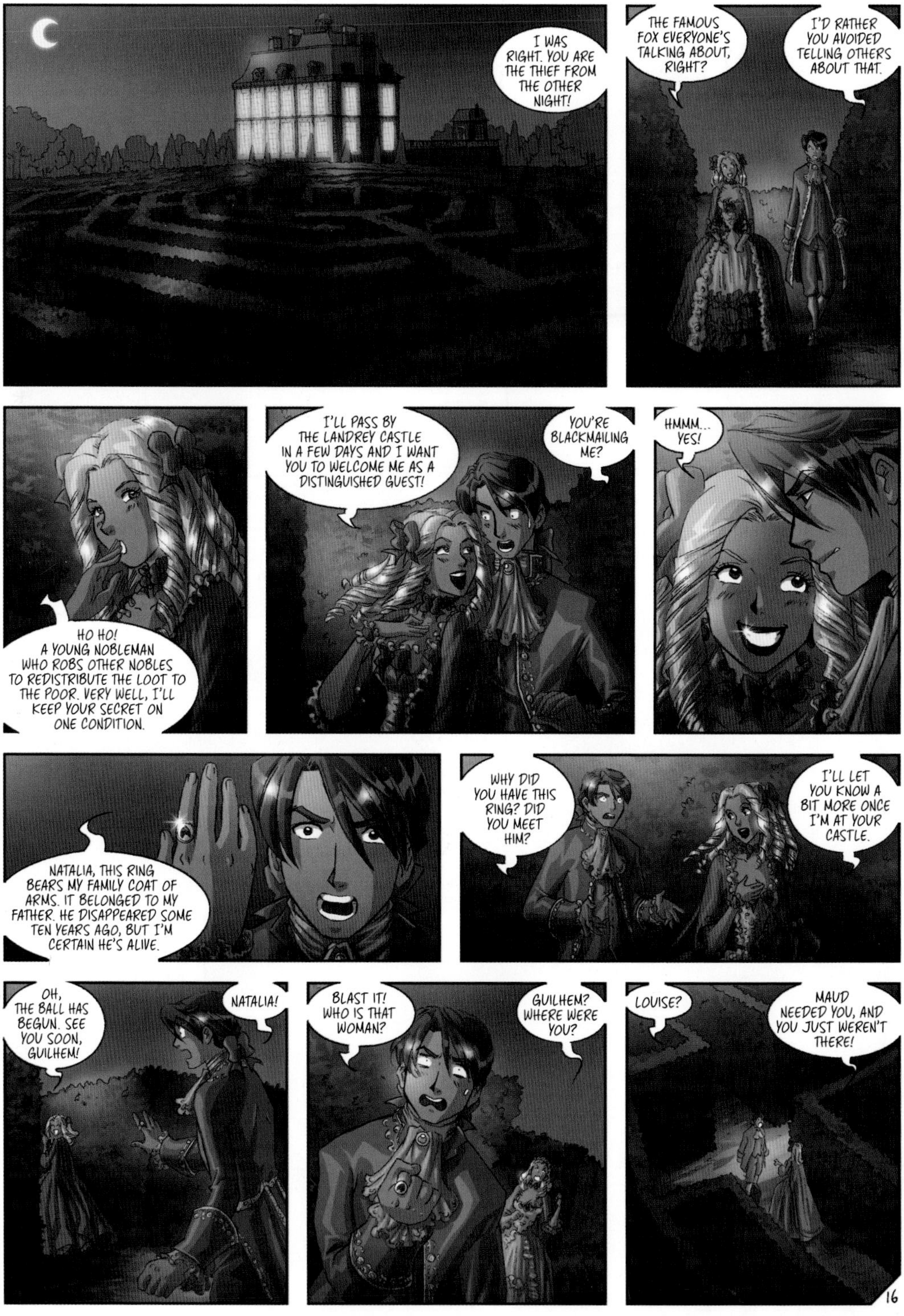
I WAS RIGHT. YOU ARE THE THIEF FROM THE OTHER NIGHT!
THE FAMOUS FOX EVERYONE'S TALKING ABOUT, RIGHT?
I'D RATHER YOU AVOIDED TELLING OTHERS ABOUT THAT.
HO HO! A YOUNG NOBLEMAN WHO ROBS OTHER NOBLES TO REDISTRIBUTE THE LOOT TO THE POOR. VERY WELL, I'LL KEEP YOUR SECRET ON ONE CONDITION.
I'LL PASS BY THE LANDREY CASTLE IN A FEW DAYS AND I WANT YOU TO WELCOME ME AS A DISTINGUISHED GUEST!
YOU'RE BLACKMAILING ME?
HMMM... YES!
NATALIA, THIS RING BEARS MY FAMILY COAT OF ARMS. IT BELONGED TO MY FATHER. HE DISAPPEARED SOME TEN YEARS AGO, BUT I'M CERTAIN HE'S ALIVE.
WHY DID YOU HAVE THIS RING? DID YOU MEET HIM?
I'LL LET YOU KNOW A BIT MORE ONCE I'M AT YOUR CASTLE.
OH, THE BALL HAS BEGUN. SEE YOU SOON, GUILHEM!
NATALIA!
BLAST IT! WHO IS THAT WOMAN?
GUILHEM? WHERE WERE YOU?
LOUISE?
MAUD NEEDED YOU, AND YOU JUST WEREN'T THERE!
16

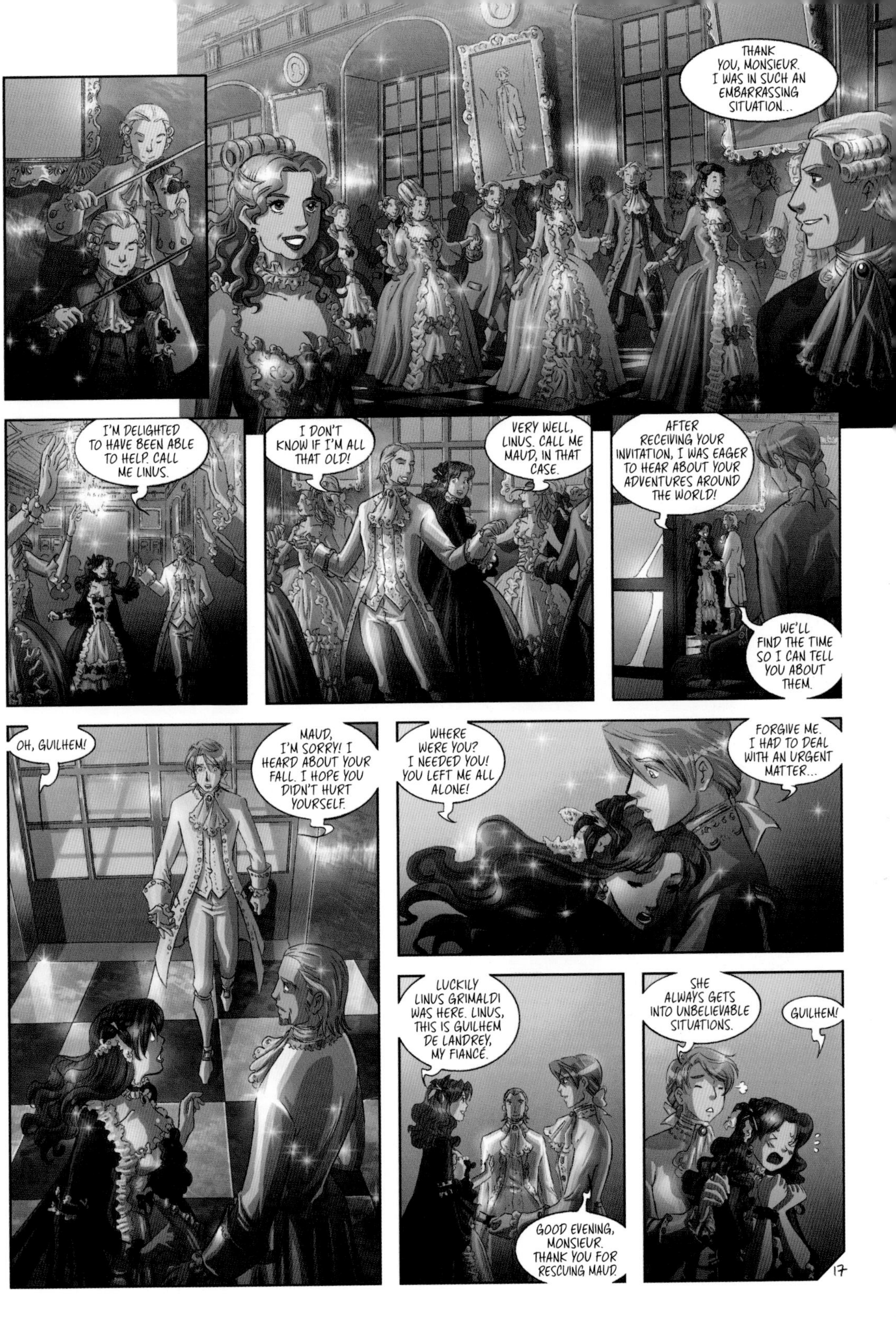
THANK YOU, MONSIEUR. I WAS IN SUCH AN EMBARRASSING SITUATION...
I'M DELIGHTED TO HAVE BEEN ABLE TO HELP. CALL ME LINUS.
I DON'T KNOW IF I'M ALL THAT OLD!
VERY WELL, LINUS. CALL ME MAUD, IN THAT CASE.
AFTER RECEIVING YOUR INVITATION, I WAS EAGER TO HEAR ABOUT YOUR ADVENTURES AROUND THE WORLD!
WE'LL FIND THE TIME SO I CAN TELL YOU ABOUT THEM.
OH, GUILHEM!
MAUD, I'M SORRY! I HEARD ABOUT YOUR FALL. I HOPE YOU DIDN'T HURT YOURSELF.
WHERE WERE YOU? I NEEDED YOU! YOU LEFT ME ALL ALONE!
FORGIVE ME. I HAD TO DEAL WITH AN URGENT MATTER...
LUCKILY LINUS GRIMALDI WAS HERE. LINUS, THIS IS GUILHEM DE LANDREY, MY FIANCÉ.
GOOD EVENING, MONSIEUR. THANK YOU FOR RESCUING MAUD.
SHE ALWAYS GETS INTO UNBELIEVABLE SITUATIONS.
GUILHEM!
17

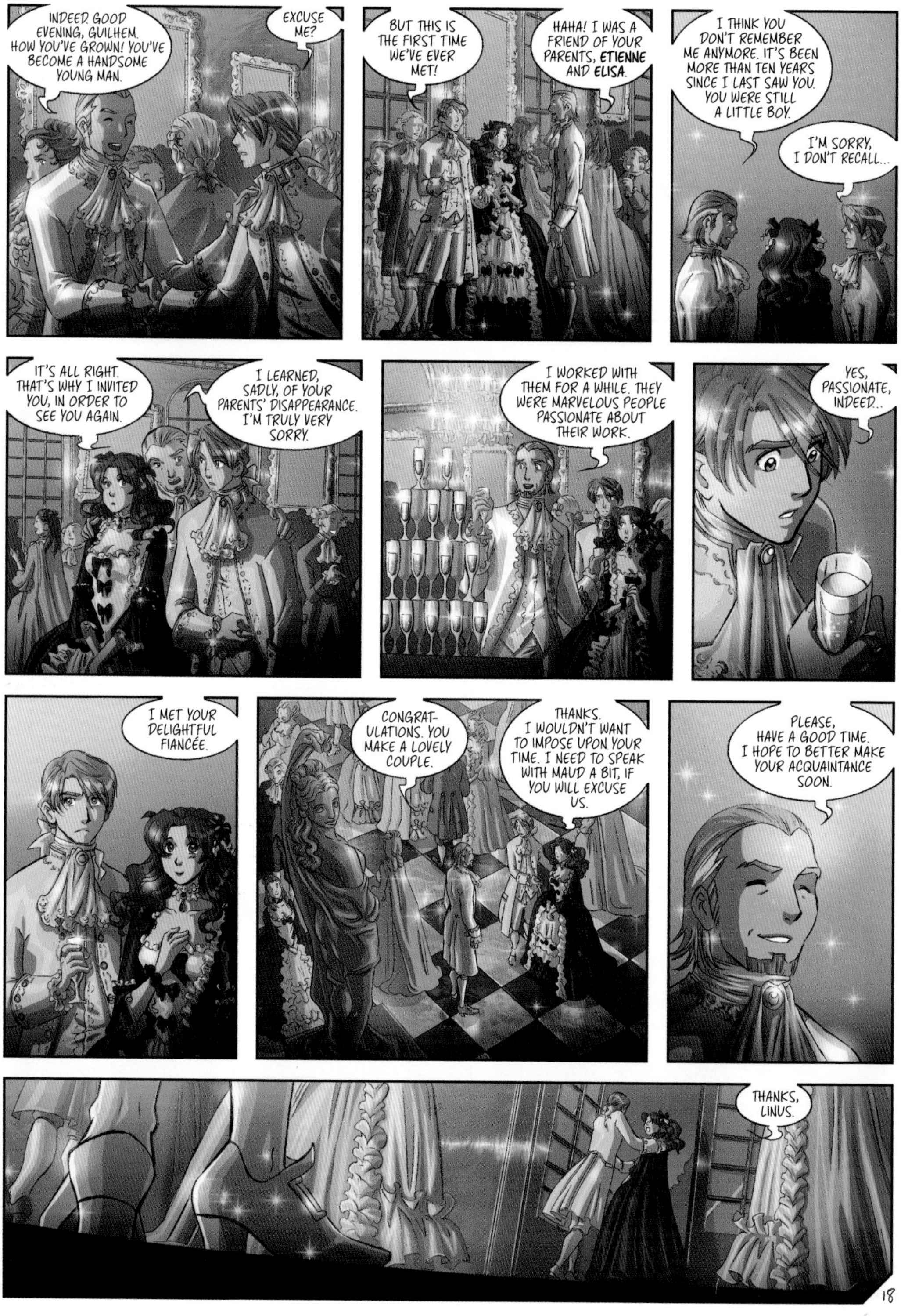
INDEED. GOOD EVENING, GUILHEM. HOW YOU'VE GROWN! YOU'VE BECOME A HANDSOME YOUNG MAN.
EXCUSE ME?
BUT THIS IS THE FIRST TIME WE'VE EVER MET!
HAHA! I WAS A FRIEND OF YOUR PARENTS, ETIENNE AND ELISA.
I THINK YOU DON'T REMEMBER ME ANYMORE. IT'S BEEN MORE THAN TEN YEARS SINCE I LAST SAW YOU. YOU WERE STILL A LITTLE BOY.
I'M SORRY, I DON'T RECALL...
IT'S ALL RIGHT. THAT'S WHY I INVITED YOU, IN ORDER TO SEE YOU AGAIN.
I LEARNED, SADLY, OF YOUR PARENTS' DISAPPEARANCE. I'M TRULY VERY SORRY.
I WORKED WITH THEM FOR A WHILE. THEY WERE MARVELOUS PEOPLE PASSIONATE ABOUT THEIR WORK.
YES, PASSIONATE, INDEED...
I MET YOUR DELIGHTFUL FIANCÉE.
CONGRATULATIONS. YOU MAKE A LOVELY COUPLE.
THANKS. I WOULDN'T WANT TO IMPOSE UPON YOUR TIME. I NEED TO SPEAK WITH MAUD A BIT, IF YOU WILL EXCUSE US.
PLEASE, HAVE A GOOD TIME. I HOPE TO BETTER MAKE YOUR ACQUAINTANCE SOON.
THANKS, LINUS.
18

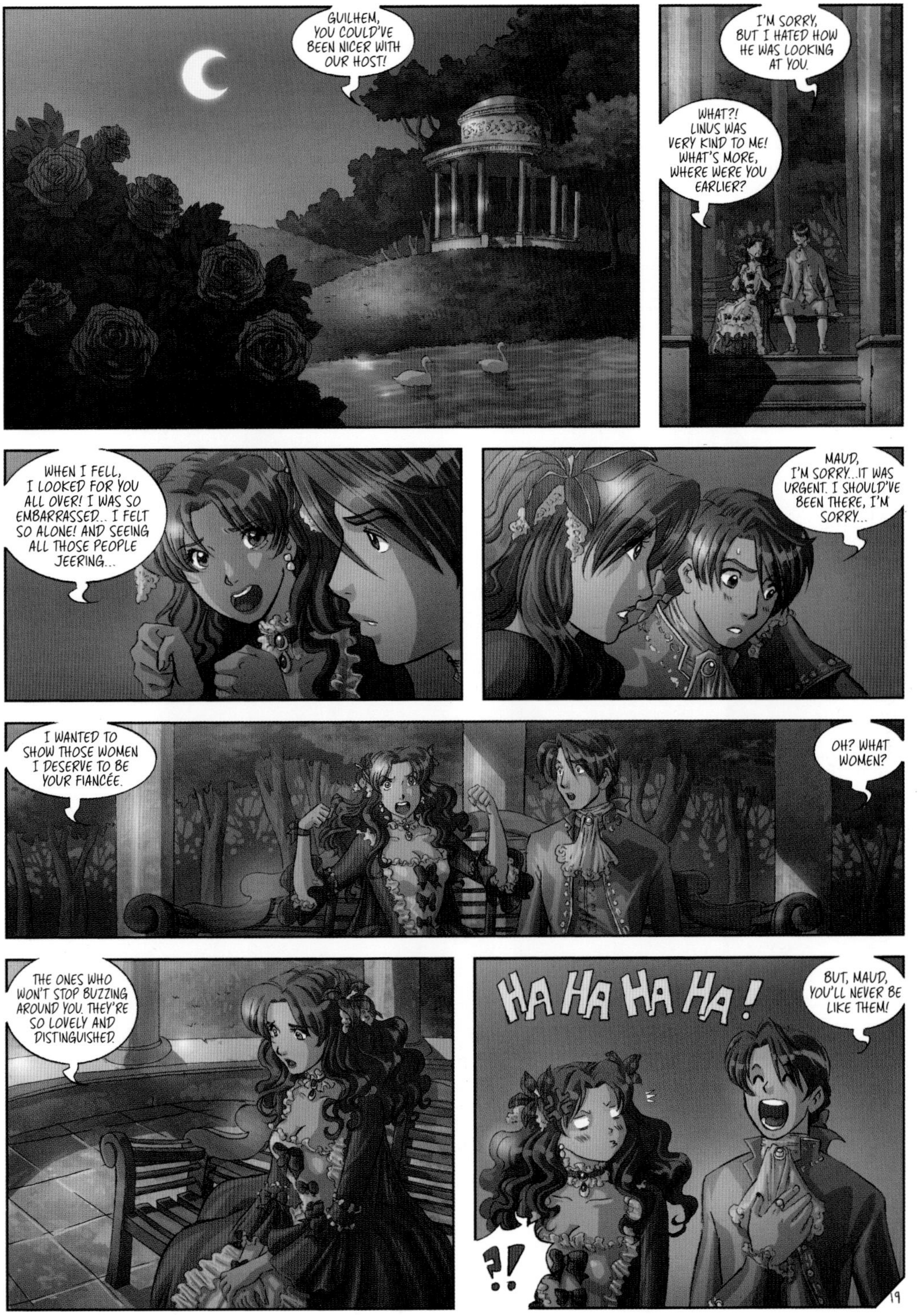
GUILHEM, YOU COULD'VE BEEN NICER WITH OUR HOST!
I'M SORRY, BUT I HATED HOW HE WAS LOOKING AT YOU.
WHAT?! LINUS WAS VERY KIND TO ME! WHAT'S MORE, WHERE WERE YOU EARLIER?
WHEN I FELL, I LOOKED FOR YOU ALL OVER! I WAS SO EMBARRASSED... I FELT SO ALONE! AND SEEING ALL THOSE PEOPLE JEERING...
MAUD, I'M SORRY...IT WAS URGENT. I SHOULD'VE BEEN THERE, I'M SORRY...
I WANTED TO SHOW THOSE WOMEN I DESERVE TO BE YOUR FIANCÉE.
OH? WHAT WOMEN?
THE ONES WHO WON'T STOP BUZZING AROUND YOU. THEY'RE SO LOVELY AND DISTINGUISHED.
HA HA HA HA!
BUT, MAUD, YOU'LL NEVER BE LIKE THEM!
?!
19

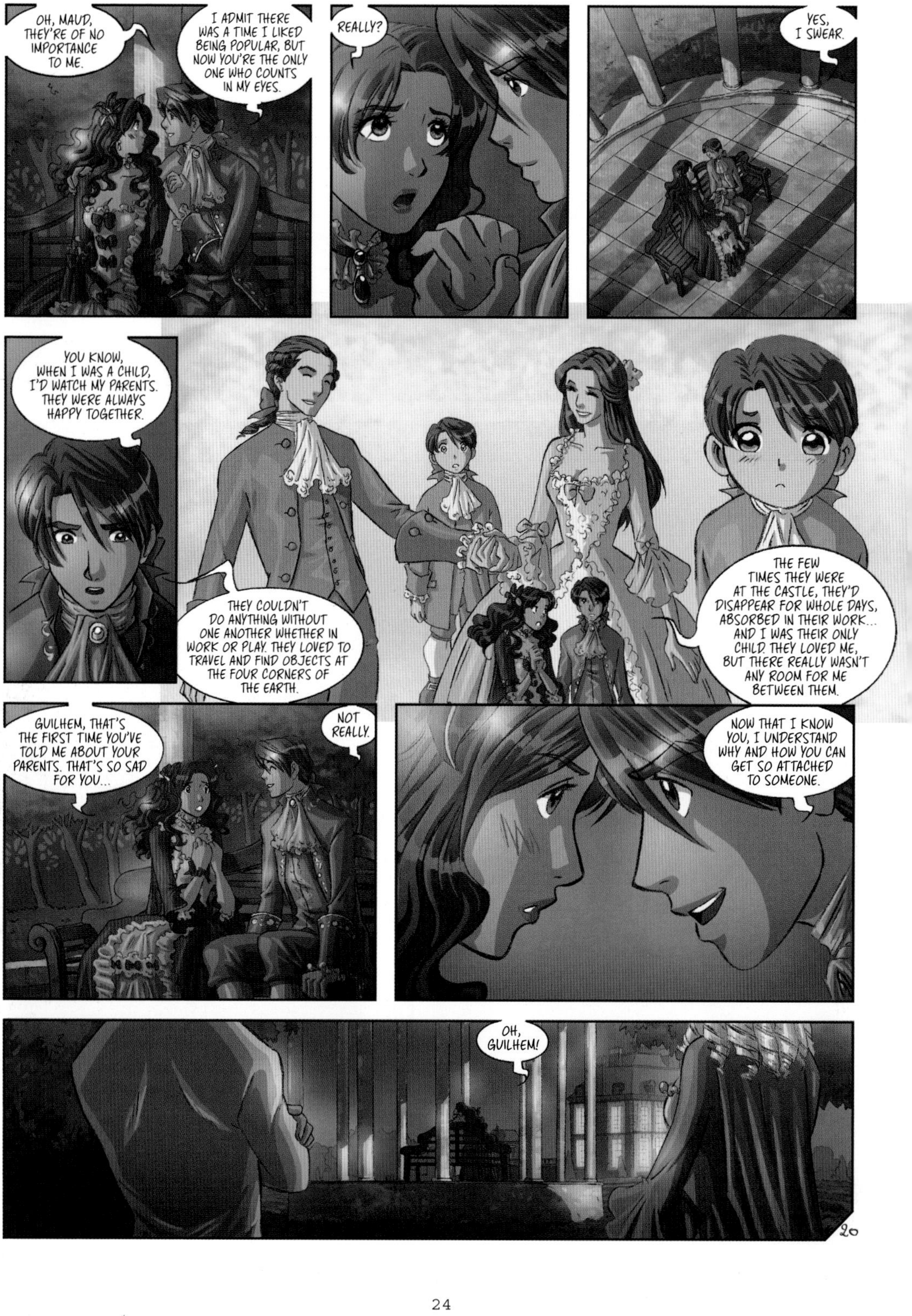
OH, MAUD, THEY'RE OF NO IMPORTANCE TO ME.
I ADMIT THERE WAS A TIME I LIKED BEING POPULAR, BUT NOW YOU'RE THE ONLY ONE WHO COUNTS IN MY EYES.
REALLY?
YES, I SWEAR.
YOU KNOW, WHEN I WAS A CHILD, I'D WATCH MY PARENTS. THEY WERE ALWAYS HAPPY TOGETHER.
THEY COULDN'T DO ANYTHING WITHOUT ONE ANOTHER WHETHER IN WORK OR PLAY. THEY LOVED TO TRAVEL AND FIND OBJECTS AT THE FOUR CORNERS OF THE EARTH.
THE FEW TIMES THEY WERE AT THE CASTLE, THEY'D DISAPPEAR FOR WHOLE DAYS, ABSORBED IN THEIR WORK... AND I WAS THEIR ONLY CHILD. THEY LOVED ME, BUT THERE REALLY WASN'T ANY ROOM FOR ME BETWEEN THEM.
GUILHEM, THAT'S THE FIRST TIME YOU'VE TOLD ME ABOUT YOUR PARENTS. THAT'S SO SAD FOR YOU...
NOT REALLY.
NOW THAT I KNOW YOU, I UNDERSTAND WHY AND HOW YOU CAN GET SO ATTACHED TO SOMEONE.
OH, GUILHEM!
20

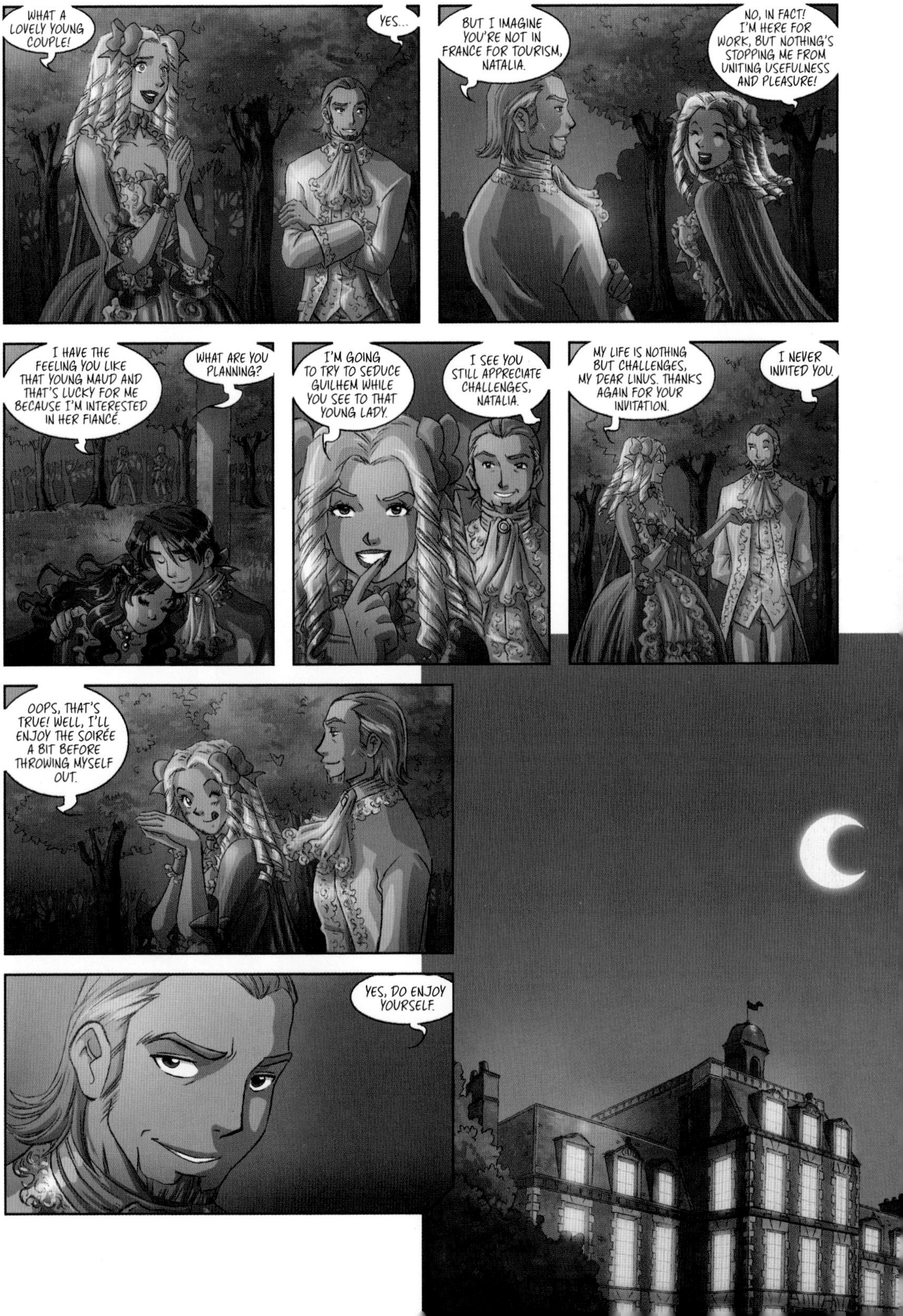
WHAT A LOVELY YOUNG COUPLE!
YES...
BUT I IMAGINE YOU'RE NOT IN FRANCE FOR TOURISM, NATALIA.
NO, IN FACT! I'M HERE FOR WORK, BUT NOTHING'S STOPPING ME FROM UNITING USEFULNESS AND PLEASURE!
I HAVE THE FEELING YOU LIKE THAT YOUNG MAUD AND THAT'S LUCKY FOR ME BECAUSE I'M INTERESTED IN HER FIANCÉ.
WHAT ARE YOU PLANNING?
I'M GOING TO TRY TO SEDUCE GUILHEM WHILE YOU SEE TO THAT YOUNG LADY.
I SEE YOU STILL APPRECIATE CHALLENGES, NATALIA.
MY LIFE IS NOTHING BUT CHALLENGES, MY DEAR LINUS. THANKS AGAIN FOR YOUR INVITATION.
I NEVER INVITED YOU.
OOPS, THAT'S TRUE! WELL, I'LL ENJOY THE SOIRÉE A BIT BEFORE THROWING MYSELF OUT.
YES, DO ENJOY YOURSELF.

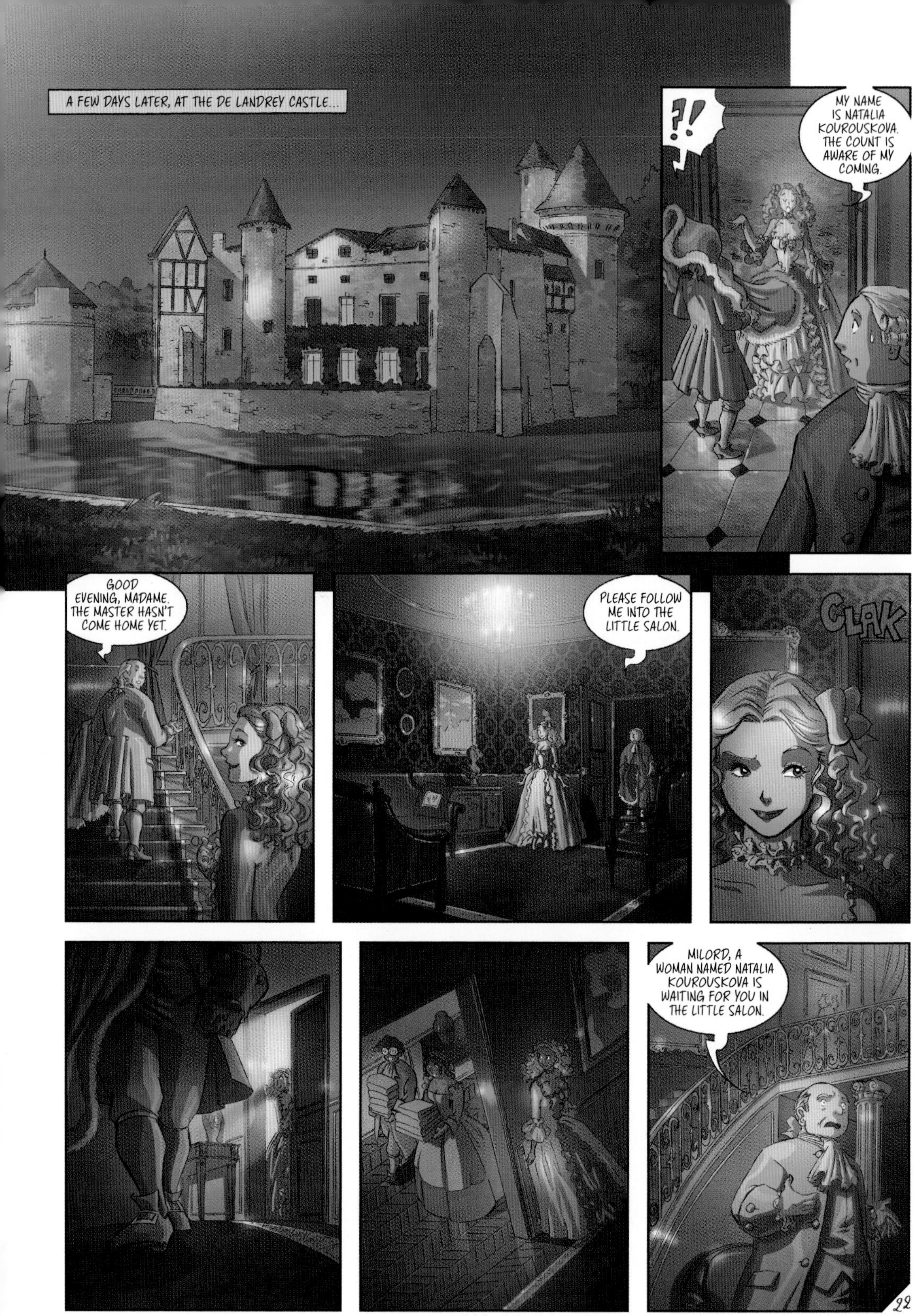

A FEW DAYS LATER, AT THE DE LANDREY CASTLE...
?!
MY NAME IS NATALIA KOUROUSKOVA. THE COUNT IS AWARE OF MY COMING.
GOOD EVENING, MADAME. THE MASTER HASN'T COME HOME YET.
PLEASE FOLLOW ME INTO THE LITTLE SALON.
CLAK
MILORD, A WOMAN NAMED NATALIA KOUROUSKOVA IS WAITING FOR YOU IN THE LITTLE SALON.
22

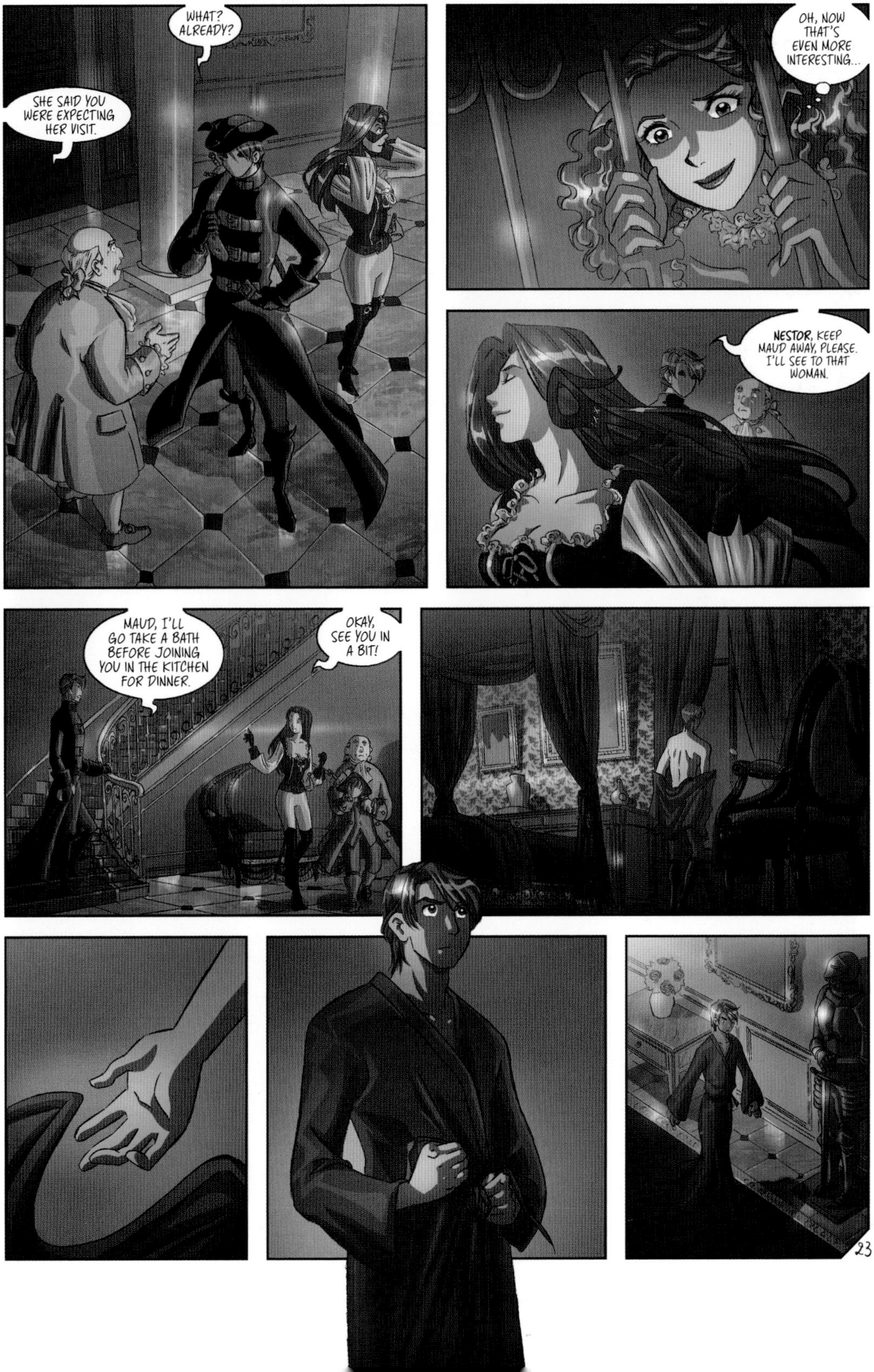
SHE SAID YOU WERE EXPECTING HER VISIT.
WHAT? ALREADY?
OH, NOW THAT'S EVEN MORE INTERESTING...
NESTOR, KEEP MAUD AWAY, PLEASE. I'LL SEE TO THAT WOMAN.
MAUD, I'LL GO TAKE A BATH BEFORE JOINING YOU IN THE KITCHEN FOR DINNER.
OKAY, SEE YOU IN A BIT!

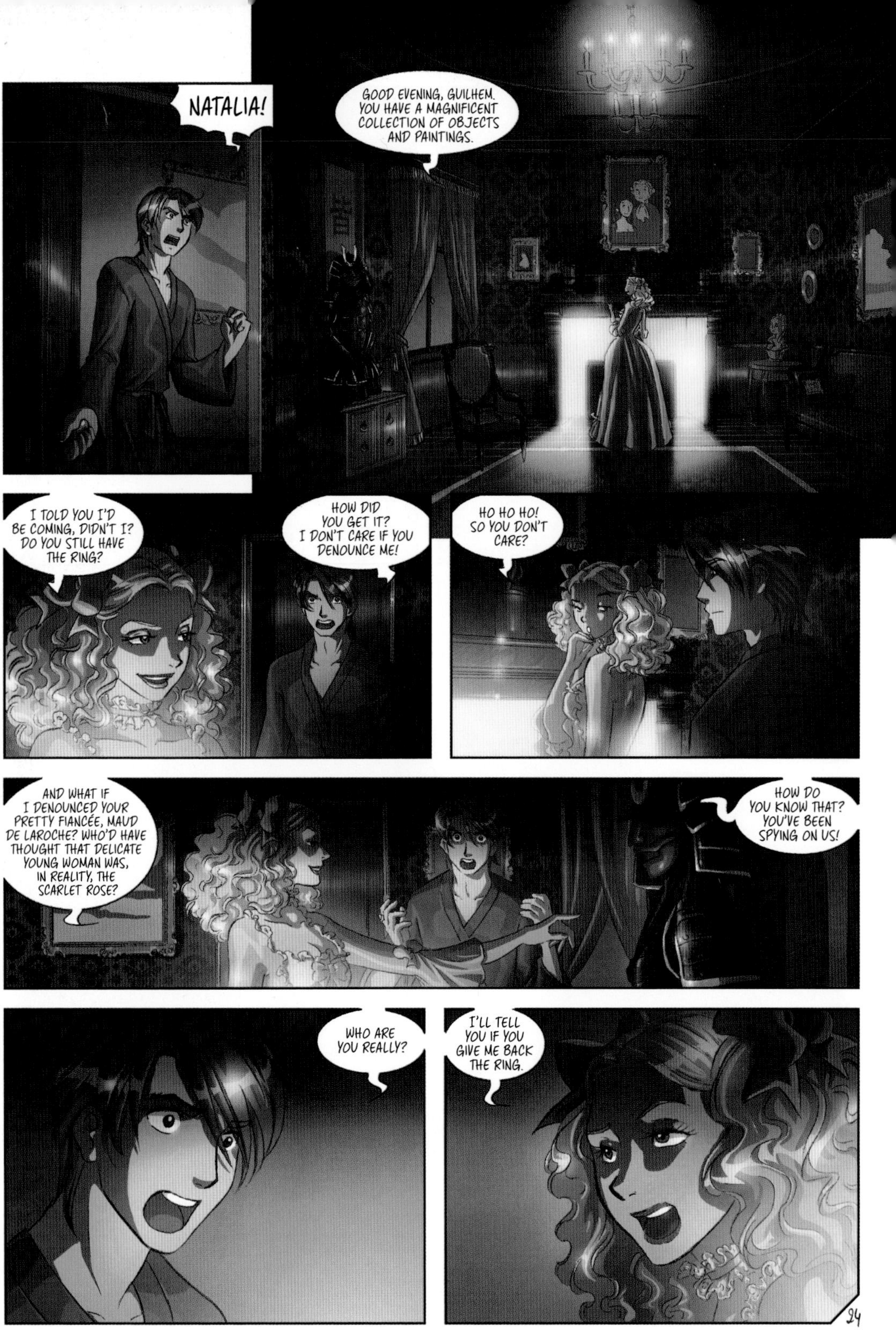
NATALIA!
GOOD EVENING, GUILHEM. YOU HAVE A MAGNIFICENT COLLECTION OF OBJECTS AND PAINTINGS.
I TOLD YOU I'D BE COMING, DIDN'T I? DO YOU STILL HAVE THE RING?
HOW DID YOU GET IT? I DON'T CARE IF YOU DENOUNCE ME!
HO HO HO! SO YOU DON'T CARE?
AND WHAT IF I DENOUNCED YOUR PRETTY FIANCÉE, MAUD DE LAROCHE? WHO'D HAVE THOUGHT THAT DELICATE YOUNG WOMAN WAS, IN REALITY, THE SCARLET ROSE?
HOW DO YOU KNOW THAT? YOU'VE BEEN SPYING ON US!
WHO ARE YOU REALLY?
I'LL TELL YOU IF YOU GIVE ME BACK THE RING.
24

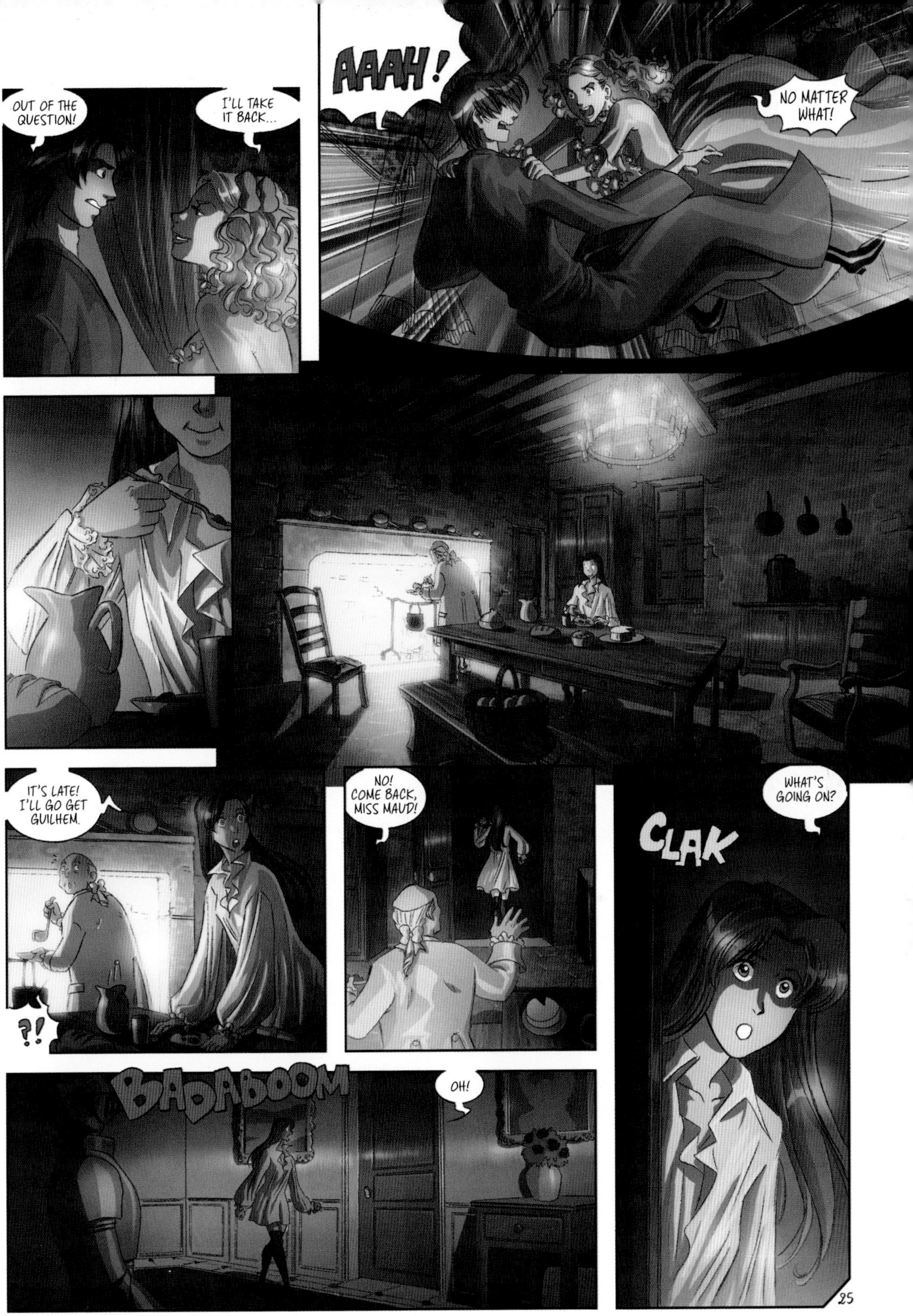
OUT OF THE QUESTION!
I'LL TAKE IT BACK...
AAAH!
NO MATTER WHAT!
IT'S LATE! I'LL GO GET GUILHEM.
?!
NO! COME BACK, MISS MAUD!
WHAT'S GOING ON?
CLAK
BADABOOM
OH!
25

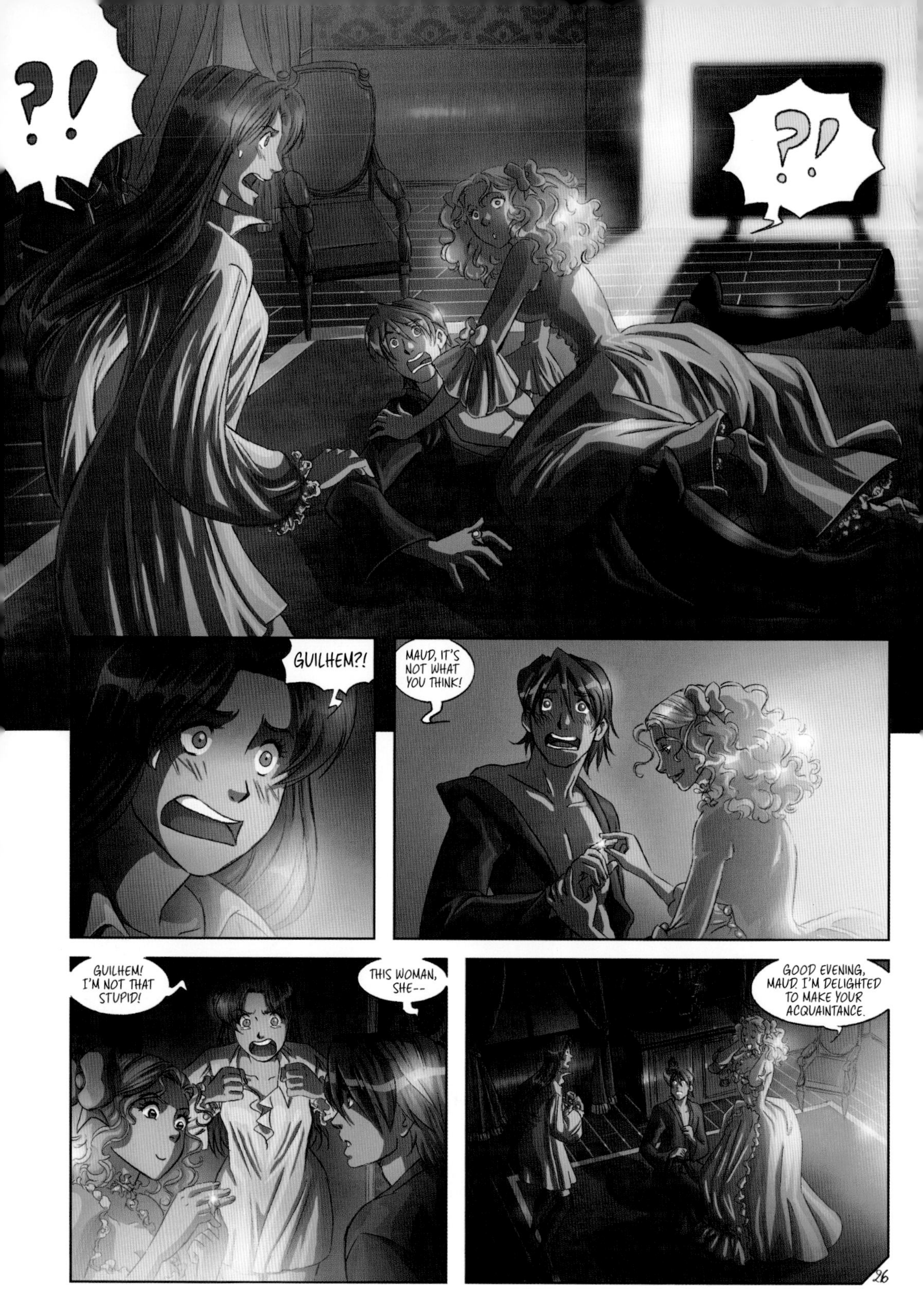
?!
?!
GUILHEM?!
MAUD, IT'S NOT WHAT YOU THINK!
GUILHEM! I'M NOT THAT STUPID!
THIS WOMAN, SHE--
GOOD EVENING, MAUD. I'M DELIGHTED TO MAKE YOUR ACQUAINTANCE.
26

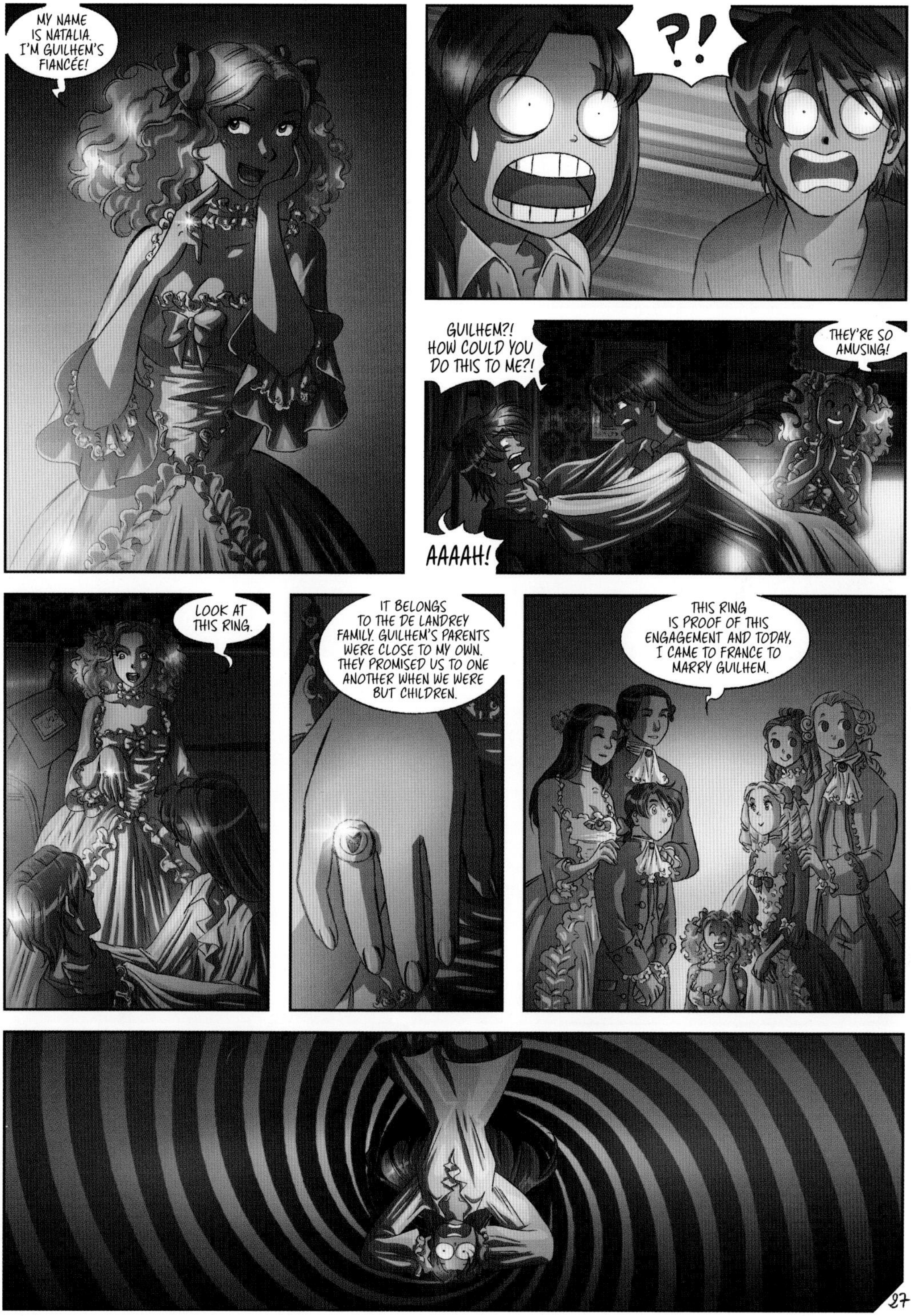
MY NAME IS NATALIA. I'M GUILHEM'S FIANCÉE!
?!
GUILHEM?! HOW COULD YOU DO THIS TO ME?!
THEY'RE SO AMUSING!
AAAAH!
LOOK AT THIS RING.
IT BELONGS TO THE DE LANDREY FAMILY. GUILHEM'S PARENTS WERE CLOSE TO MY OWN. THEY PROMISED US TO ONE ANOTHER WHEN WE WERE BUT CHILDREN.
THIS RING IS PROOF OF THIS ENGAGEMENT AND TODAY, I CAME TO FRANCE TO MARRY GUILHEM.
27

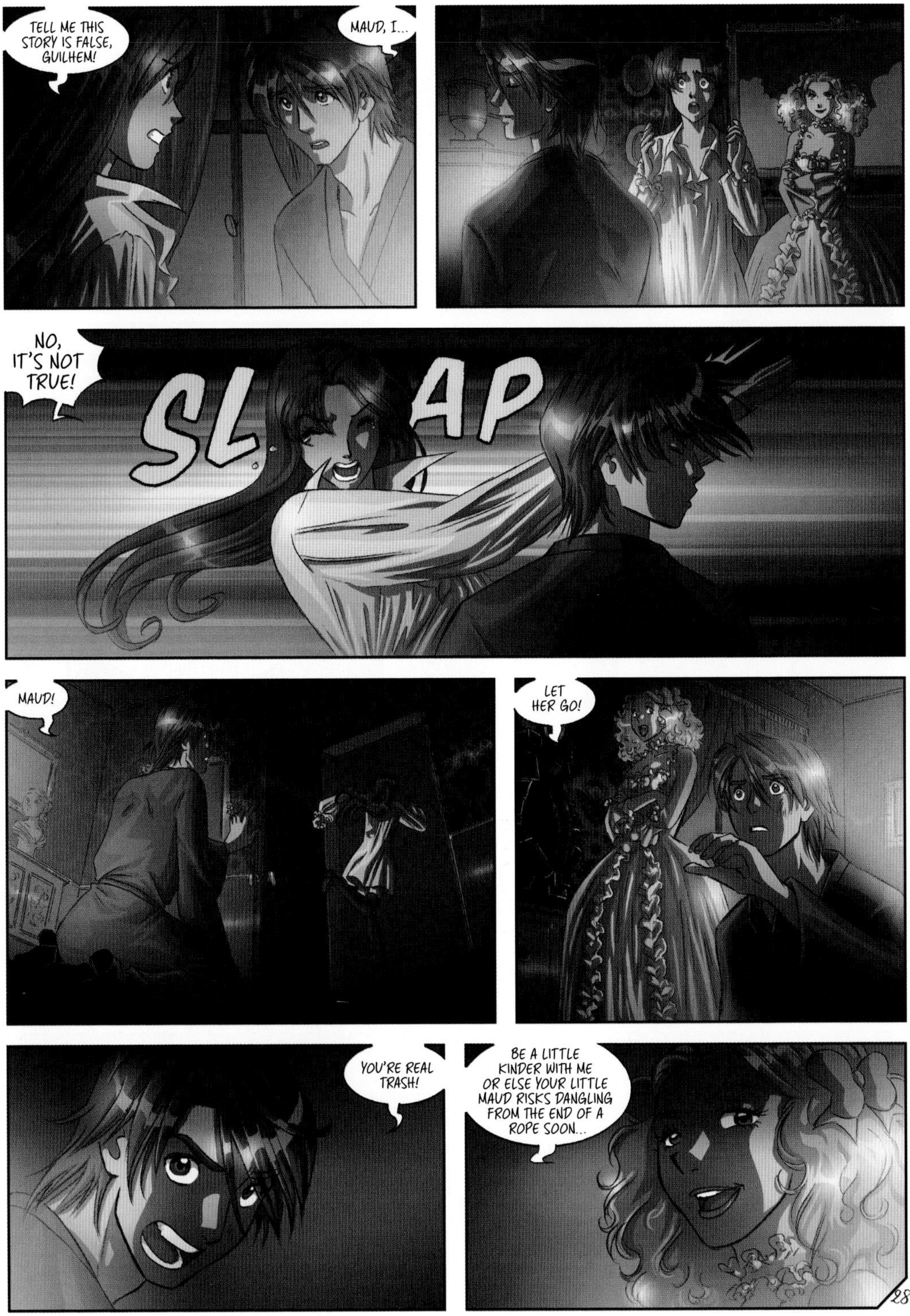
TELL ME THIS STORY IS FALSE, GUILHEM!
MAUD, I...
NO, IT'S NOT TRUE!
SLAP
MAUD!
LET HER GO!
YOU'RE REAL TRASH!
BE A LITTLE KINDER WITH ME OR ELSE YOUR LITTLE MAUD RISKS DANGLING FROM THE END OF A ROPE SOON...
28

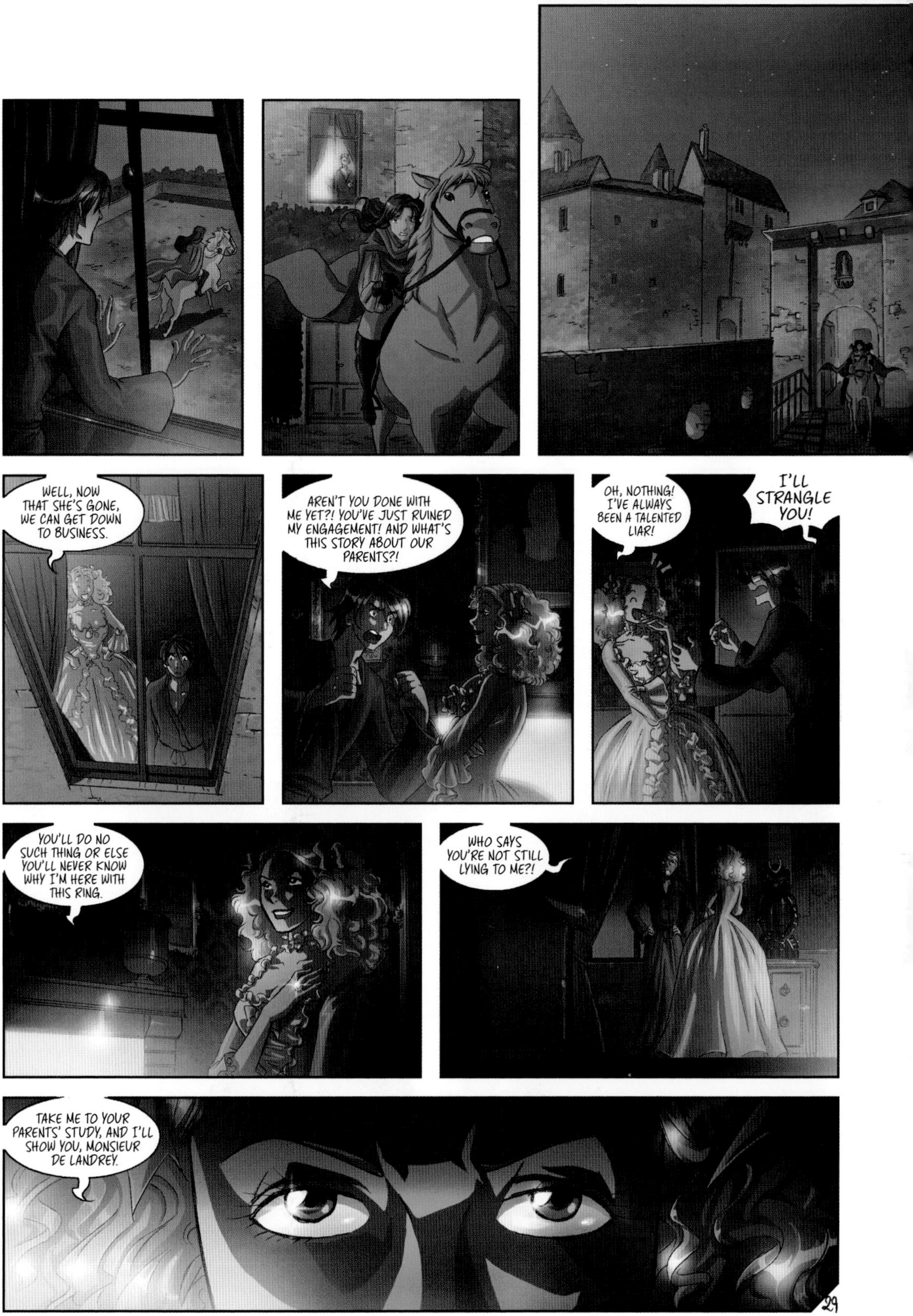
WELL, NOW THAT SHE'S GONE, WE CAN GET DOWN TO BUSINESS.
AREN'T YOU DONE WITH ME YET?! YOU'VE JUST RUINED MY ENGAGEMENT! AND WHAT'S THIS STORY ABOUT OUR PARENTS?!
OH, NOTHING! I'VE ALWAYS BEEN A TALENTED LIAR!
I'LL STRANGLE YOU!
YOU'LL DO NO SUCH THING OR ELSE YOU'LL NEVER KNOW WHY I'M HERE WITH THIS RING.
WHO SAYS YOU'RE NOT STILL LYING TO ME?!
TAKE ME TO YOUR PARENTS' STUDY, AND I'LL SHOW YOU, MONSIEUR DE LANDREY.
29

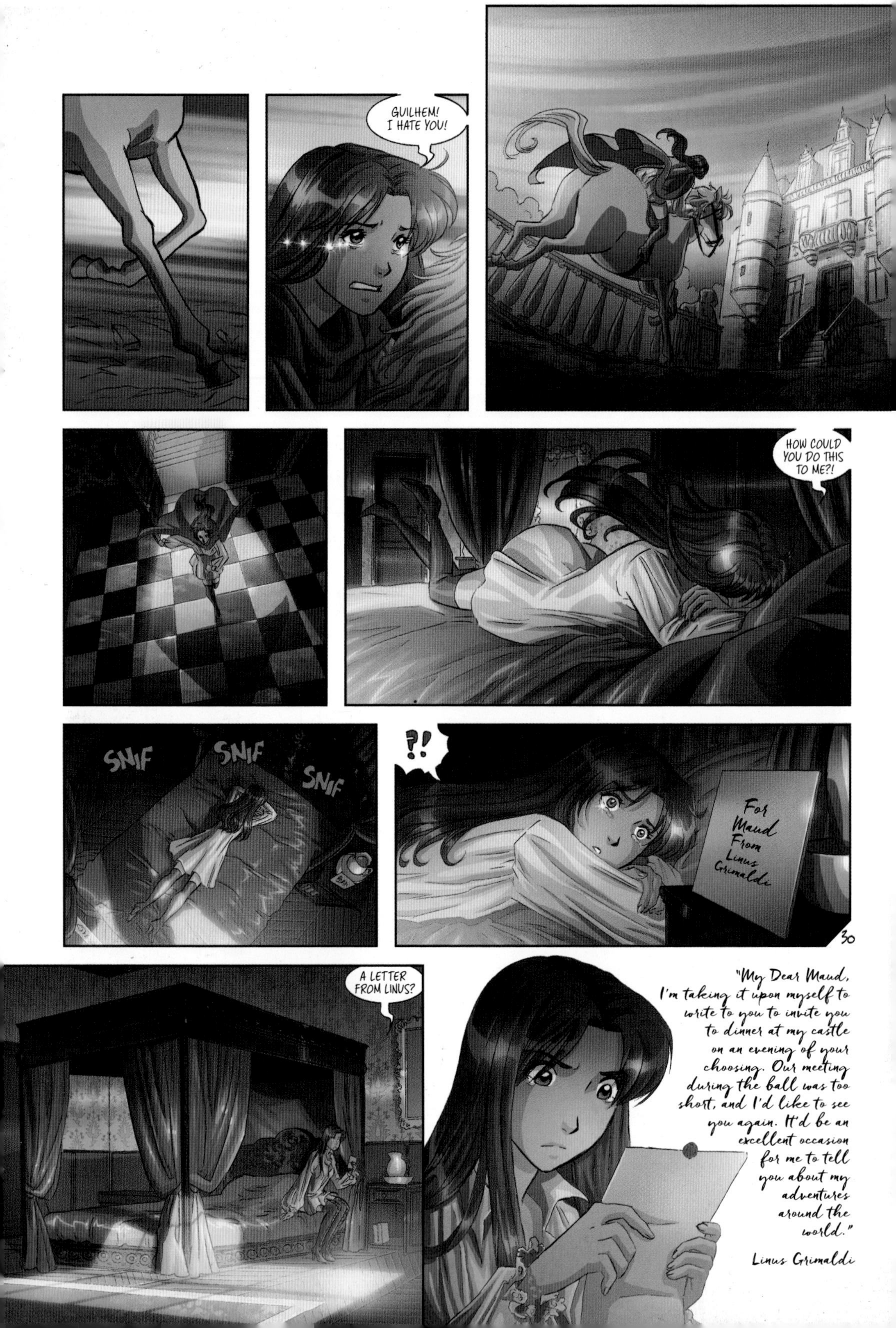
GUILHEM! I HATE YOU!
HOW COULD YOU DO THIS TO ME?!
SNIF
SNIF
SNIF
?!
For Maud From Linus Grimaldi
30
A LETTER FROM LINUS?
"My Dear Maud,
I'm taking it upon myself to write to you to invite you to dinner at my castle on an evening of your choosing. Our meeting during the ball was too short, and I'd like to see you again. It'd be an excellent occasion for me to tell you about my adventures around the world."
Linus Grimaldi

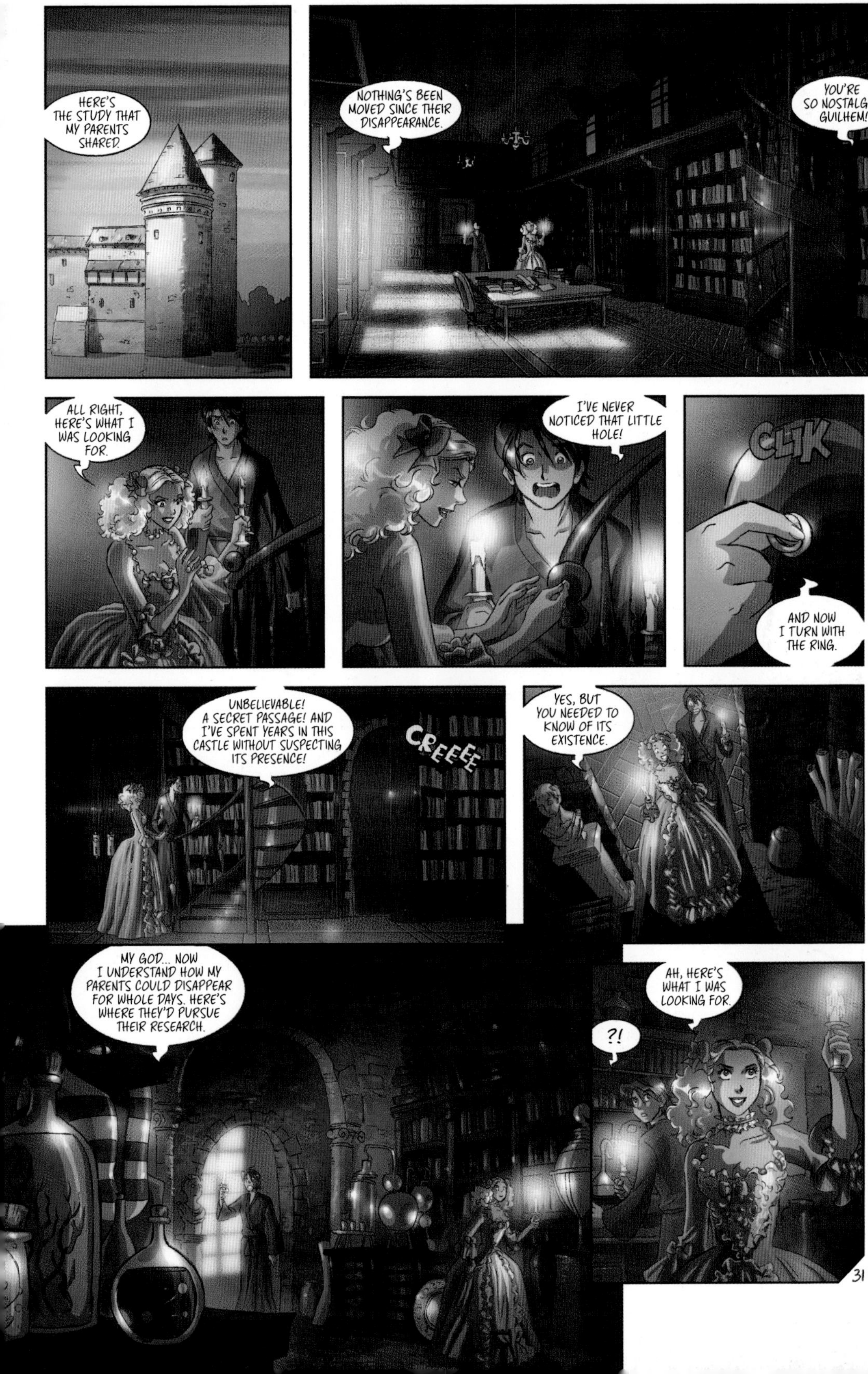
HERE'S THE STUDY THAT MY PARENTS SHARED.
NOTHING'S BEEN MOVED SINCE THEIR DISAPPEARANCE.
YOU'RE SO NOSTALGIC, GUILHEM!
ALL RIGHT, HERE'S WHAT I WAS LOOKING FOR.
I'VE NEVER NOTICED THAT LITTLE HOLE!
CLIK
AND NOW I TURN WITH THE RING.
UNBELIEVABLE! A SECRET PASSAGE! AND I'VE SPENT YEARS IN THIS CASTLE WITHOUT SUSPECTING ITS PRESENCE!
CREEEE
YES, BUT YOU NEEDED TO KNOW OF ITS EXISTENCE.
MY GOD... NOW I UNDERSTAND HOW MY PARENTS COULD DISAPPEAR FOR WHOLE DAYS. HERE'S WHERE THEY'D PURSUE THEIR RESEARCH.
AH, HERE'S WHAT I WAS LOOKING FOR.
?!

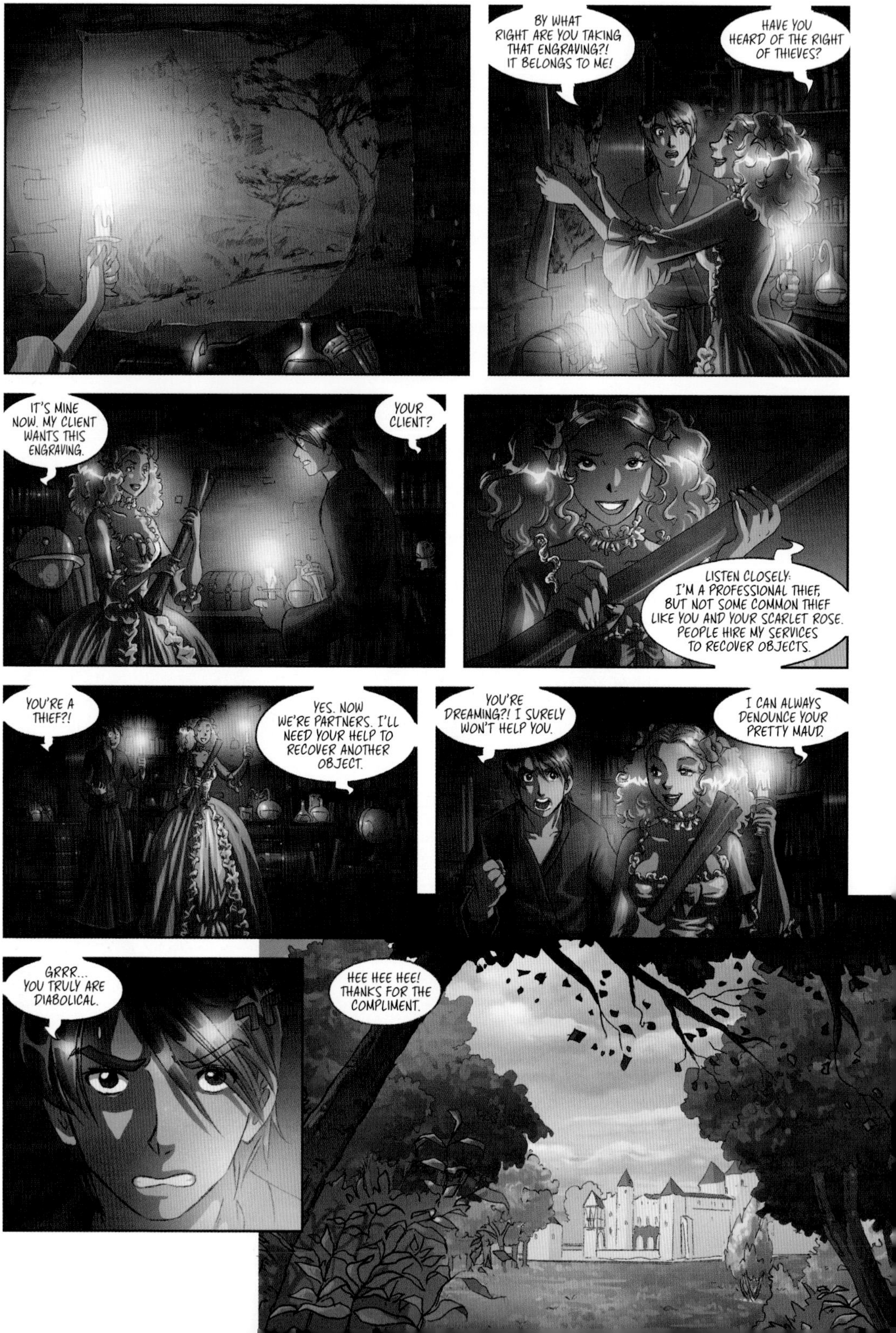
BY WHAT RIGHT ARE YOU TAKING THAT ENGRAVING?! IT BELONGS TO ME!
HAVE YOU HEARD OF THE RIGHT OF THIEVES?
IT'S MINE NOW. MY CLIENT WANTS THIS ENGRAVING.
YOUR CLIENT?
LISTEN CLOSELY: I'M A PROFESSIONAL THIEF, BUT NOT SOME COMMON THIEF LIKE YOU AND YOUR SCARLET ROSE. PEOPLE HIRE MY SERVICES TO RECOVER OBJECTS.
YOU'RE A THIEF?!
YES. NOW WE'RE PARTNERS. I'LL NEED YOUR HELP TO RECOVER ANOTHER OBJECT.
YOU'RE DREAMING?! I SURELY WON'T HELP YOU.
I CAN ALWAYS DENOUNCE YOUR PRETTY MAUD.
GRRR... YOU TRULY ARE DIABOLICAL.
HEE HEE HEE! THANKS FOR THE COMPLIMENT.

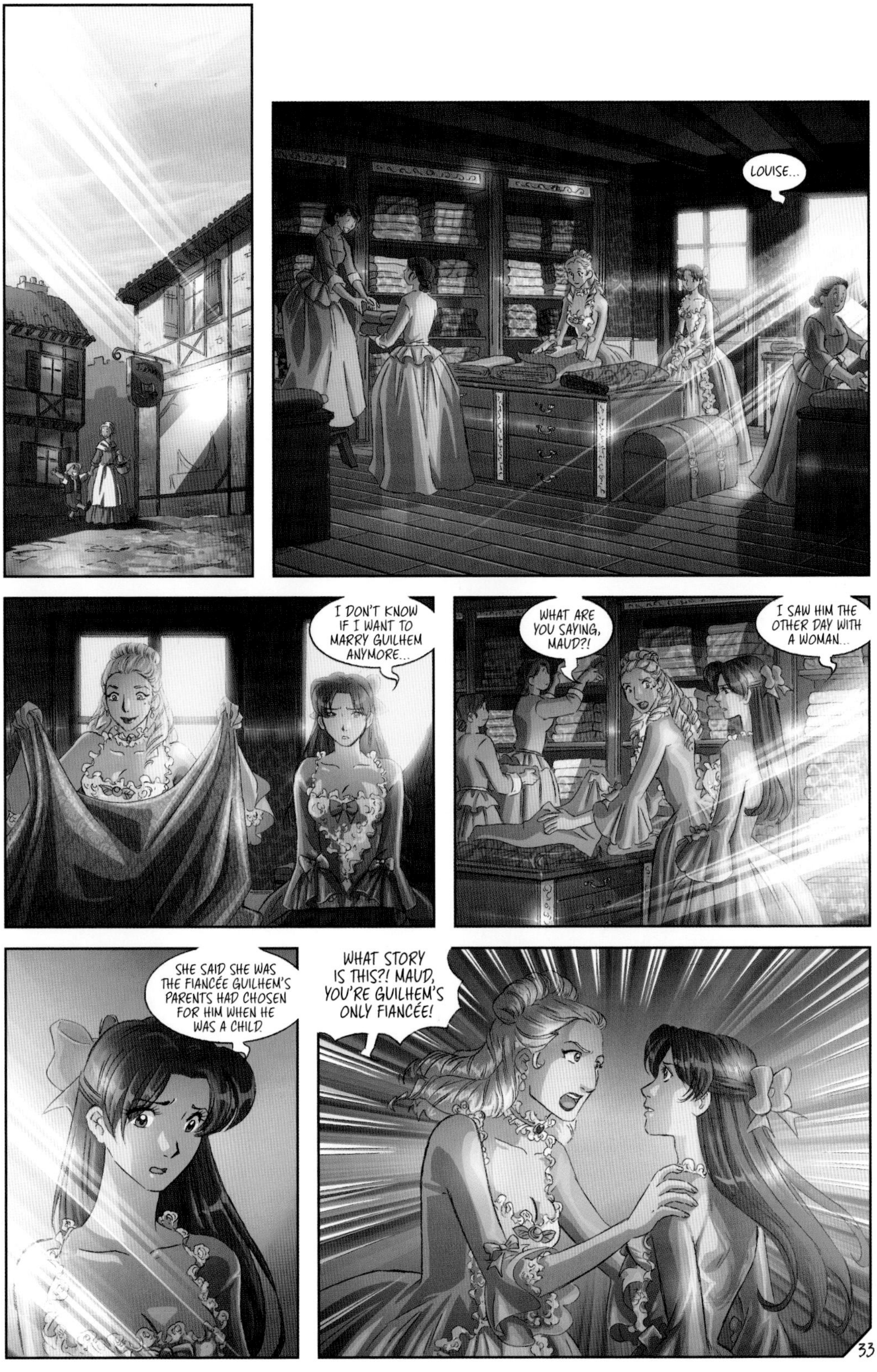
LOUISE...
I DON'T KNOW IF I WANT TO MARRY GUILHEM ANYMORE...
WHAT ARE YOU SAYING, MAUD?!
I SAW HIM THE OTHER DAY WITH A WOMAN...
SHE SAID SHE WAS THE FIANCÉE GUILHEM'S PARENTS HAD CHOSEN FOR HIM WHEN HE WAS A CHILD.
WHAT STORY IS THIS?! MAUD, YOU'RE GUILHEM'S ONLY FIANCÉE!
33

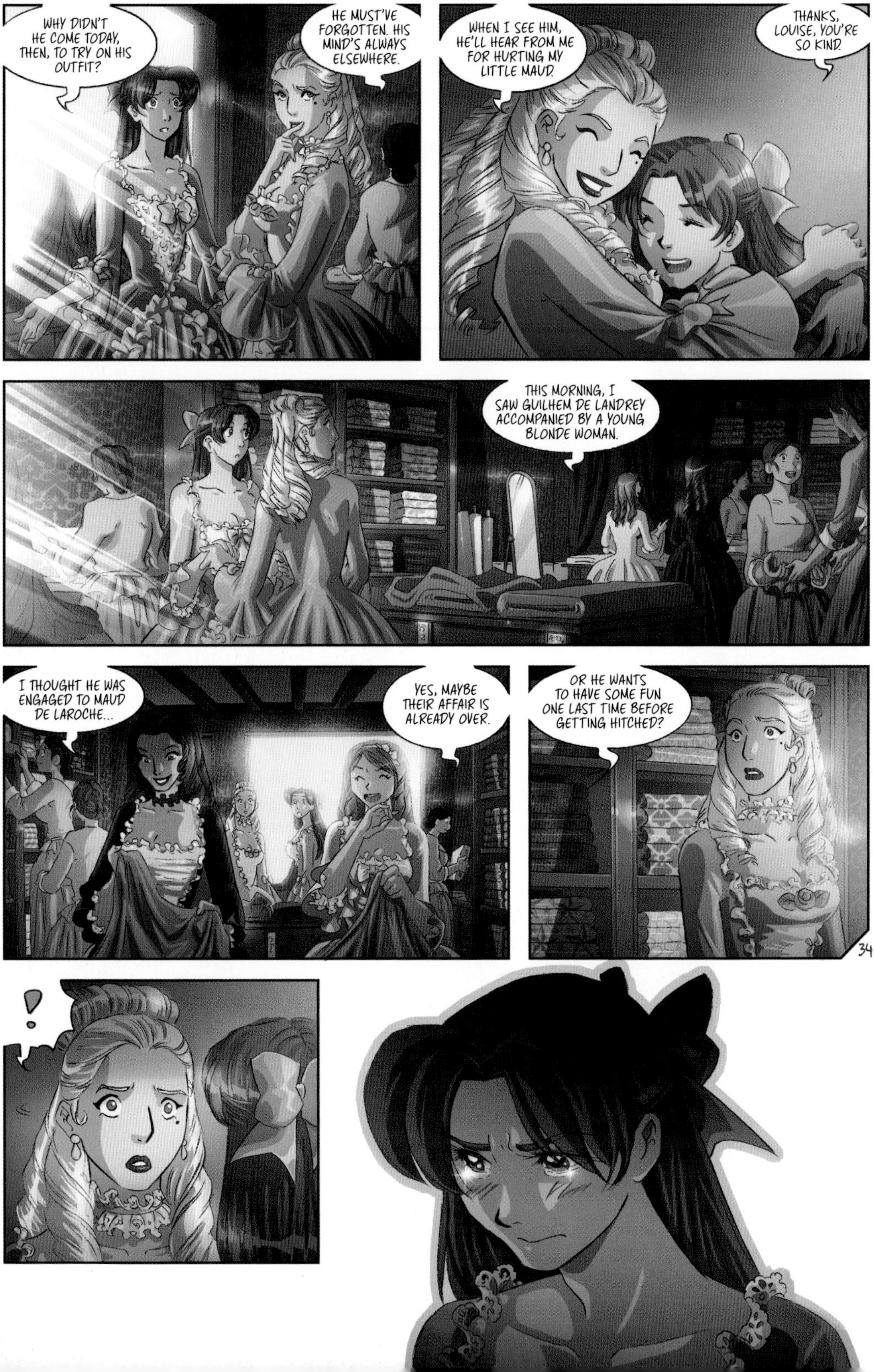
WHY DIDN'T HE COME TODAY, THEN, TO TRY ON HIS OUTFIT?
HE MUST'VE FORGOTTEN. HIS MIND'S ALWAYS ELSEWHERE.
WHEN I SEE HIM, HE'LL HEAR FROM ME FOR HURTING MY LITTLE MAUD.
THANKS, LOUISE, YOU'RE SO KIND.
THIS MORNING, I SAW GUILHEM DE LANDREY ACCOMPANIED BY A YOUNG BLONDE WOMAN.
I THOUGHT HE WAS ENGAGED TO MAUD DE LAROCHE...
YES, MAYBE THEIR AFFAIR IS ALREADY OVER.
OR HE WANTS TO HAVE SOME FUN ONE LAST TIME BEFORE GETTING HITCHED?
!

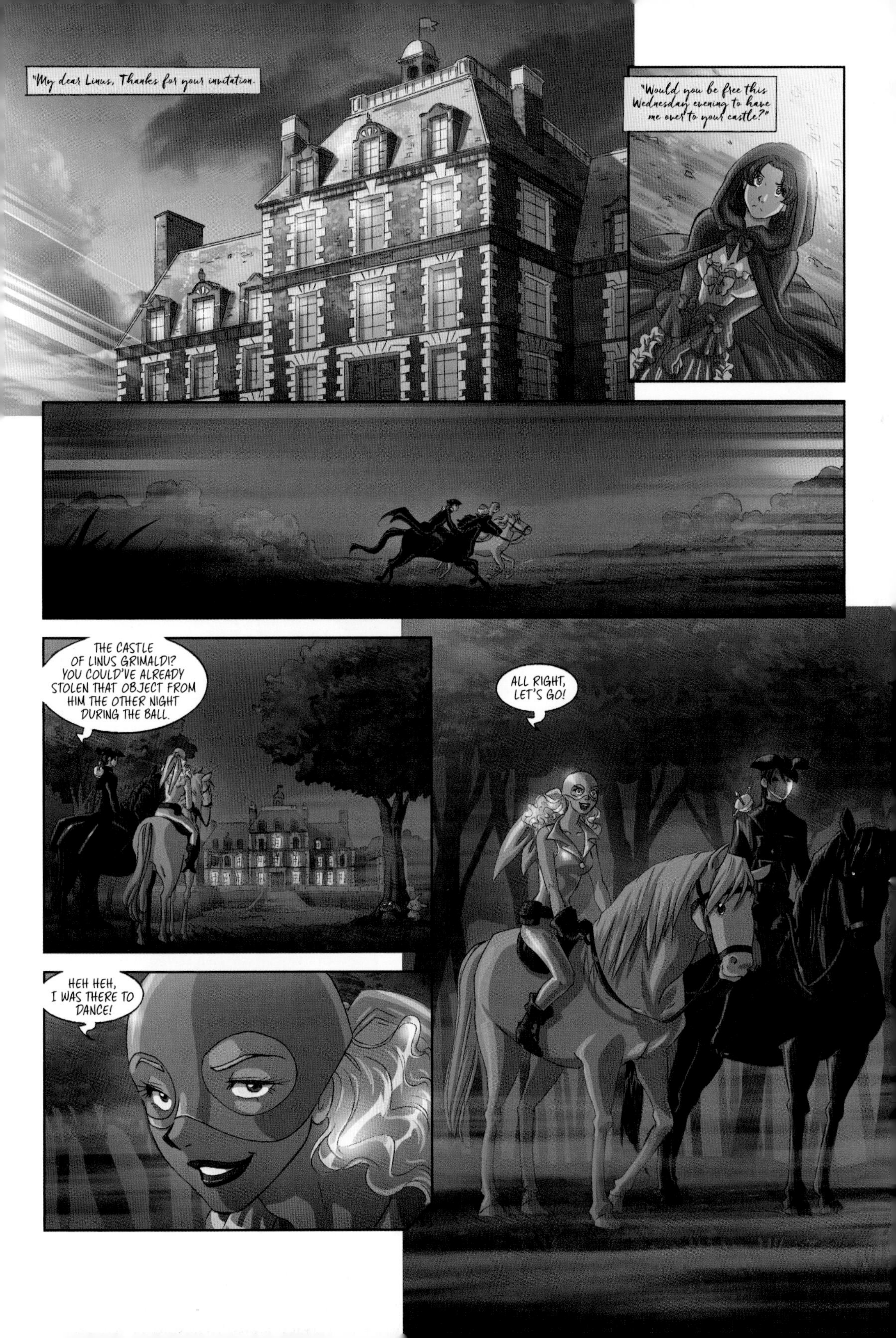
"My dear Linus, Thanks for your invitation.
"Would you be free this Wednesday evening to have me over to your castle?"
THE CASTLE OF LINUS GRIMALDI? YOU COULD'VE ALREADY STOLEN THAT OBJECT FROM HIM THE OTHER NIGHT DURING THE BALL.
HEH HEH, I WAS THERE TO DANCE!
ALL RIGHT, LET'S GO!

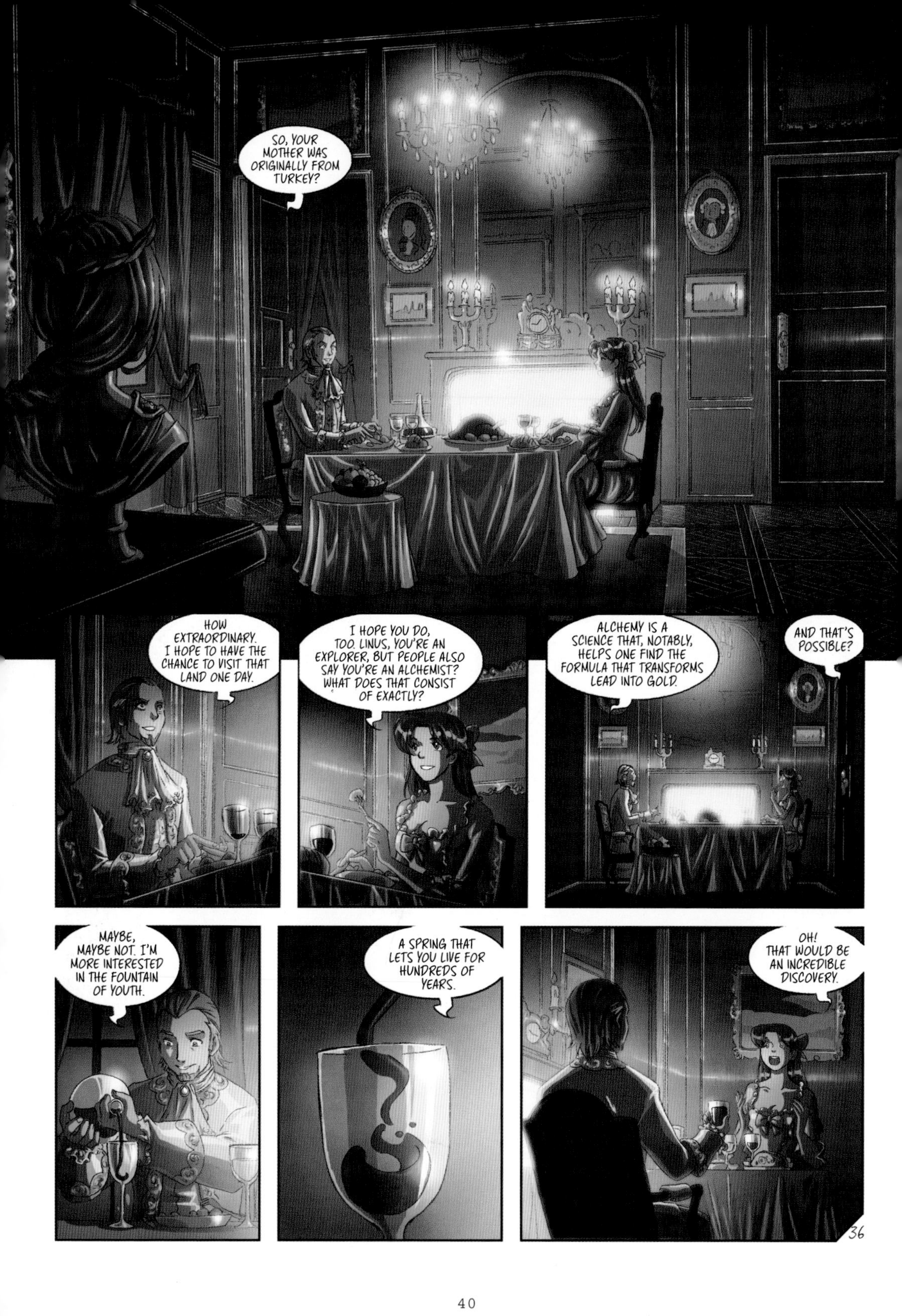
SO, YOUR MOTHER WAS ORIGINALLY FROM TURKEY?
HOW EXTRAORDINARY. I HOPE TO HAVE THE CHANCE TO VISIT THAT LAND ONE DAY.
I HOPE YOU DO, TOO. LINUS, YOU'RE AN EXPLORER, BUT PEOPLE ALSO SAY YOU'RE AN ALCHEMIST? WHAT DOES THAT CONSIST OF EXACTLY?
ALCHEMY IS A SCIENCE THAT, NOTABLY, HELPS ONE FIND THE FORMULA THAT TRANSFORMS LEAD INTO GOLD.
AND THAT'S POSSIBLE?
MAYBE, MAYBE NOT. I'M MORE INTERESTED IN THE FOUNTAIN OF YOUTH.
A SPRING THAT LETS YOU LIVE FOR HUNDREDS OF YEARS.
OH! THAT WOULD BE AN INCREDIBLE DISCOVERY.
36

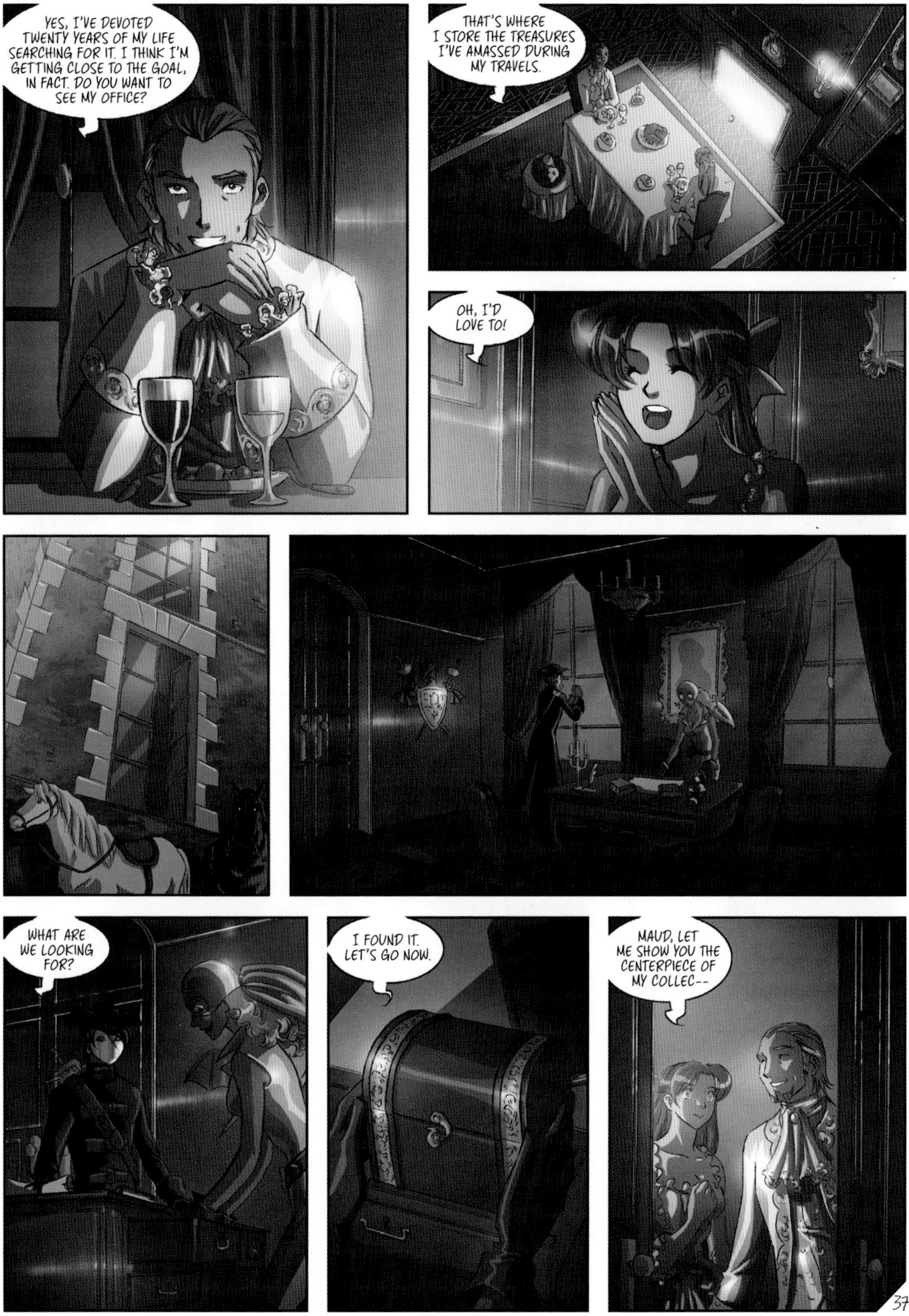
YES, I'VE DEVOTED TWENTY YEARS OF MY LIFE SEARCHING FOR IT. I THINK I'M GETTING CLOSE TO THE GOAL, IN FACT. DO YOU WANT TO SEE MY OFFICE?
THAT'S WHERE I STORE THE TREASURES I'VE AMASSED DURING MY TRAVELS.
OH, I'D LOVE TO!
WHAT ARE WE LOOKING FOR?
I FOUND IT. LET'S GO NOW.
MAUD, LET ME SHOW YOU THE CENTERPIECE OF MY COLLEC--
37

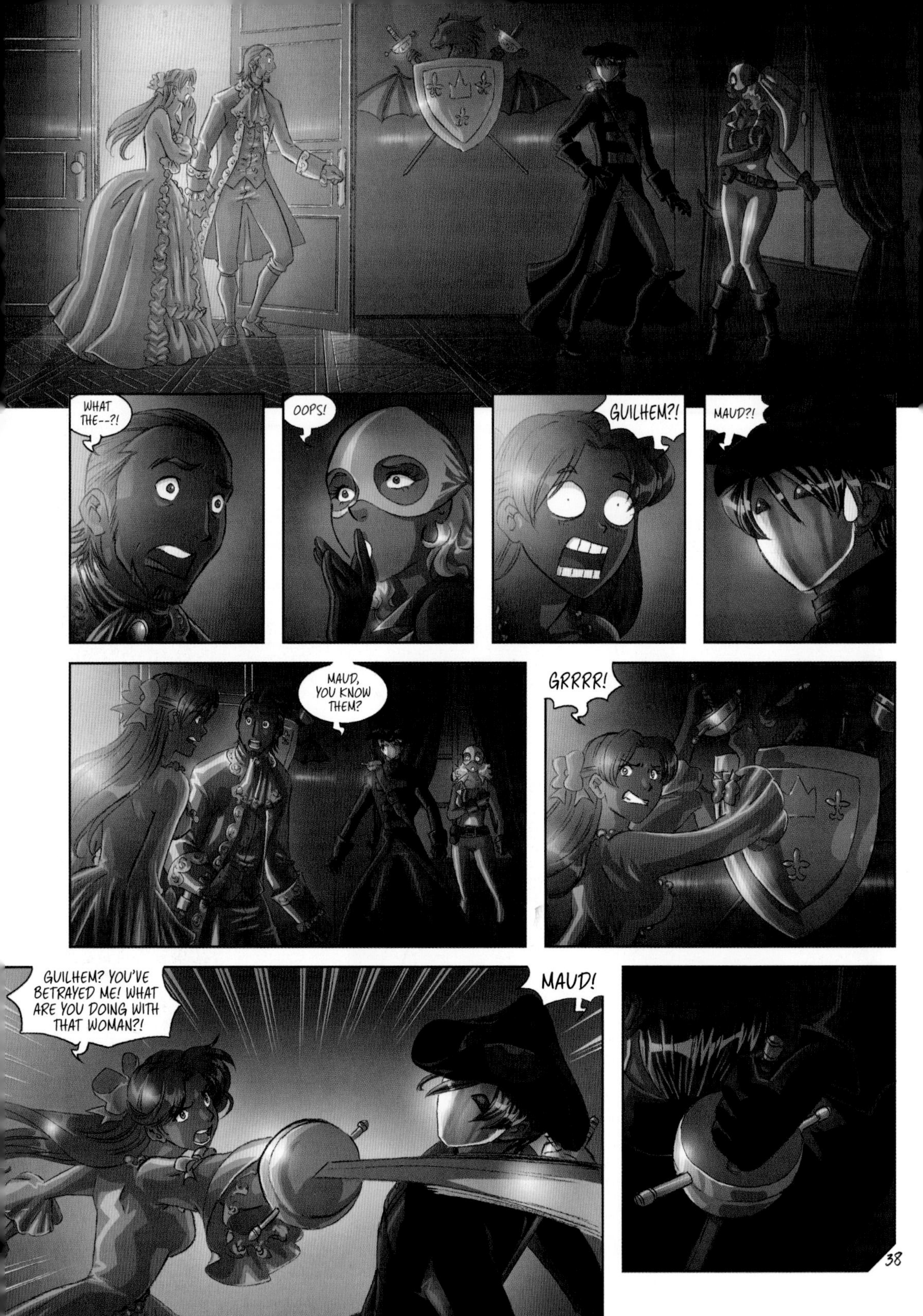
WHAT THE--?!
OOPS!
GUILHEM?!
MAUD?!
MAUD, YOU KNOW THEM?
GRRRR!
GUILHEM? YOU'VE BETRAYED ME! WHAT ARE YOU DOING WITH THAT WOMAN?!
MAUD!

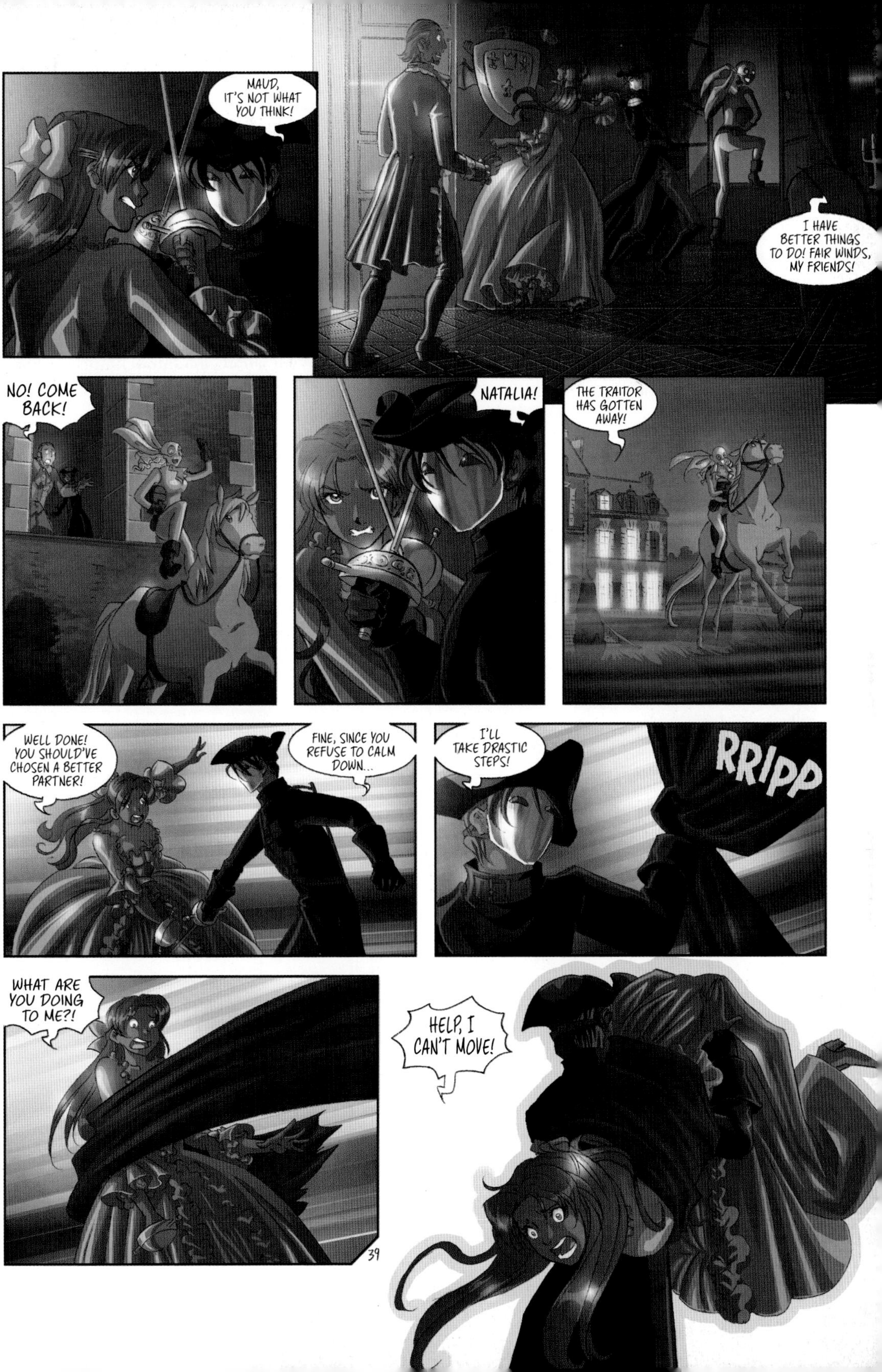
MAUD, IT'S NOT WHAT YOU THINK!
I HAVE BETTER THINGS TO DO! FAIR WINDS, MY FRIENDS!
NO! COME BACK!
NATALIA!
THE TRAITOR HAS GOTTEN AWAY!
WELL DONE! YOU SHOULD'VE CHOSEN A BETTER PARTNER!
FINE, SINCE YOU REFUSE TO CALM DOWN...
I'LL TAKE DRASTIC STEPS!
RRIPP
WHAT ARE YOU DOING TO ME?!
HELP, I CAN'T MOVE!

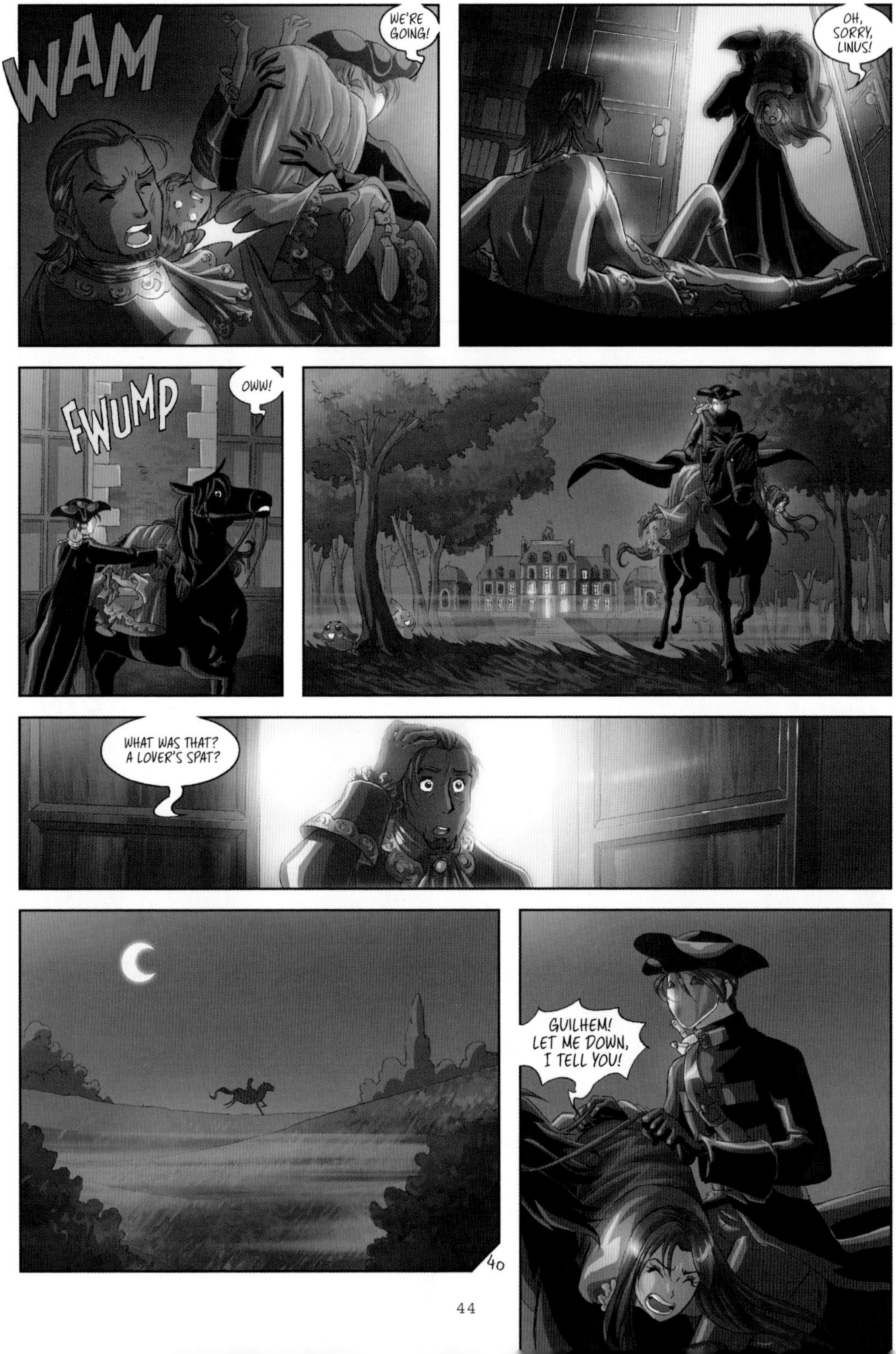
WAM
WE'RE GOING!
OH, SORRY, LINUS!
FWUMP
OWW!
WHAT WAS THAT? A LOVER'S SPAT?
GUILHEM! LET ME DOWN, I TELL YOU!
40

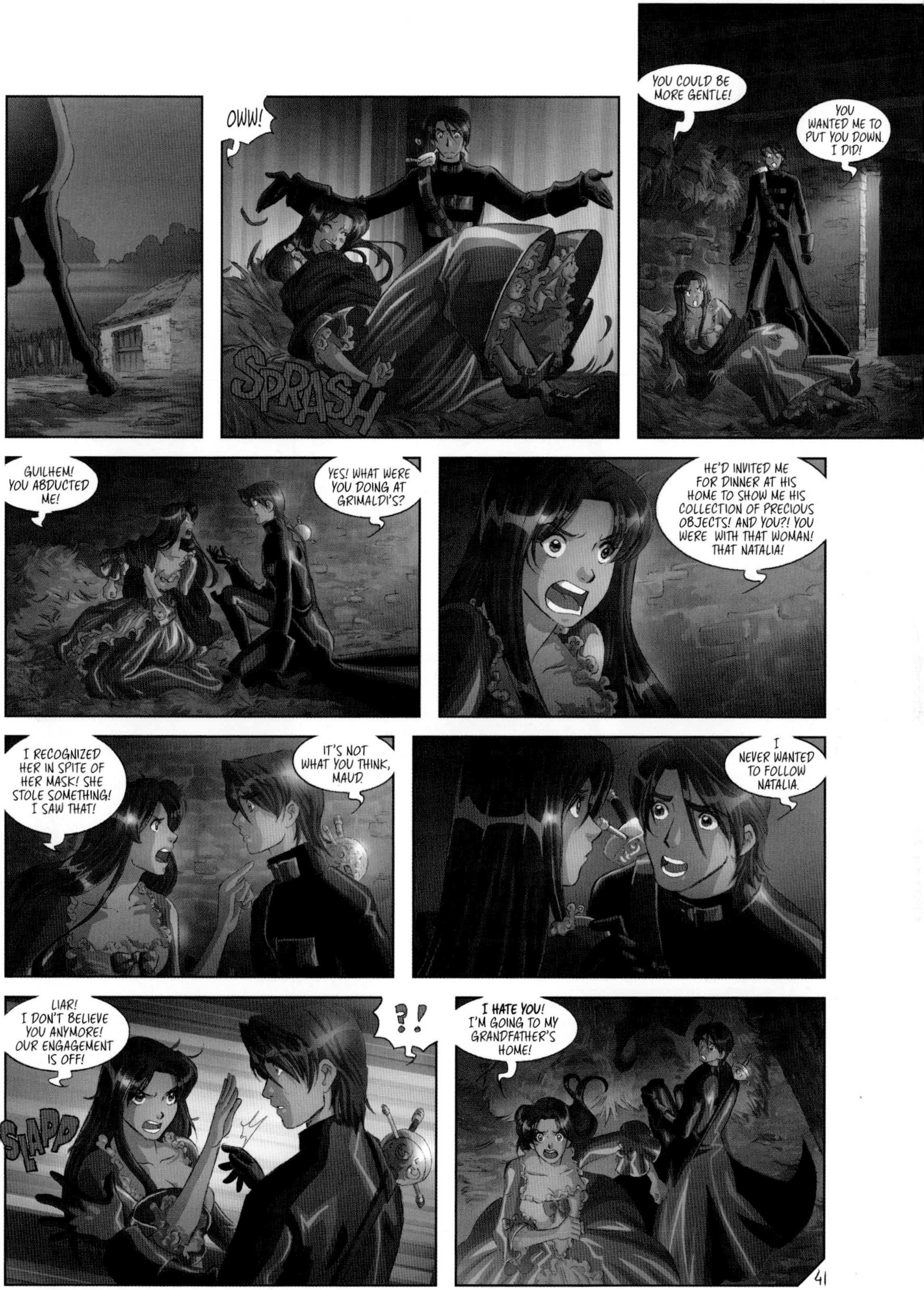
OWW!
SPRASH
YOU COULD BE MORE GENTLE!
YOU WANTED ME TO PUT YOU DOWN. I DID!
GUILHEM! YOU ABDUCTED ME!
YES! WHAT WERE YOU DOING AT GRIMALDI'S?
HE'D INVITED ME FOR DINNER AT HIS HOME TO SHOW ME HIS COLLECTION OF PRECIOUS OBJECTS! AND YOU?! YOU WERE WITH THAT WOMAN! THAT NATALIA!
I RECOGNIZED HER IN SPITE OF HER MASK! SHE STOLE SOMETHING! I SAW THAT!
IT'S NOT WHAT YOU THINK, MAUD.
I NEVER WANTED TO FOLLOW NATALIA.
LIAR! I DON'T BELIEVE YOU ANYMORE! OUR ENGAGEMENT IS OFF!
?!
SLAPP
I HATE YOU! I'M GOING TO MY GRANDFATHER'S HOME!
41

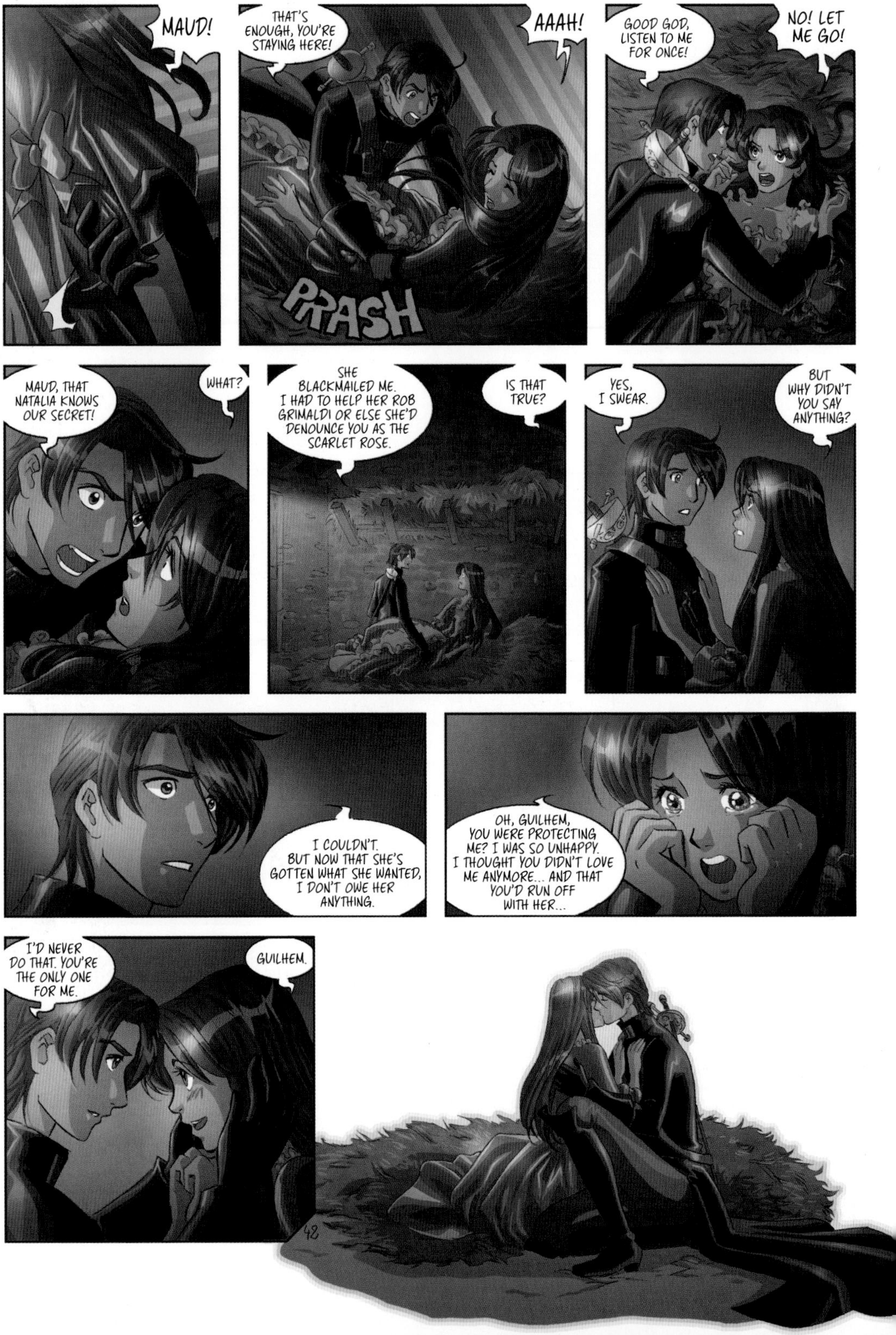
MAUD!
THAT'S ENOUGH, YOU'RE STAYING HERE!
AAAH!
PRASH
GOOD GOD, LISTEN TO ME FOR ONCE!
NO! LET ME GO!
MAUD, THAT NATALIA KNOWS OUR SECRET!
WHAT?
SHE BLACKMAILED ME. I HAD TO HELP HER ROB GRIMALDI OR ELSE SHE'D DENOUNCE YOU AS THE SCARLET ROSE.
IS THAT TRUE?
YES, I SWEAR.
BUT WHY DIDN'T YOU SAY ANYTHING?
I COULDN'T. BUT NOW THAT SHE'S GOTTEN WHAT SHE WANTED, I DON'T OWE HER ANYTHING.
OH, GUILHEM, YOU WERE PROTECTING ME? I WAS SO UNHAPPY. I THOUGHT YOU DIDN'T LOVE ME ANYMORE... AND THAT YOU'D RUN OFF WITH HER...
I'D NEVER DO THAT. YOU'RE THE ONLY ONE FOR ME.
GUILHEM.

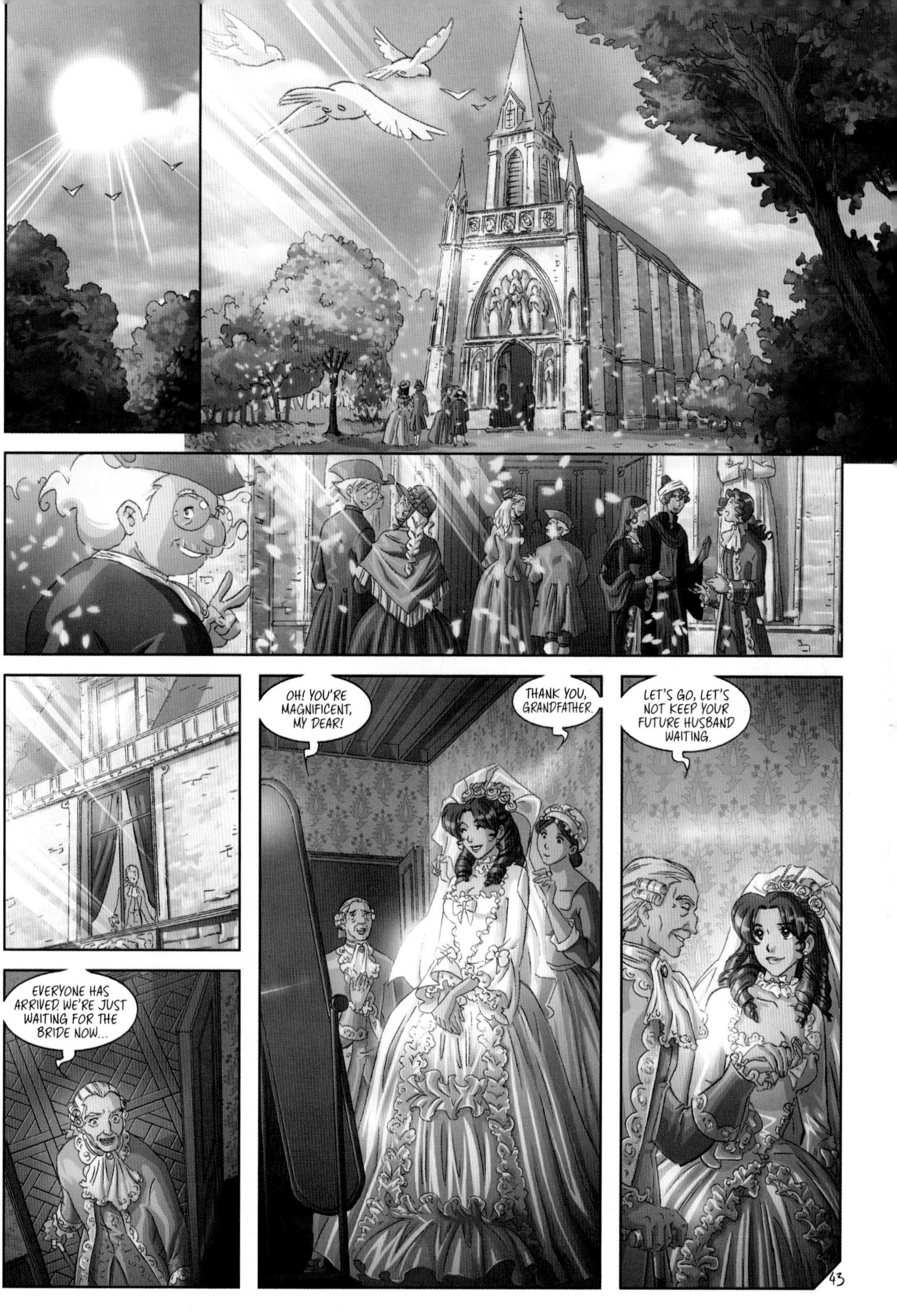
EVERYONE HAS ARRIVED. WE'RE JUST WAITING FOR THE BRIDE NOW...
OH! YOU'RE MAGNIFICENT, MY DEAR!
THANK YOU, GRANDFATHER.
LET'S GO, LET'S NOT KEEP YOUR FUTURE HUSBAND WAITING.
43

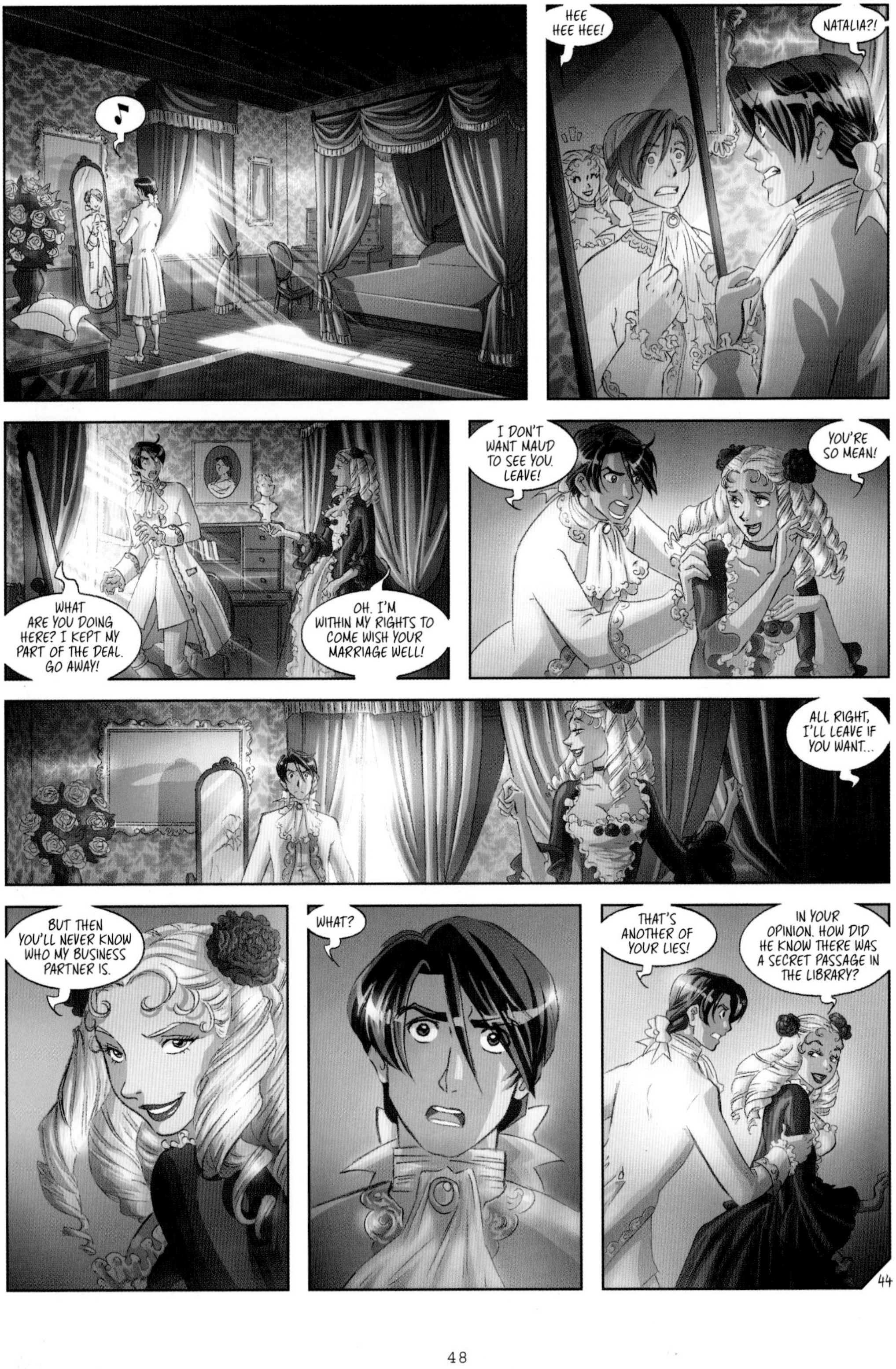
♪
HEE HEE HEE!
NATALIA?!
WHAT ARE YOU DOING HERE? I KEPT MY PART OF THE DEAL. GO AWAY!
OH. I'M WITHIN MY RIGHTS TO COME WISH YOUR MARRIAGE WELL!
I DON'T WANT MAUD TO SEE YOU. LEAVE!
YOU'RE SO MEAN!
ALL RIGHT, I'LL LEAVE IF YOU WANT...
BUT THEN YOU'LL NEVER KNOW WHO MY BUSINESS PARTNER IS.
WHAT?
THAT'S ANOTHER OF YOUR LIES!
IN YOUR OPINION. HOW DID HE KNOW THERE WAS A SECRET PASSAGE IN THE LIBRARY?
44

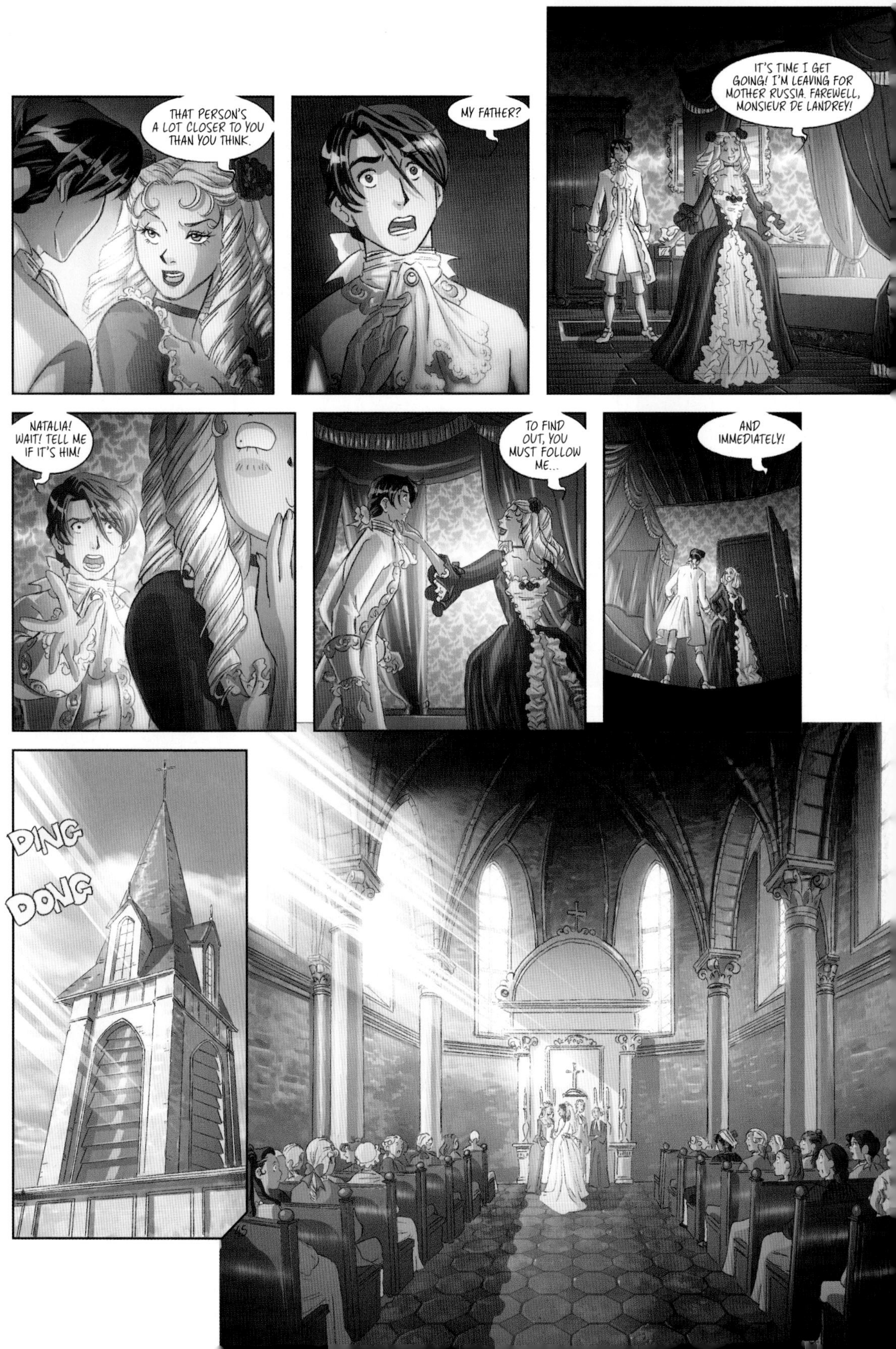
THAT PERSON'S A LOT CLOSER TO YOU THAN YOU THINK.
MY FATHER?
IT'S TIME I GET GOING! I'M LEAVING FOR MOTHER RUSSIA. FAREWELL, MONSIEUR DE LANDREY!
NATALIA! WAIT! TELL ME IF IT'S HIM!
TO FIND OUT, YOU MUST FOLLOW ME...
AND IMMEDIATELY!
DING
DONG

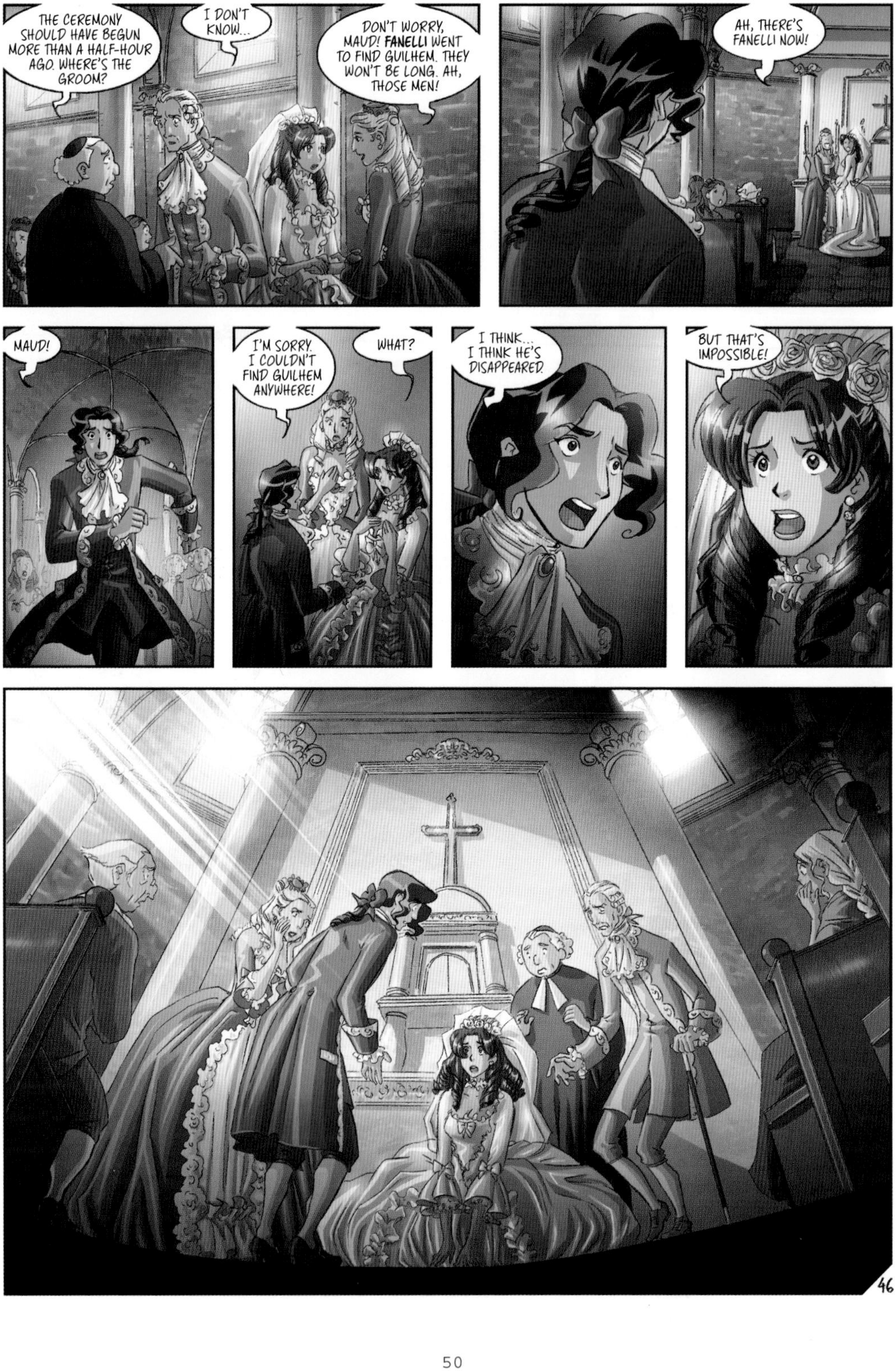
THE CEREMONY SHOULD HAVE BEGUN MORE THAN A HALF-HOUR AGO. WHERE'S THE GROOM?
I DON'T KNOW...
DON'T WORRY, MAUD! FANELLI WENT TO FIND GUILHEM. THEY WON'T BE LONG. AH, THOSE MEN!
AH, THERE'S FANELLI NOW!
MAUD!
I'M SORRY. I COULDN'T FIND GUILHEM ANYWHERE!
WHAT?
I THINK... I THINK HE'S DISAPPEARED.
BUT THAT'S IMPOSSIBLE!
46

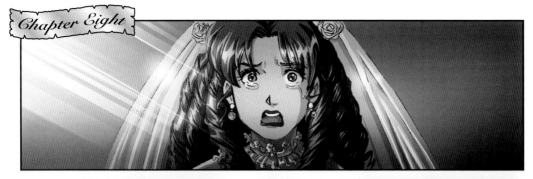

Chapter Eight

GUILHEM IS GONE...

IT'S IMPOSSIBLE...

MAUD, I'M SORRY...

MY POOR MAUD... WHAT'S GOTTEN INTO GUILHEM'S HEAD?

THE NERVE! JILTING MY GRANDDAUGHTER ON HER WEDDING DAY! AND I TRUSTED HIM!

WHAT A SCOUNDREL! I'LL FIND HIM AND MAKE HIM PAY DEARLY...

NO! GRAND-FATHER...

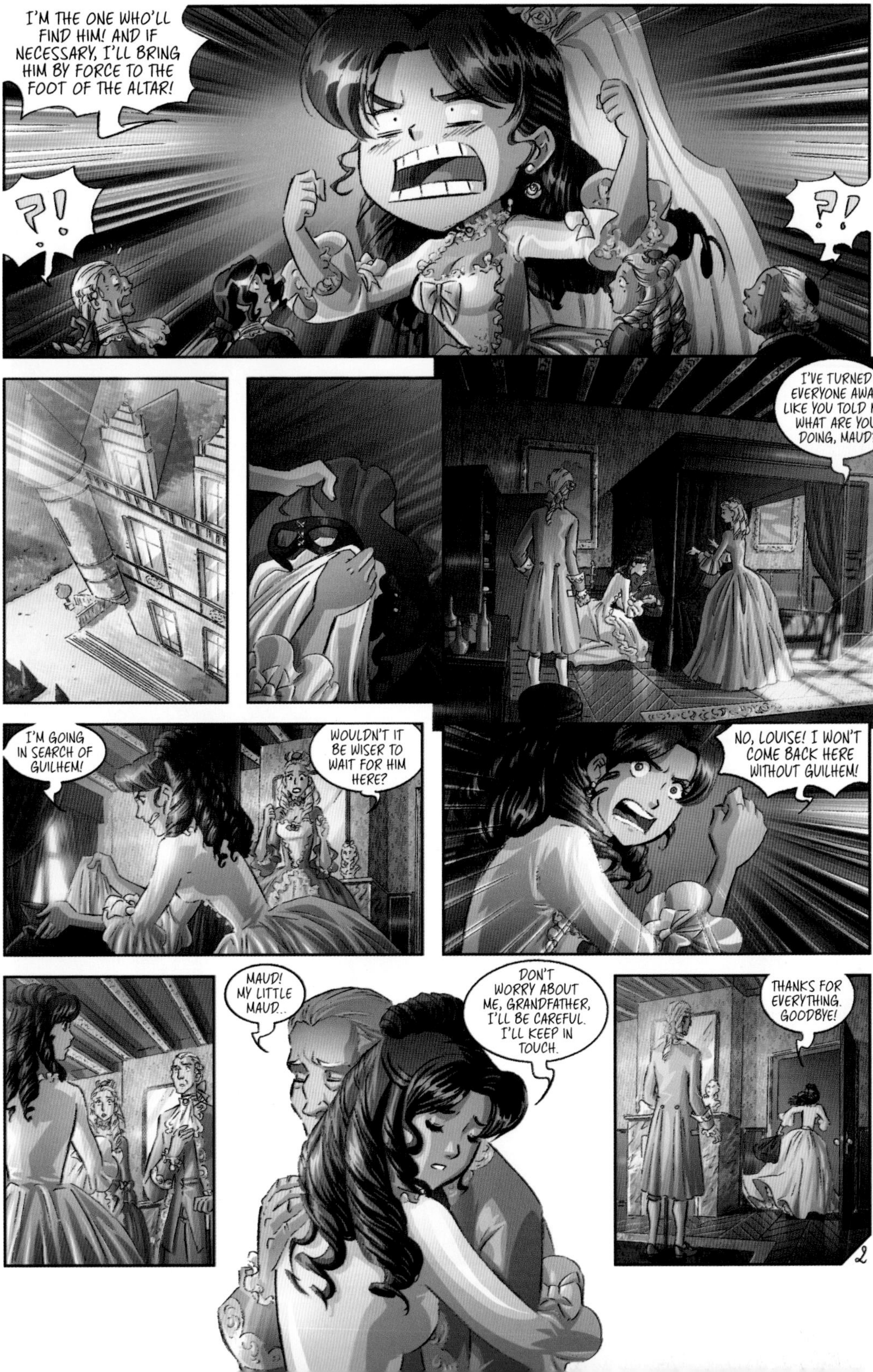
I'M THE ONE WHO'LL FIND HIM! AND IF NECESSARY, I'LL BRING HIM BY FORCE TO THE FOOT OF THE ALTAR!
?!
?!
I'VE TURNED EVERYONE AWAY, LIKE YOU TOLD ME. WHAT ARE YOU DOING, MAUD?
I'M GOING IN SEARCH OF GUILHEM!
WOULDN'T IT BE WISER TO WAIT FOR HIM HERE?
NO, LOUISE! I WON'T COME BACK HERE WITHOUT GUILHEM!
MAUD! MY LITTLE MAUD...
DON'T WORRY ABOUT ME, GRANDFATHER, I'LL BE CAREFUL. I'LL KEEP IN TOUCH.
THANKS FOR EVERYTHING. GOODBYE!

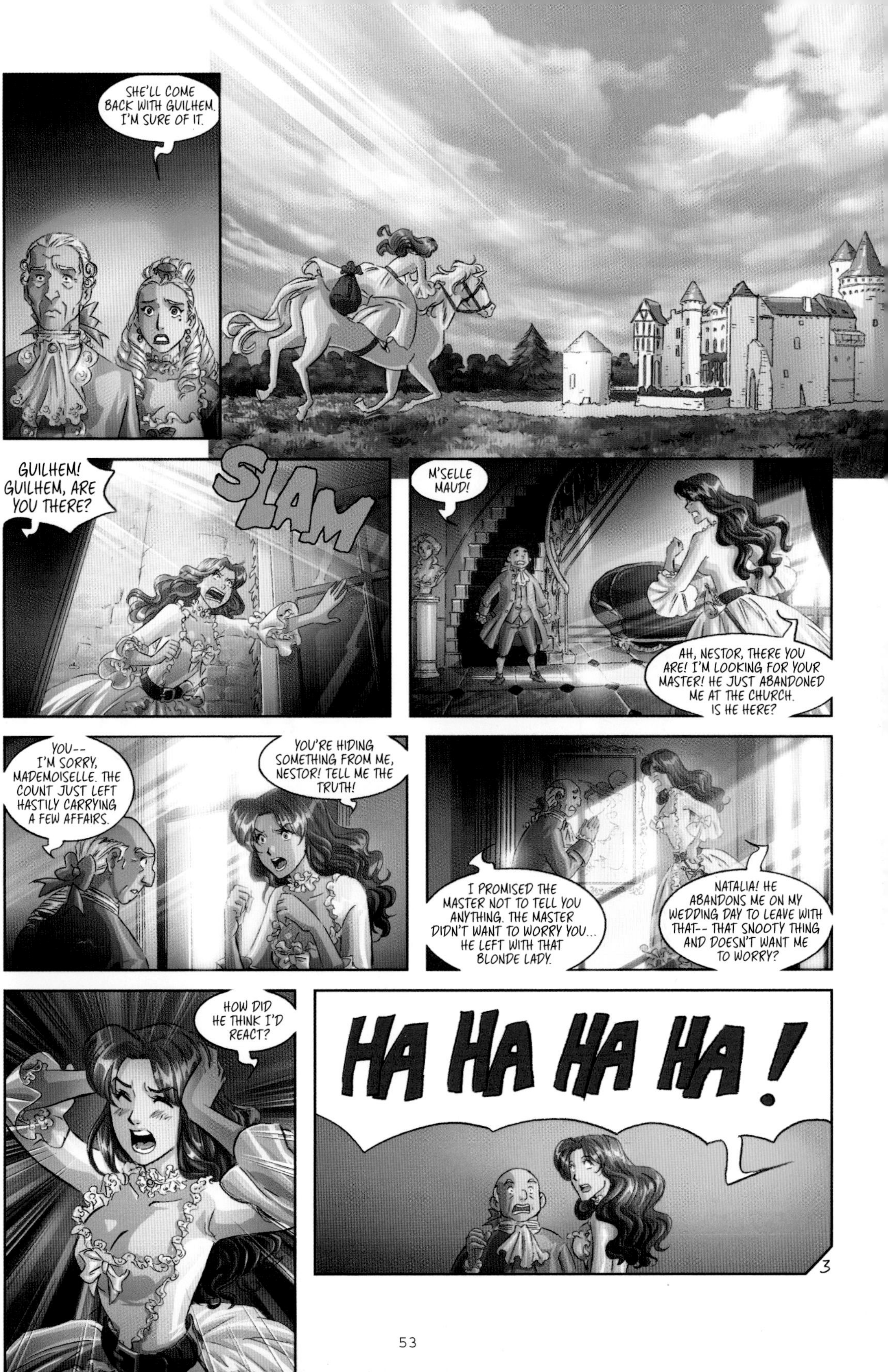
SHE'LL COME BACK WITH GUILHEM. I'M SURE OF IT.
GUILHEM! GUILHEM, ARE YOU THERE?
SLAM
M'SELLE MAUD!
AH, NESTOR, THERE YOU ARE! I'M LOOKING FOR YOUR MASTER! HE JUST ABANDONED ME AT THE CHURCH. IS HE HERE?
YOU-- I'M SORRY, MADEMOISELLE. THE COUNT JUST LEFT HASTILY CARRYING A FEW AFFAIRS.
YOU'RE HIDING SOMETHING FROM ME, NESTOR! TELL ME THE TRUTH!
I PROMISED THE MASTER NOT TO TELL YOU ANYTHING. THE MASTER DIDN'T WANT TO WORRY YOU... HE LEFT WITH THAT BLONDE LADY.
NATALIA! HE ABANDONS ME ON MY WEDDING DAY TO LEAVE WITH THAT-- THAT SNOOTY THING AND DOESN'T WANT ME TO WORRY?
HOW DID HE THINK I'D REACT?
HA HA HA HA!
3

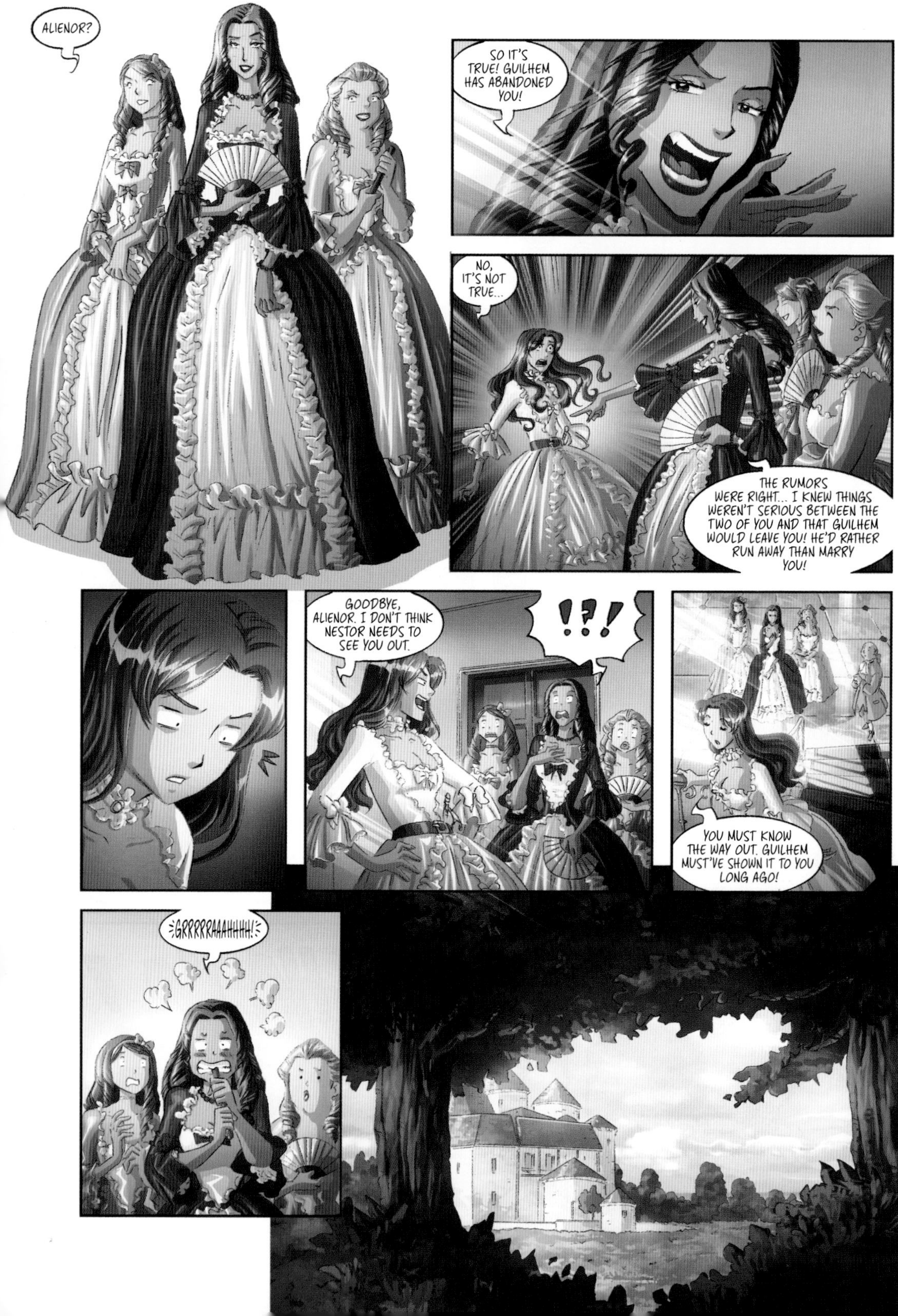
ALIENOR?
SO IT'S TRUE! GUILHEM HAS ABANDONED YOU!
NO, IT'S NOT TRUE...
THE RUMORS WERE RIGHT... I KNEW THINGS WEREN'T SERIOUS BETWEEN THE TWO OF YOU AND THAT GUILHEM WOULD LEAVE YOU! HE'D RATHER RUN AWAY THAN MARRY YOU!
GOODBYE, ALIENOR. I DON'T THINK NESTOR NEEDS TO SEE YOU OUT.
!?!
YOU MUST KNOW THE WAY OUT. GUILHEM MUST'VE SHOWN IT TO YOU LONG AGO!
GRRRRRAAAHHHH!

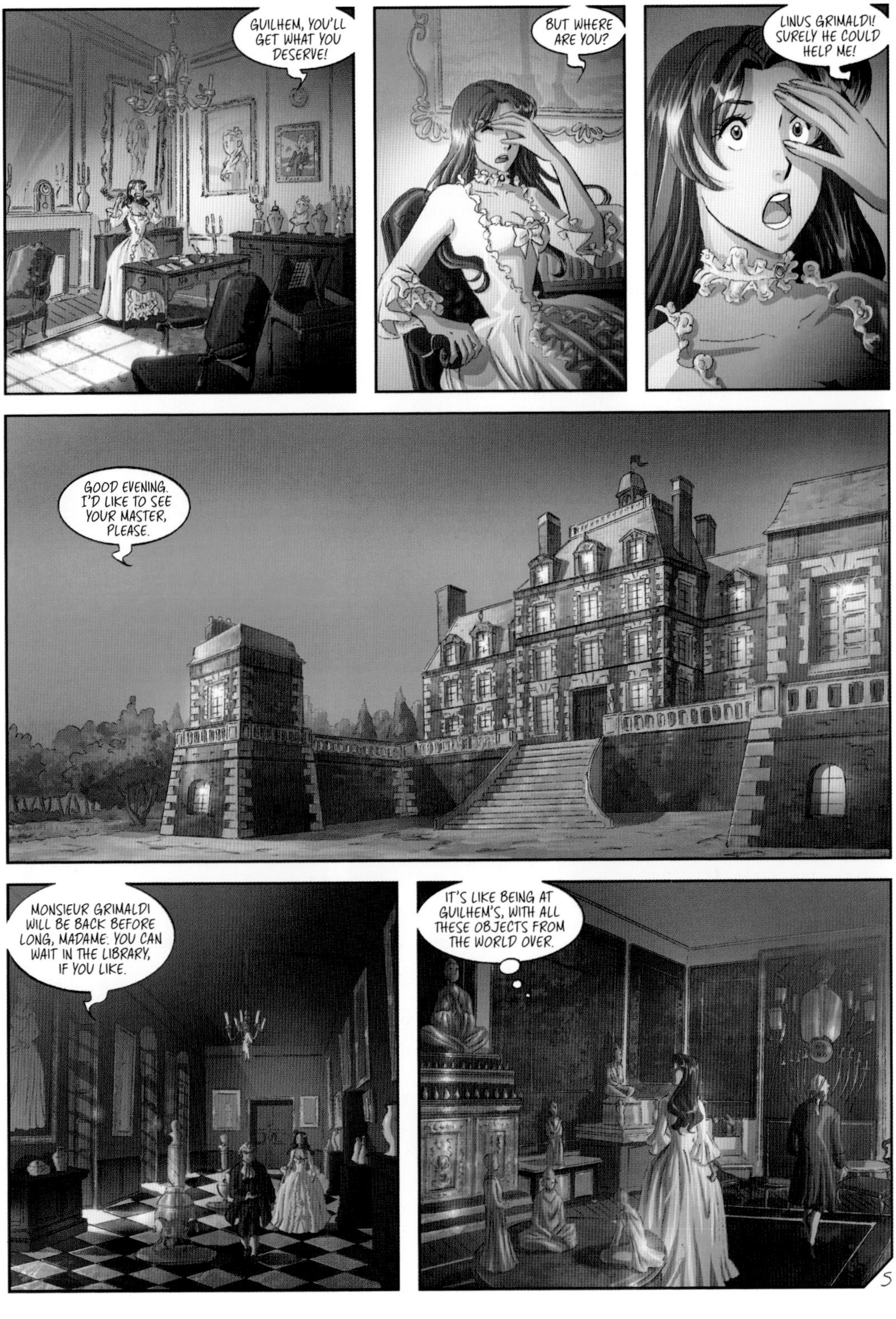
GUILHEM, YOU'LL GET WHAT YOU DESERVE!
BUT WHERE ARE YOU?
LINUS GRIMALDI! SURELY HE COULD HELP ME!
GOOD EVENING. I'D LIKE TO SEE YOUR MASTER, PLEASE.
MONSIEUR GRIMALDI WILL BE BACK BEFORE LONG, MADAME. YOU CAN WAIT IN THE LIBRARY, IF YOU LIKE.
IT'S LIKE BEING AT GUILHEM'S, WITH ALL THESE OBJECTS FROM THE WORLD OVER.
5

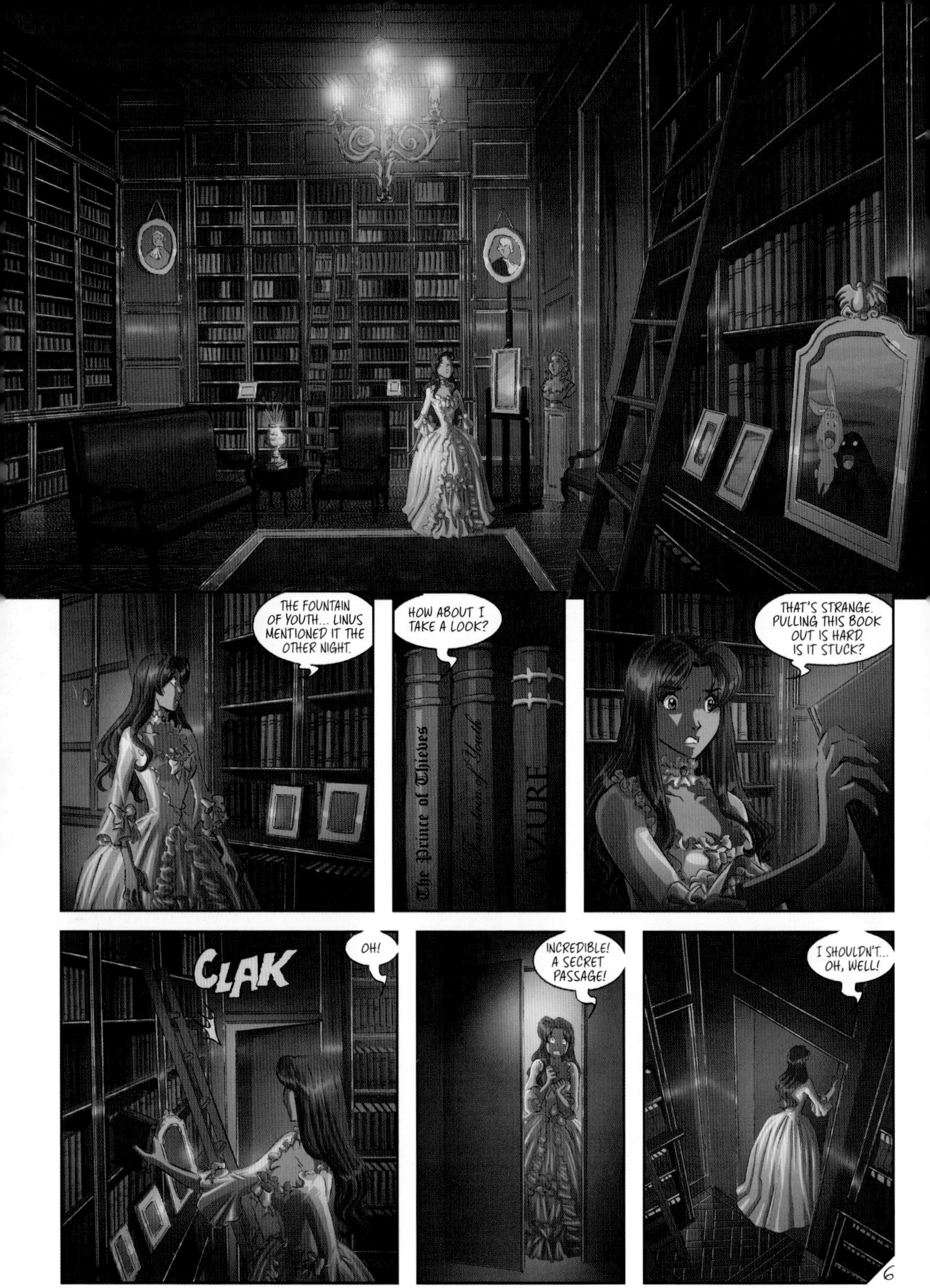
THE FOUNTAIN OF YOUTH... LINUS MENTIONED IT THE OTHER NIGHT.
HOW ABOUT I TAKE A LOOK?
The Prince of Thieves
AZURE
THAT'S STRANGE. PULLING THIS BOOK OUT IS HARD. IS IT STUCK?
CLAK
OH!
INCREDIBLE! A SECRET PASSAGE!
I SHOULDN'T... OH, WELL!

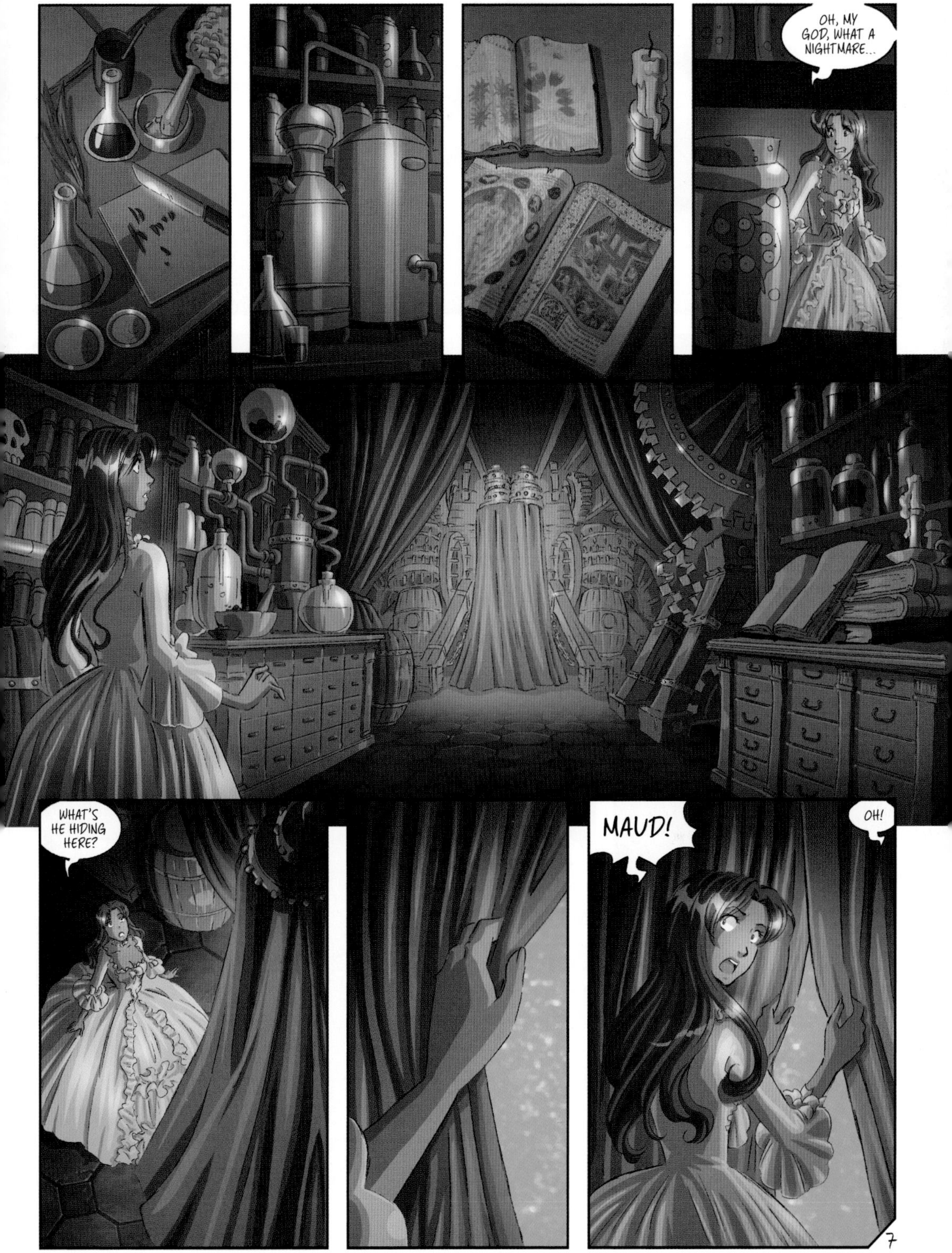
OH, MY GOD, WHAT A NIGHTMARE...
WHAT'S HE HIDING HERE?
MAUD!
OH!
7

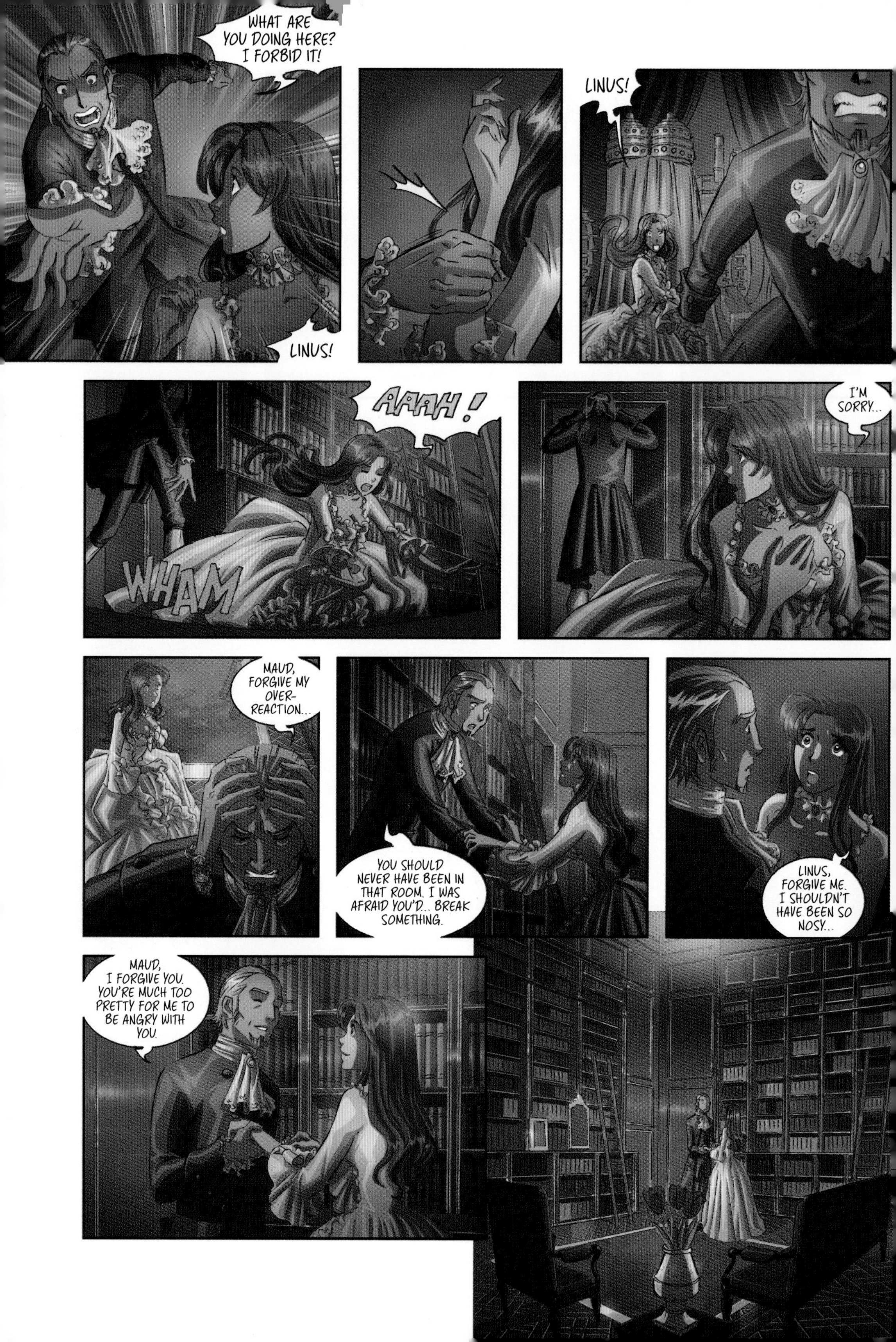
WHAT ARE YOU DOING HERE? I FORBID IT!
LINUS!
LINUS!
AAAH!
WHAM
I'M SORRY...
MAUD, FORGIVE MY OVER-REACTION...
YOU SHOULD NEVER HAVE BEEN IN THAT ROOM. I WAS AFRAID YOU'D... BREAK SOMETHING.
LINUS, FORGIVE ME. I SHOULDN'T HAVE BEEN SO NOSY...
MAUD, I FORGIVE YOU. YOU'RE MUCH TOO PRETTY FOR ME TO BE ANGRY WITH YOU.

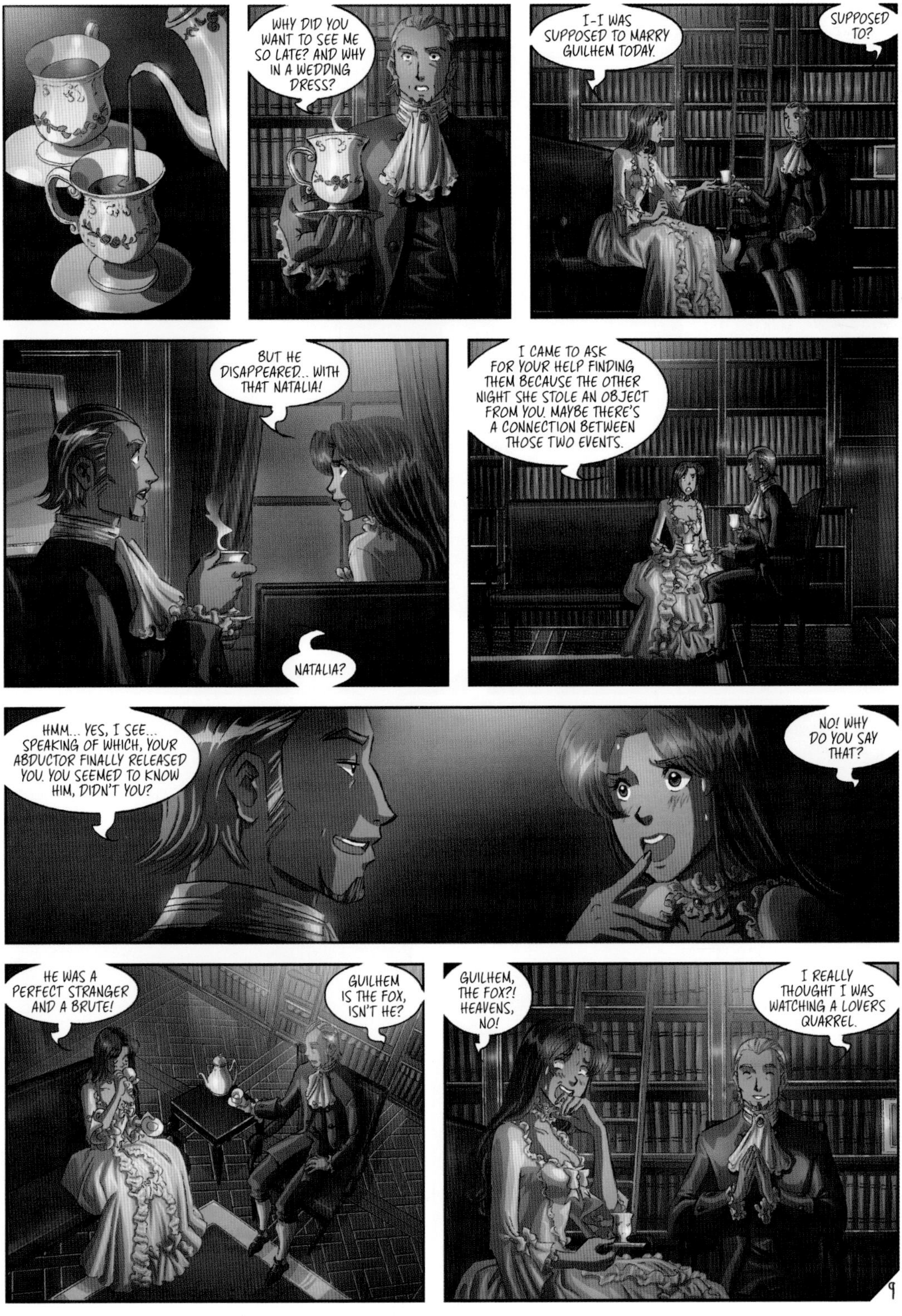
WHY DID YOU WANT TO SEE ME SO LATE? AND WHY IN A WEDDING DRESS?
I-I WAS SUPPOSED TO MARRY GUILHEM TODAY.
SUPPOSED TO?
BUT HE DISAPPEARED... WITH THAT NATALIA!
NATALIA?
I CAME TO ASK FOR YOUR HELP FINDING THEM BECAUSE THE OTHER NIGHT SHE STOLE AN OBJECT FROM YOU. MAYBE THERE'S A CONNECTION BETWEEN THOSE TWO EVENTS.
HMM... YES, I SEE... SPEAKING OF WHICH, YOUR ABDUCTOR FINALLY RELEASED YOU. YOU SEEMED TO KNOW HIM, DIDN'T YOU?
NO! WHY DO YOU SAY THAT?
HE WAS A PERFECT STRANGER AND A BRUTE!
GUILHEM IS THE FOX, ISN'T HE?
GUILHEM, THE FOX?! HEAVENS, NO!
I REALLY THOUGHT I WAS WATCHING A LOVERS QUARREL.
9

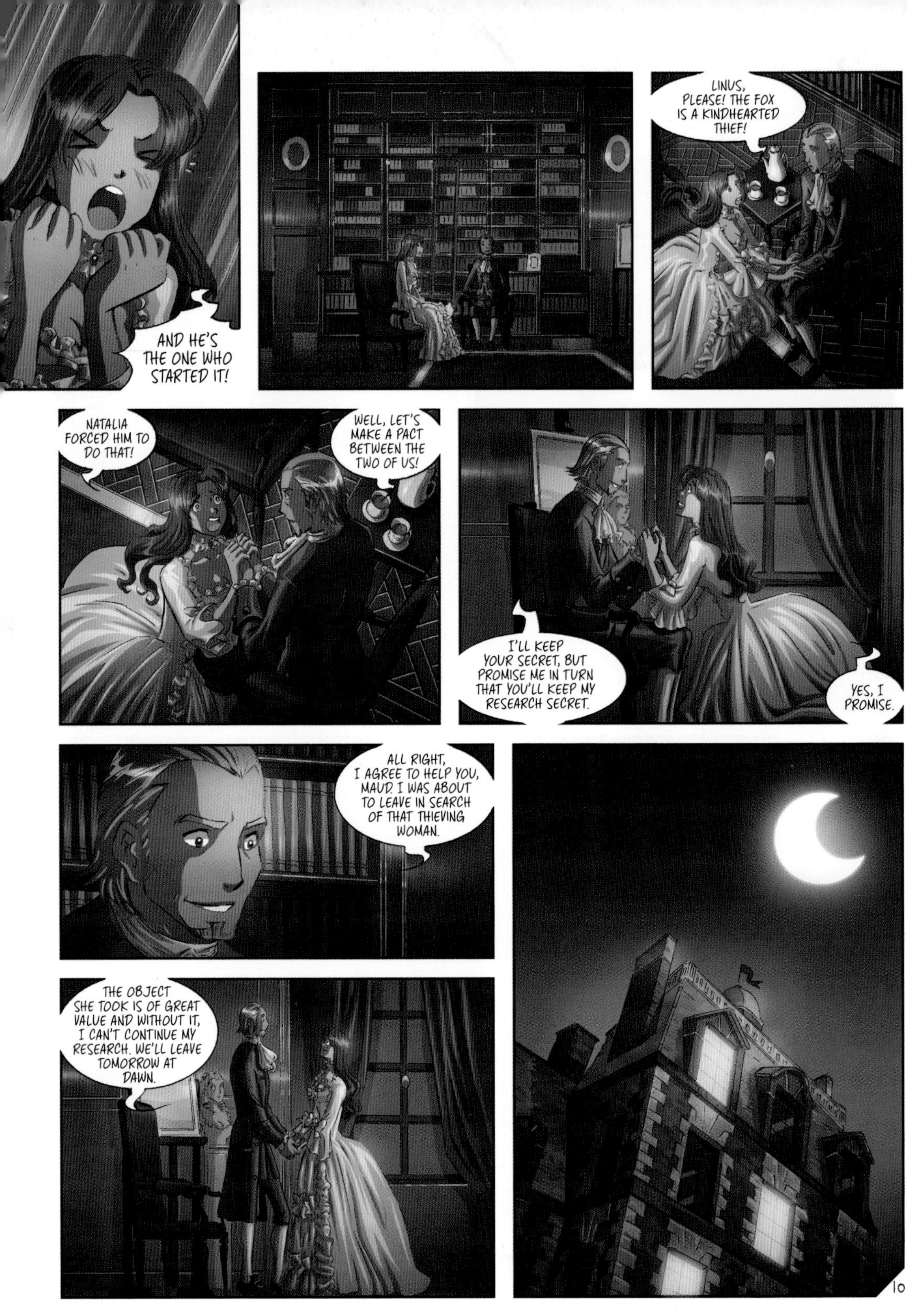
AND HE'S THE ONE WHO STARTED IT!
LINUS, PLEASE! THE FOX IS A KINDHEARTED THIEF!
NATALIA FORCED HIM TO DO THAT!
WELL, LET'S MAKE A PACT BETWEEN THE TWO OF US!
I'LL KEEP YOUR SECRET, BUT PROMISE ME IN TURN THAT YOU'LL KEEP MY RESEARCH SECRET.
YES, I PROMISE.
ALL RIGHT, I AGREE TO HELP YOU, MAUD. I WAS ABOUT TO LEAVE IN SEARCH OF THAT THIEVING WOMAN.
THE OBJECT SHE TOOK IS OF GREAT VALUE AND WITHOUT IT, I CAN'T CONTINUE MY RESEARCH. WE'LL LEAVE TOMORROW AT DAWN.
10

HOW MUCH OF MY TIME ARE YOU GOING TO WASTE? I WANT TO SEE MY FATHER!

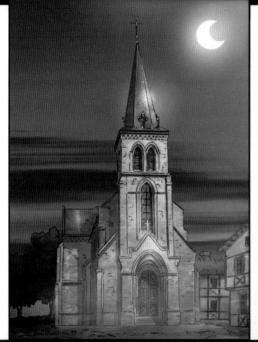

MY STOMACH'S COMPLETELY IN KNOTS FROM ABANDONING MAUD...

DON'T YOU FRET! IF SHE LOVES YOU, SHE'LL WAIT FOR YOU.

UNFORTUNATELY, PATIENCE ISN'T ONE OF HER VIRTUES. YOU KEPT ME FROM EXPLAINING TO HER THIS SUDDEN DEPARTURE. THE POOR THING, SHE'LL IMAGINE ALL SORTS OF THINGS.

WHAT'S DONE IS DONE!

YOU TRULY ARE-- ≥GRRR!≤ WHAT ARE WE DOING HERE?

WE'RE IN THE CAPUCHINS' CHURCH.

11

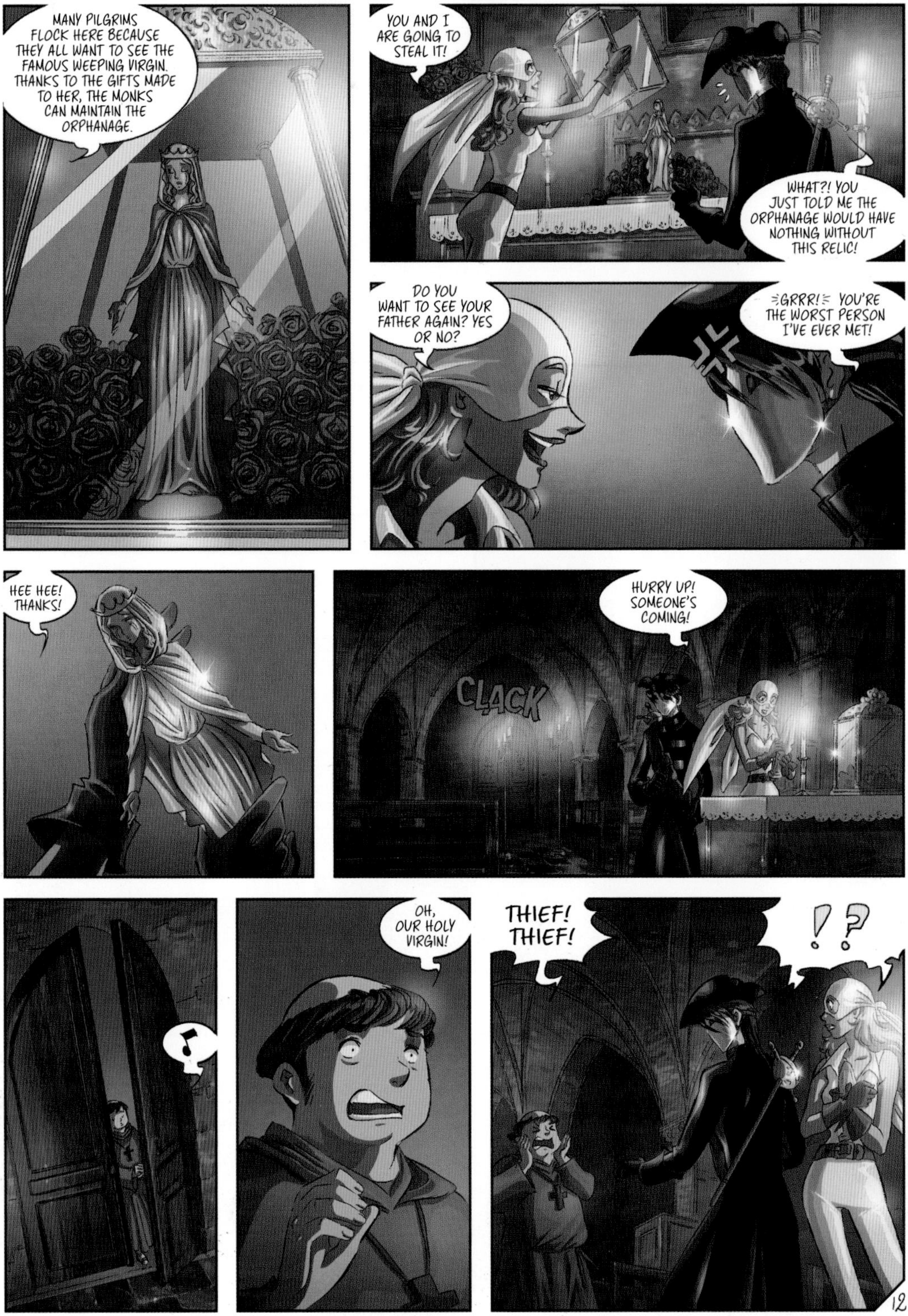
MANY PILGRIMS FLOCK HERE BECAUSE THEY ALL WANT TO SEE THE FAMOUS WEEPING VIRGIN. THANKS TO THE GIFTS MADE TO HER, THE MONKS CAN MAINTAIN THE ORPHANAGE.
YOU AND I ARE GOING TO STEAL IT!
WHAT?! YOU JUST TOLD ME THE ORPHANAGE WOULD HAVE NOTHING WITHOUT THIS RELIC!
DO YOU WANT TO SEE YOUR FATHER AGAIN? YES OR NO?
GRRR! YOU'RE THE WORST PERSON I'VE EVER MET!
HEE HEE! THANKS!
CLACK
HURRY UP! SOMEONE'S COMING!
OH, OUR HOLY VIRGIN!
THIEF! THIEF!
!?
12

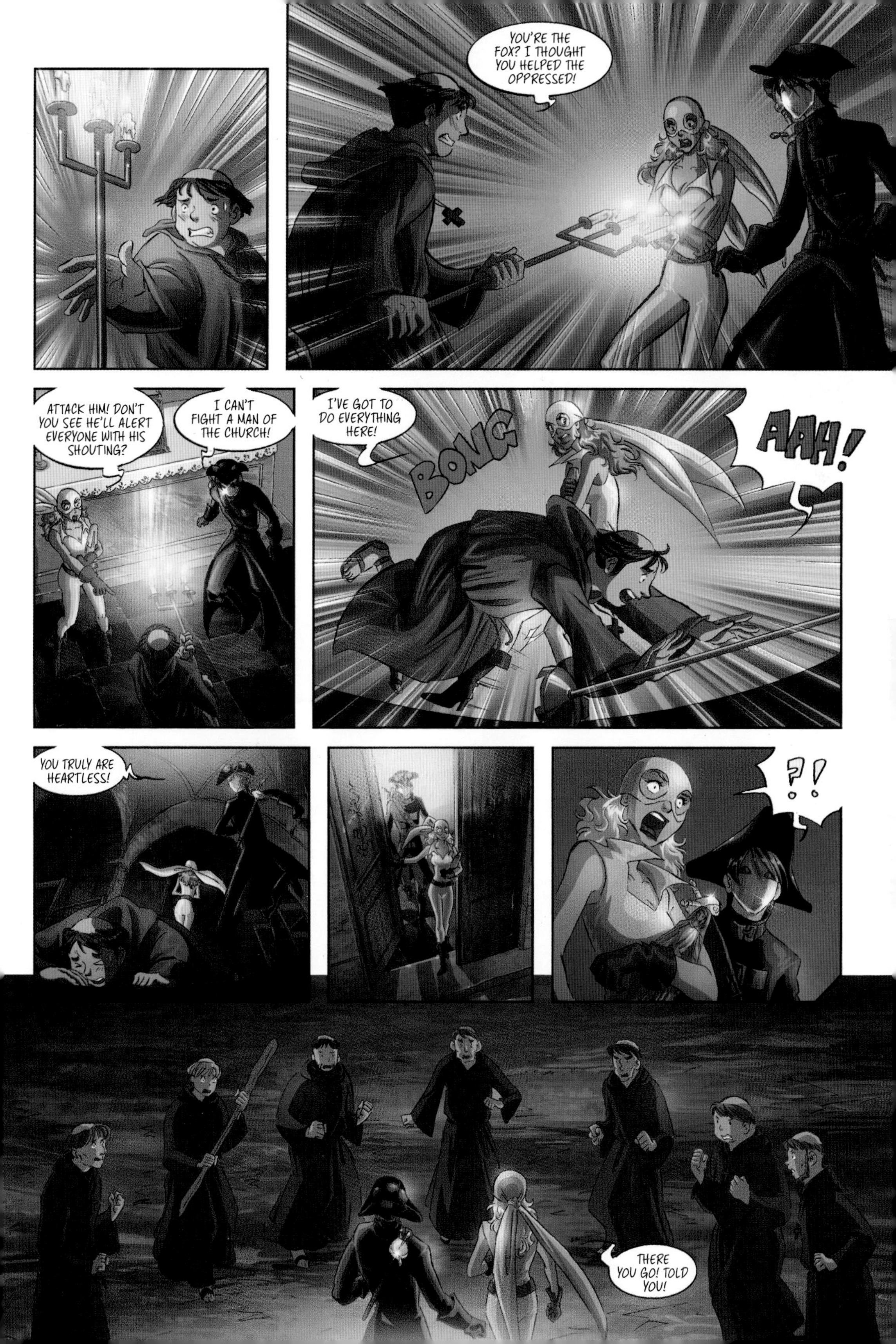
YOU'RE THE FOX? I THOUGHT YOU HELPED THE OPPRESSED!
ATTACK HIM! DON'T YOU SEE HE'LL ALERT EVERYONE WITH HIS SHOUTING?
I CAN'T FIGHT A MAN OF THE CHURCH!
I'VE GOT TO DO EVERYTHING HERE!
BONG
AAH!
YOU TRULY ARE HEARTLESS!
?!
THERE YOU GO! TOLD YOU!

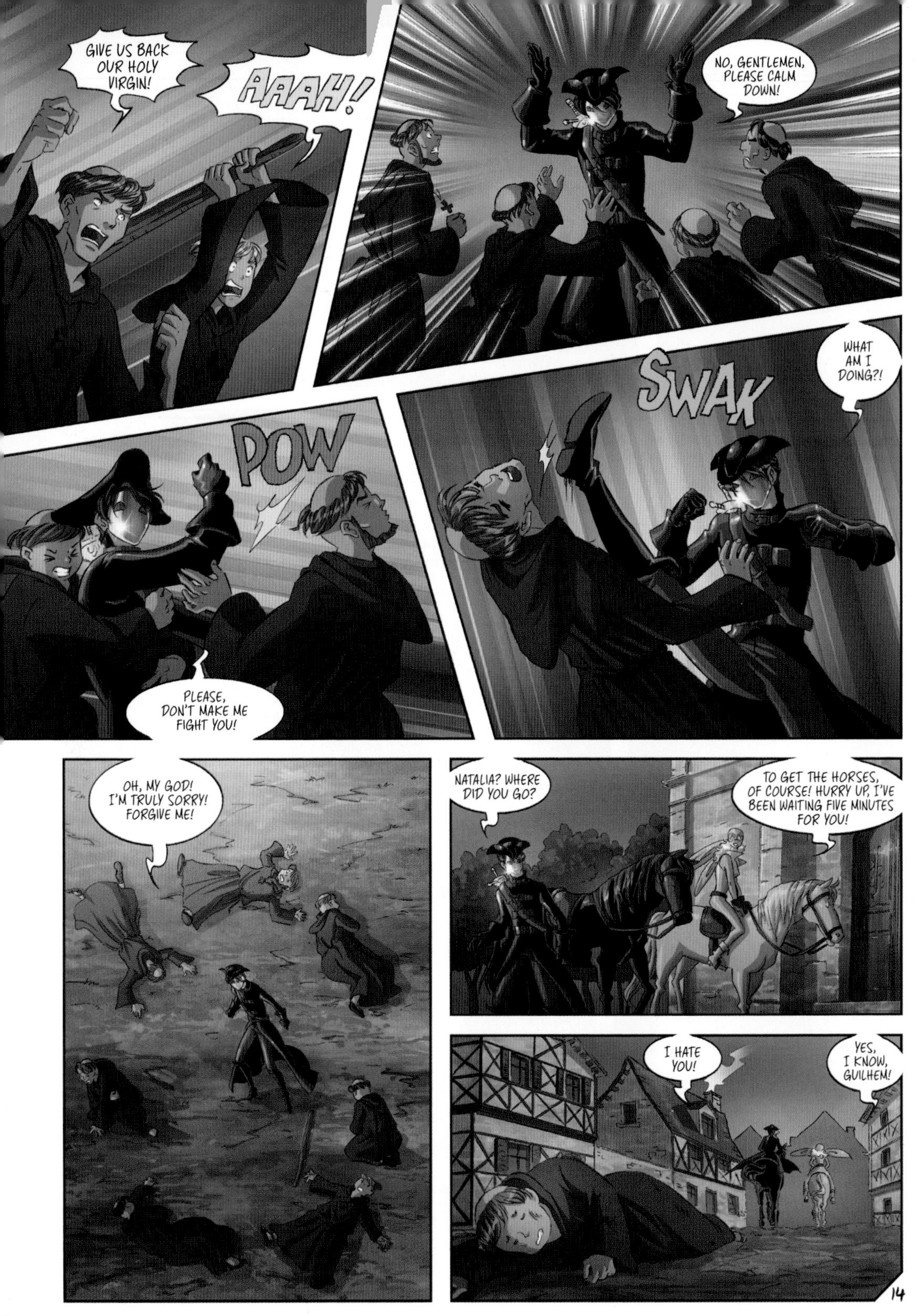
GIVE US BACK OUR HOLY VIRGIN!
AAAH!
NO, GENTLEMEN, PLEASE CALM DOWN!
POW
PLEASE, DON'T MAKE ME FIGHT YOU!
SWAK
WHAT AM I DOING?!
OH, MY GOD! I'M TRULY SORRY! FORGIVE ME!
NATALIA? WHERE DID YOU GO?
TO GET THE HORSES, OF COURSE! HURRY UP, I'VE BEEN WAITING FIVE MINUTES FOR YOU!
I HATE YOU!
YES, I KNOW, GUILHEM!
14

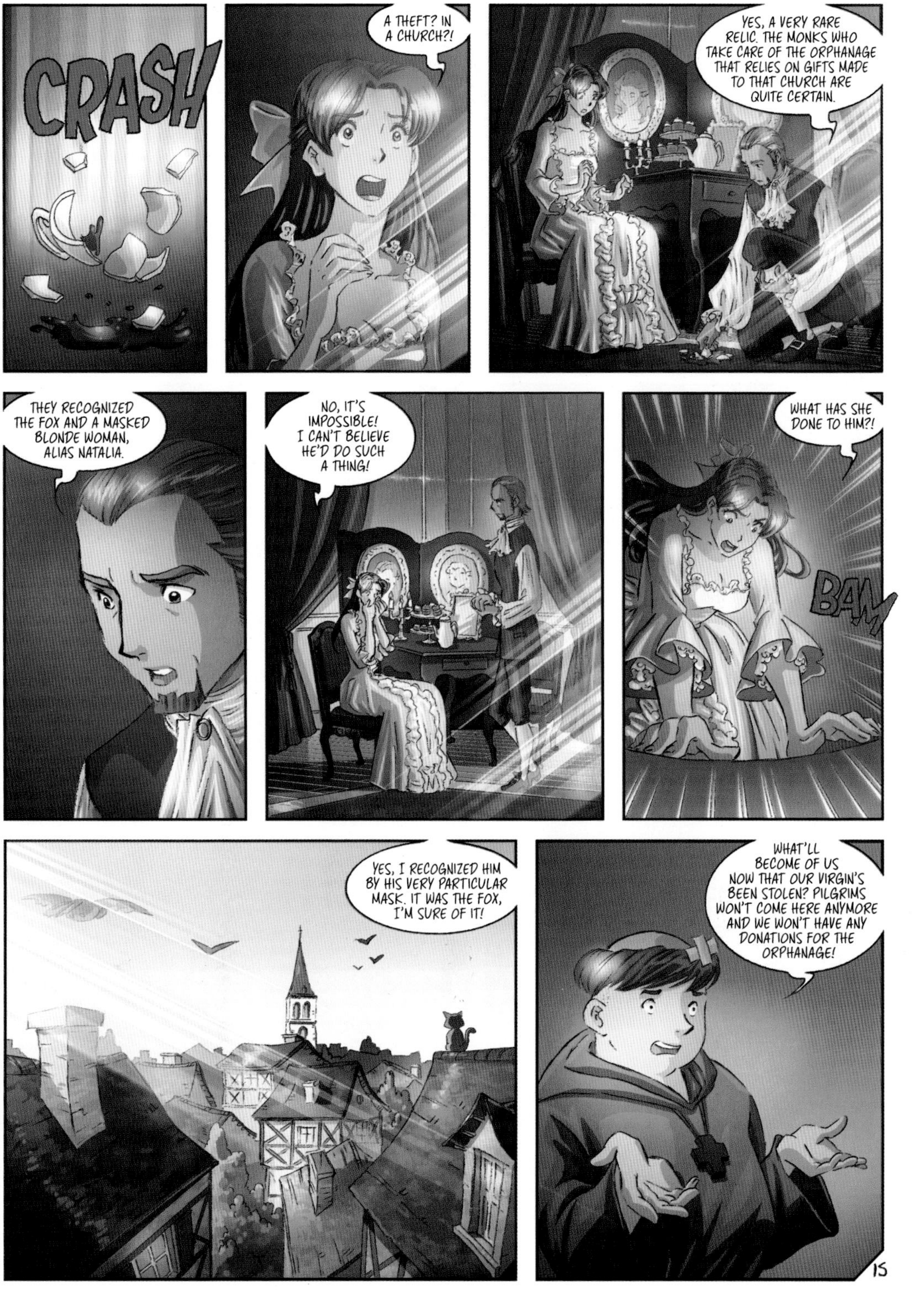
CRASH
A THEFT? IN A CHURCH?!
YES, A VERY RARE RELIC. THE MONKS WHO TAKE CARE OF THE ORPHANAGE THAT RELIES ON GIFTS MADE TO THAT CHURCH ARE QUITE CERTAIN.
THEY RECOGNIZED THE FOX AND A MASKED BLONDE WOMAN, ALIAS NATALIA.
NO, IT'S IMPOSSIBLE! I CAN'T BELIEVE HE'D DO SUCH A THING!
WHAT HAS SHE DONE TO HIM?!
BAM
YES, I RECOGNIZED HIM BY HIS VERY PARTICULAR MASK. IT WAS THE FOX, I'M SURE OF IT!
WHAT'LL BECOME OF US NOW THAT OUR VIRGIN'S BEEN STOLEN? PILGRIMS WON'T COME HERE ANYMORE AND WE WON'T HAVE ANY DONATIONS FOR THE ORPHANAGE!
15

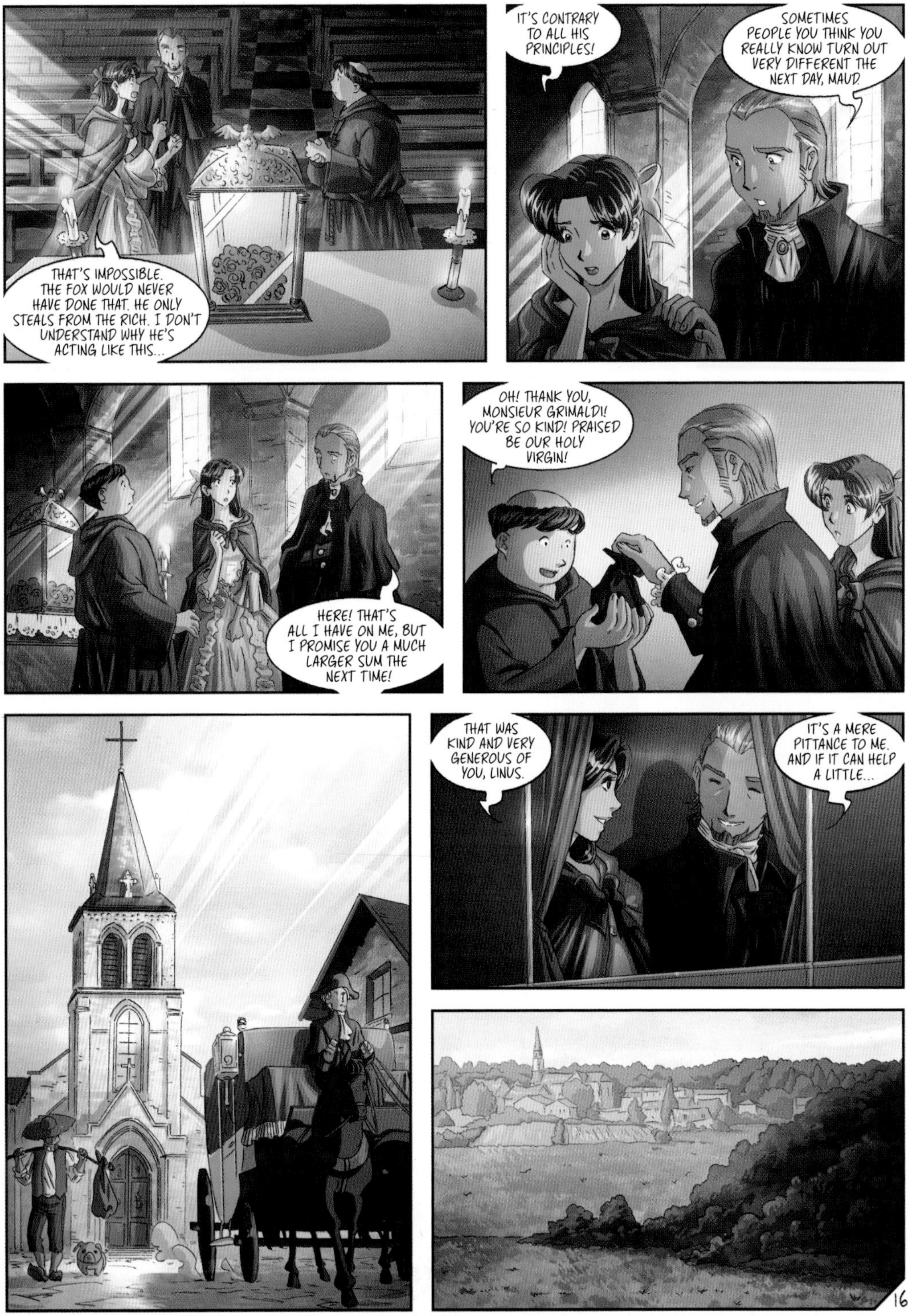
THAT'S IMPOSSIBLE. THE FOX WOULD NEVER HAVE DONE THAT. HE ONLY STEALS FROM THE RICH. I DON'T UNDERSTAND WHY HE'S ACTING LIKE THIS...
IT'S CONTRARY TO ALL HIS PRINCIPLES!
SOMETIMES PEOPLE YOU THINK YOU REALLY KNOW TURN OUT VERY DIFFERENT THE NEXT DAY, MAUD.
HERE! THAT'S ALL I HAVE ON ME, BUT I PROMISE YOU A MUCH LARGER SUM THE NEXT TIME!
OH! THANK YOU, MONSIEUR GRIMALDI! YOU'RE SO KIND! PRAISED BE OUR HOLY VIRGIN!
THAT WAS KIND AND VERY GENEROUS OF YOU, LINUS.
IT'S A MERE PITTANCE TO ME. AND IF IT CAN HELP A LITTLE...
16

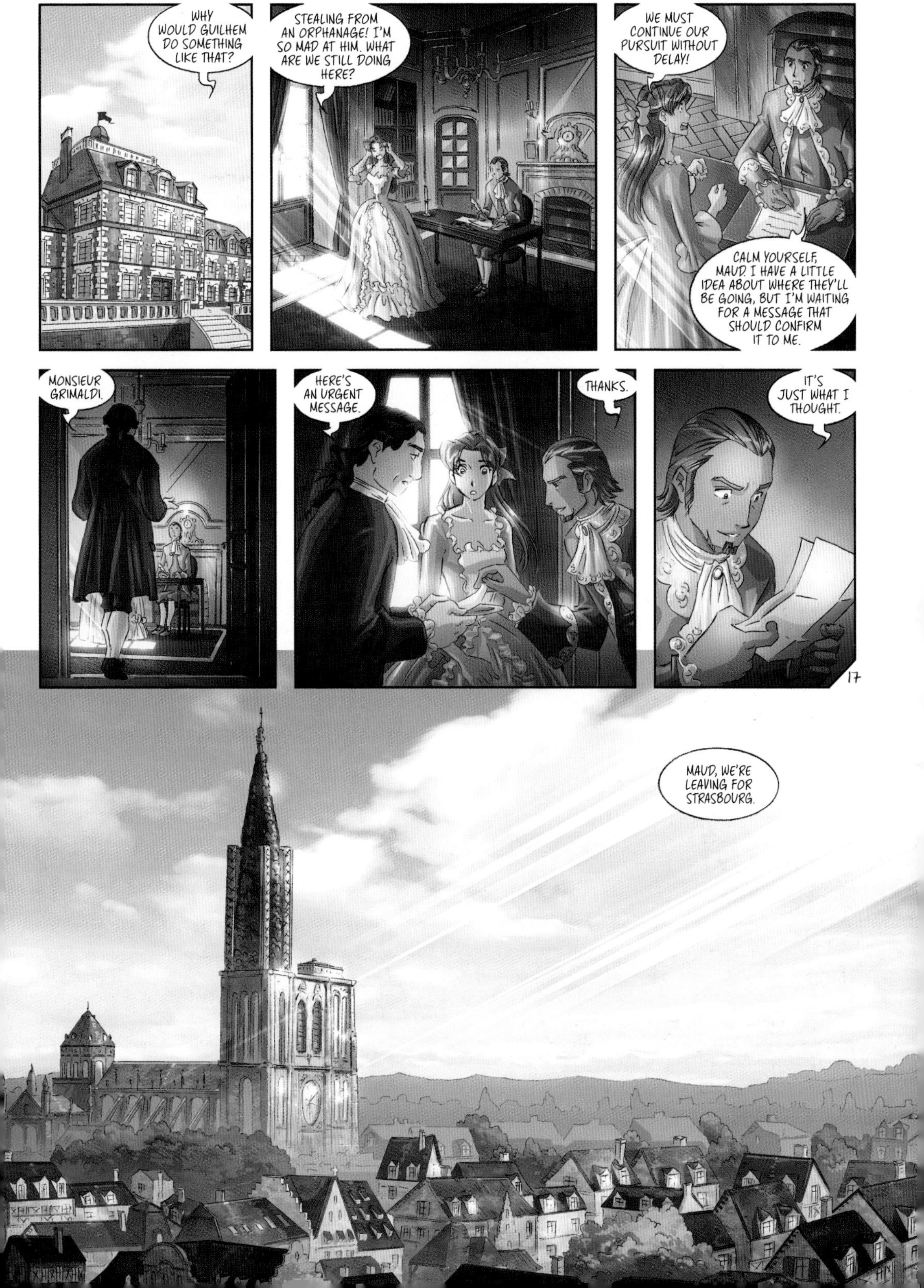
WHY WOULD GUILHEM DO SOMETHING LIKE THAT?
STEALING FROM AN ORPHANAGE! I'M SO MAD AT HIM. WHAT ARE WE STILL DOING HERE?
WE MUST CONTINUE OUR PURSUIT WITHOUT DELAY!
CALM YOURSELF, MAUD. I HAVE A LITTLE IDEA ABOUT WHERE THEY'LL BE GOING, BUT I'M WAITING FOR A MESSAGE THAT SHOULD CONFIRM IT TO ME.
MONSIEUR GRIMALDI.
HERE'S AN URGENT MESSAGE.
THANKS.
IT'S JUST WHAT I THOUGHT.
MAUD, WE'RE LEAVING FOR STRASBOURG.

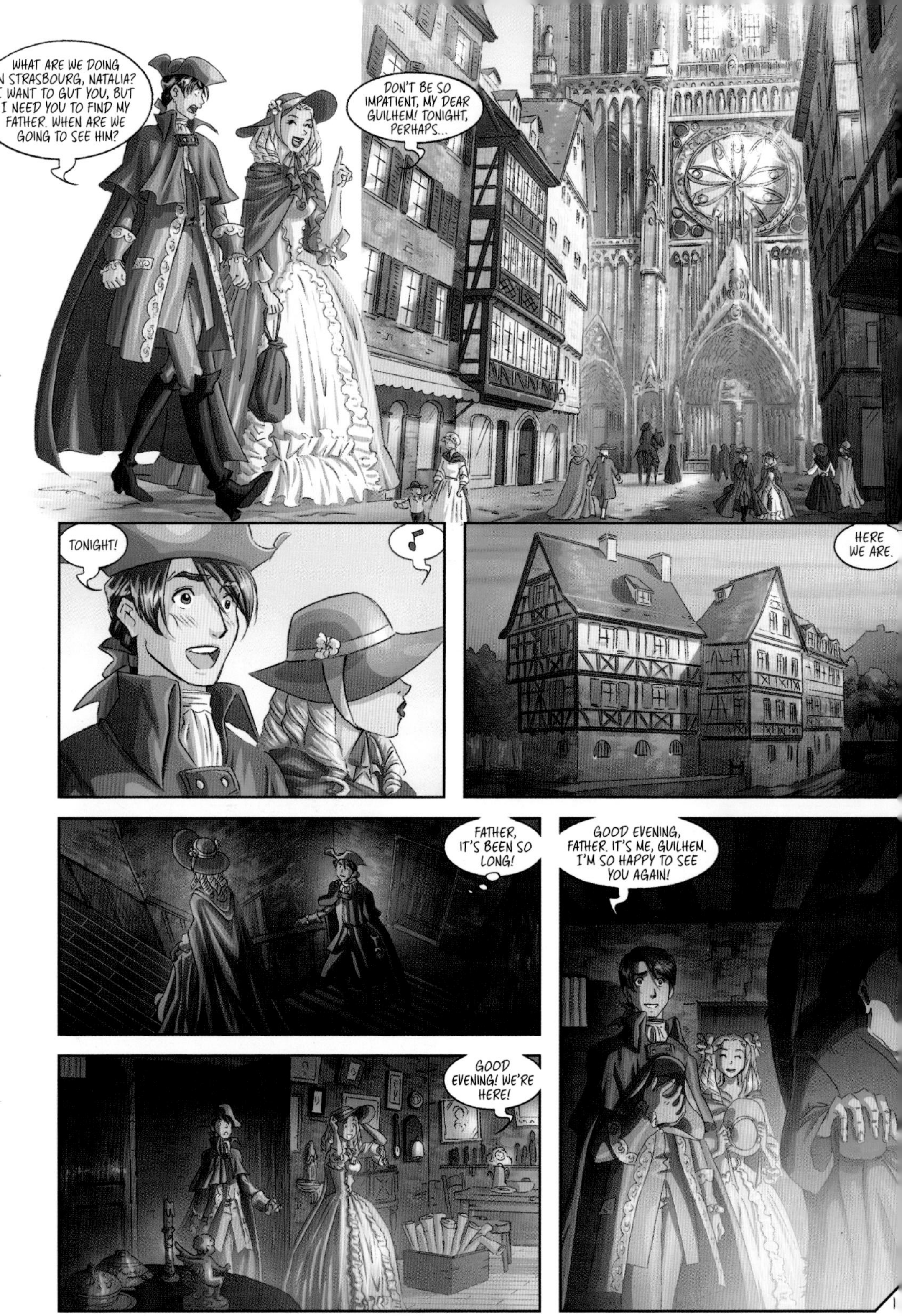
WHAT ARE WE DOING IN STRASBOURG, NATALIA? I WANT TO GUT YOU, BUT I NEED YOU TO FIND MY FATHER. WHEN ARE WE GOING TO SEE HIM?
DON'T BE SO IMPATIENT, MY DEAR GUILHEM! TONIGHT, PERHAPS...
TONIGHT!
♪
HERE WE ARE.
FATHER, IT'S BEEN SO LONG!
GOOD EVENING! WE'RE HERE!
GOOD EVENING, FATHER. IT'S ME, GUILHEM. I'M SO HAPPY TO SEE YOU AGAIN!

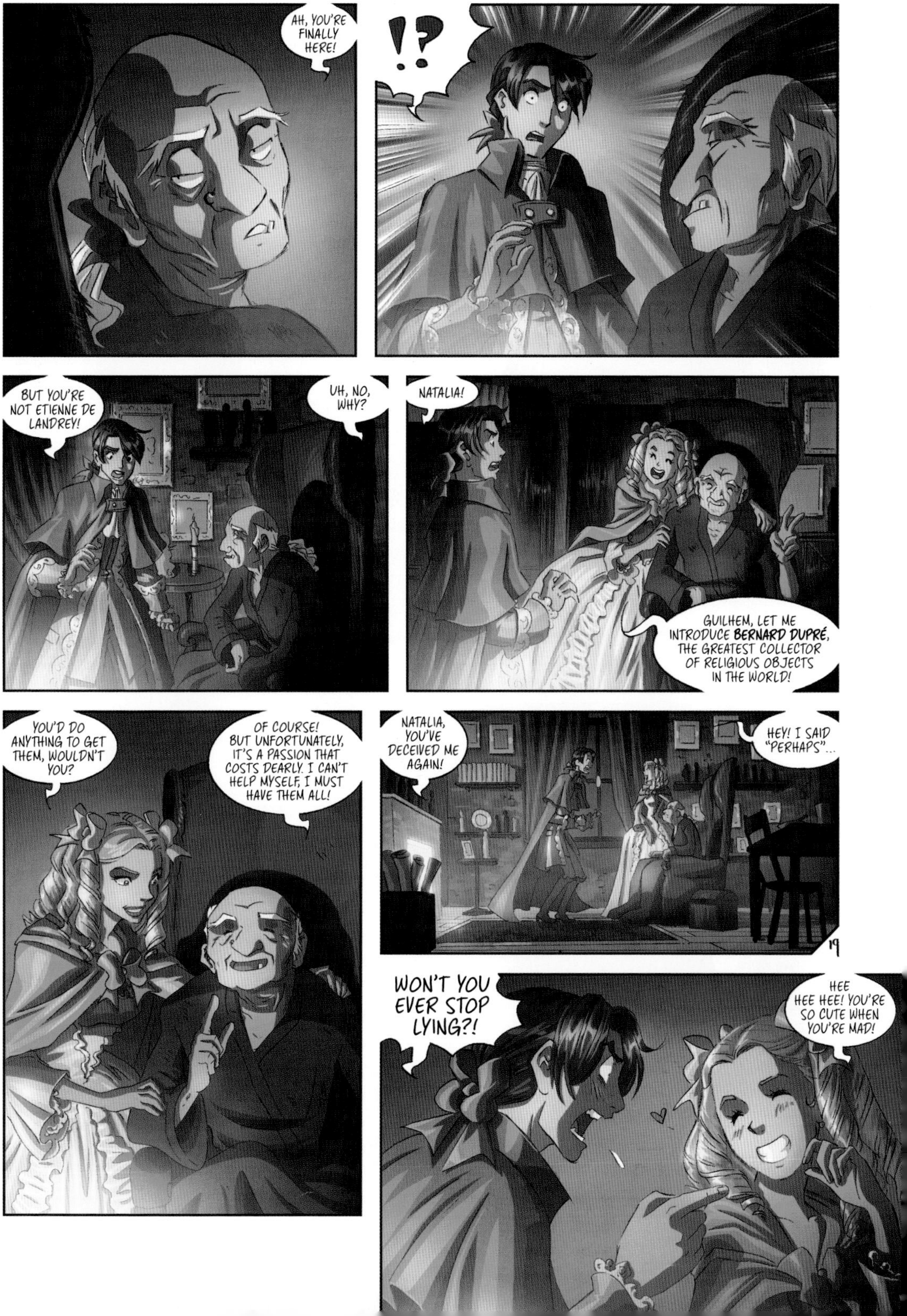
AH, YOU'RE FINALLY HERE!
!?
BUT YOU'RE NOT ETIENNE DE LANDREY!
UH, NO, WHY?
NATALIA!
GUILHEM, LET ME INTRODUCE **BERNARD DUPRÉ**, THE GREATEST COLLECTOR OF RELIGIOUS OBJECTS IN THE WORLD!
YOU'D DO ANYTHING TO GET THEM, WOULDN'T YOU?
OF COURSE! BUT UNFORTUNATELY, IT'S A PASSION THAT COSTS DEARLY. I CAN'T HELP MYSELF, I MUST HAVE THEM ALL!
NATALIA, YOU'VE DECEIVED ME AGAIN!
HEY! I SAID "PERHAPS"...
WON'T YOU EVER STOP LYING?!
HEE HEE HEE! YOU'RE SO CUTE WHEN YOU'RE MAD!

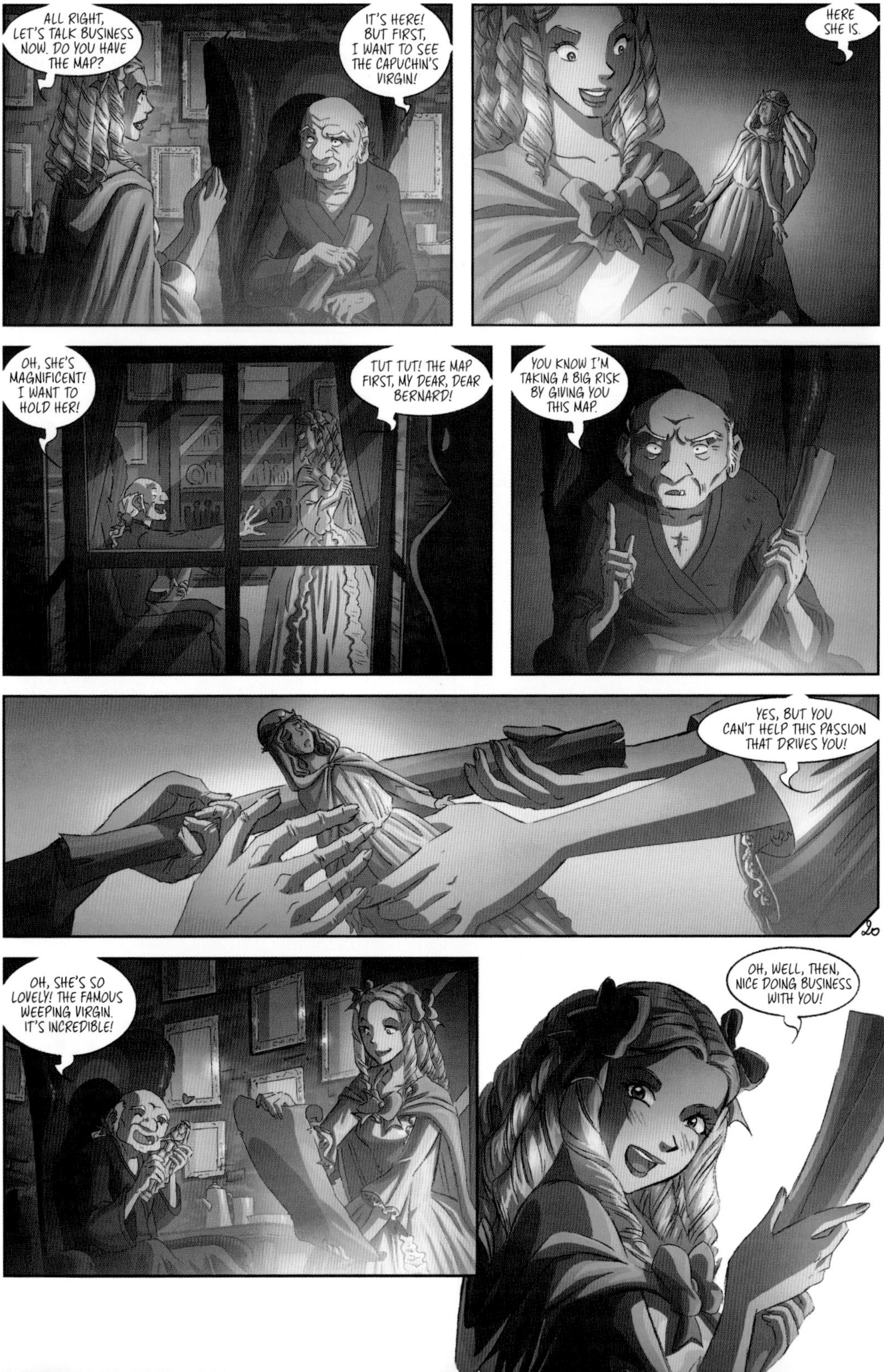
ALL RIGHT, LET'S TALK BUSINESS NOW. DO YOU HAVE THE MAP?
IT'S HERE! BUT FIRST, I WANT TO SEE THE CAPUCHIN'S VIRGIN!
HERE SHE IS.
OH, SHE'S MAGNIFICENT! I WANT TO HOLD HER!
TUT TUT! THE MAP FIRST, MY DEAR, DEAR BERNARD!
YOU KNOW I'M TAKING A BIG RISK BY GIVING YOU THIS MAP.
YES, BUT YOU CAN'T HELP THIS PASSION THAT DRIVES YOU!
OH, SHE'S SO LOVELY! THE FAMOUS WEEPING VIRGIN. IT'S INCREDIBLE!
OH, WELL, THEN, NICE DOING BUSINESS WITH YOU!

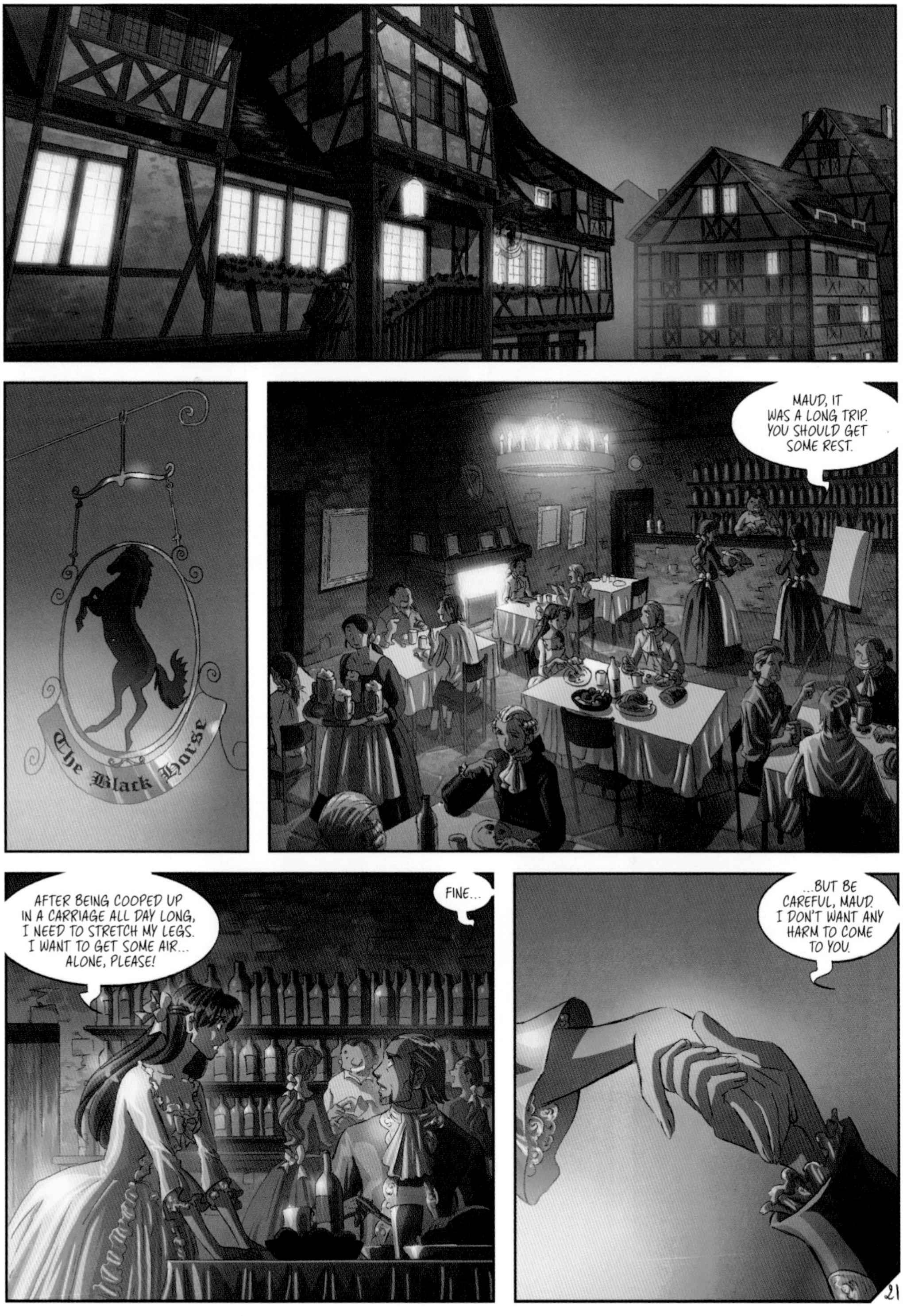
The Black Horse
MAUD, IT WAS A LONG TRIP. YOU SHOULD GET SOME REST.
AFTER BEING COOPED UP IN A CARRIAGE ALL DAY LONG, I NEED TO STRETCH MY LEGS. I WANT TO GET SOME AIR... ALONE, PLEASE!
FINE...
...BUT BE CAREFUL, MAUD. I DON'T WANT ANY HARM TO COME TO YOU.
21

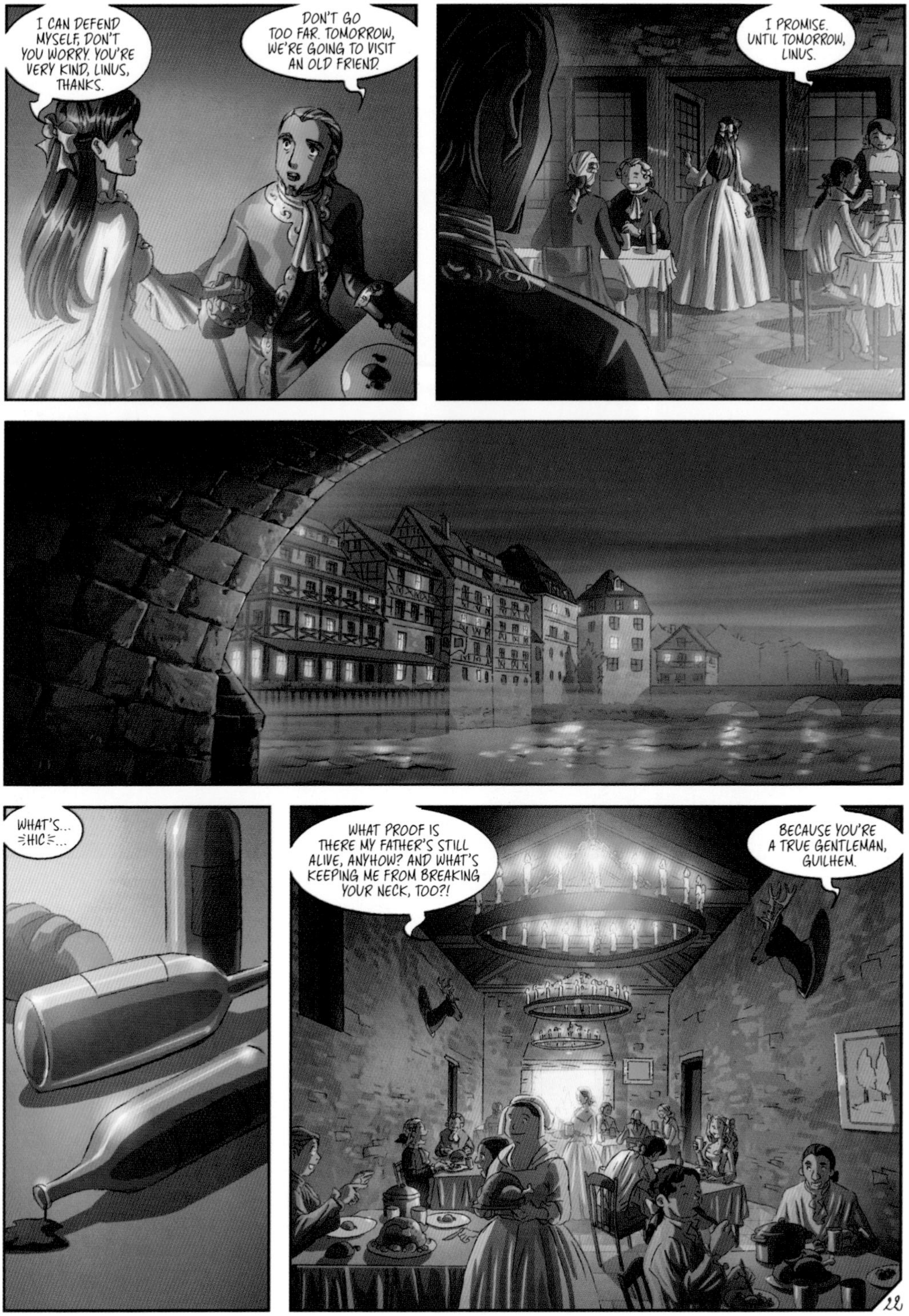
I CAN DEFEND MYSELF, DON'T YOU WORRY. YOU'RE VERY KIND, LINUS, THANKS.
DON'T GO TOO FAR. TOMORROW, WE'RE GOING TO VISIT AN OLD FRIEND.
I PROMISE. UNTIL TOMORROW, LINUS.
WHAT'S... HIC...
WHAT PROOF IS THERE MY FATHER'S STILL ALIVE, ANYHOW? AND WHAT'S KEEPING ME FROM BREAKING YOUR NECK, TOO?!
BECAUSE YOU'RE A TRUE GENTLEMAN, GUILHEM.
22

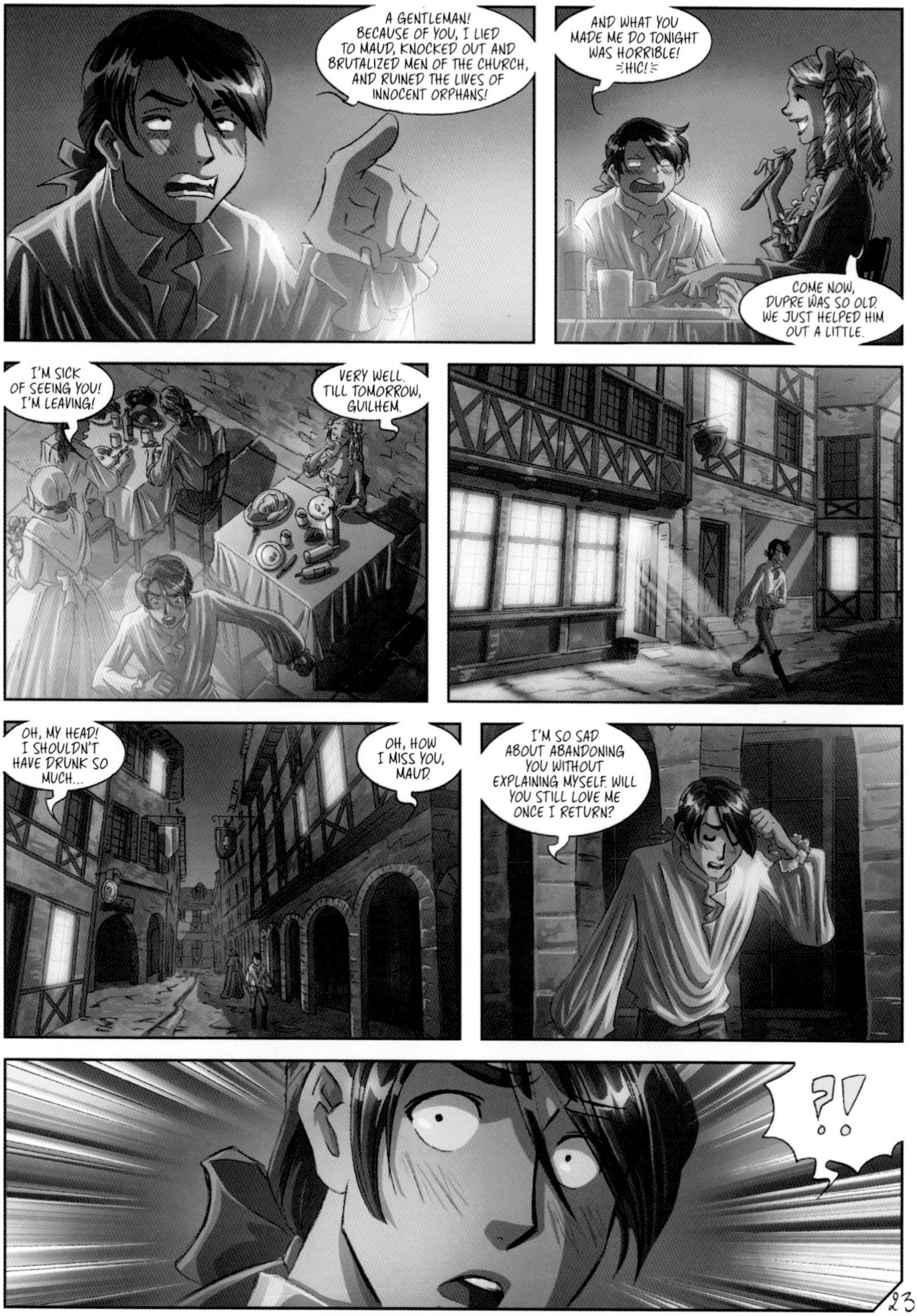
A GENTLEMAN! BECAUSE OF YOU, I LIED TO MAUD, KNOCKED OUT AND BRUTALIZED MEN OF THE CHURCH, AND RUINED THE LIVES OF INNOCENT ORPHANS!
AND WHAT YOU MADE ME DO TONIGHT WAS HORRIBLE! HIC!
COME NOW, DUPRE WAS SO OLD. WE JUST HELPED HIM OUT A LITTLE.
I'M SICK OF SEEING YOU! I'M LEAVING!
VERY WELL. TILL TOMORROW, GUILHEM.
OH, MY HEAD! I SHOULDN'T HAVE DRUNK SO MUCH...
OH, HOW I MISS YOU, MAUD.
I'M SO SAD ABOUT ABANDONING YOU WITHOUT EXPLAINING MYSELF. WILL YOU STILL LOVE ME ONCE I RETURN?
?!
23

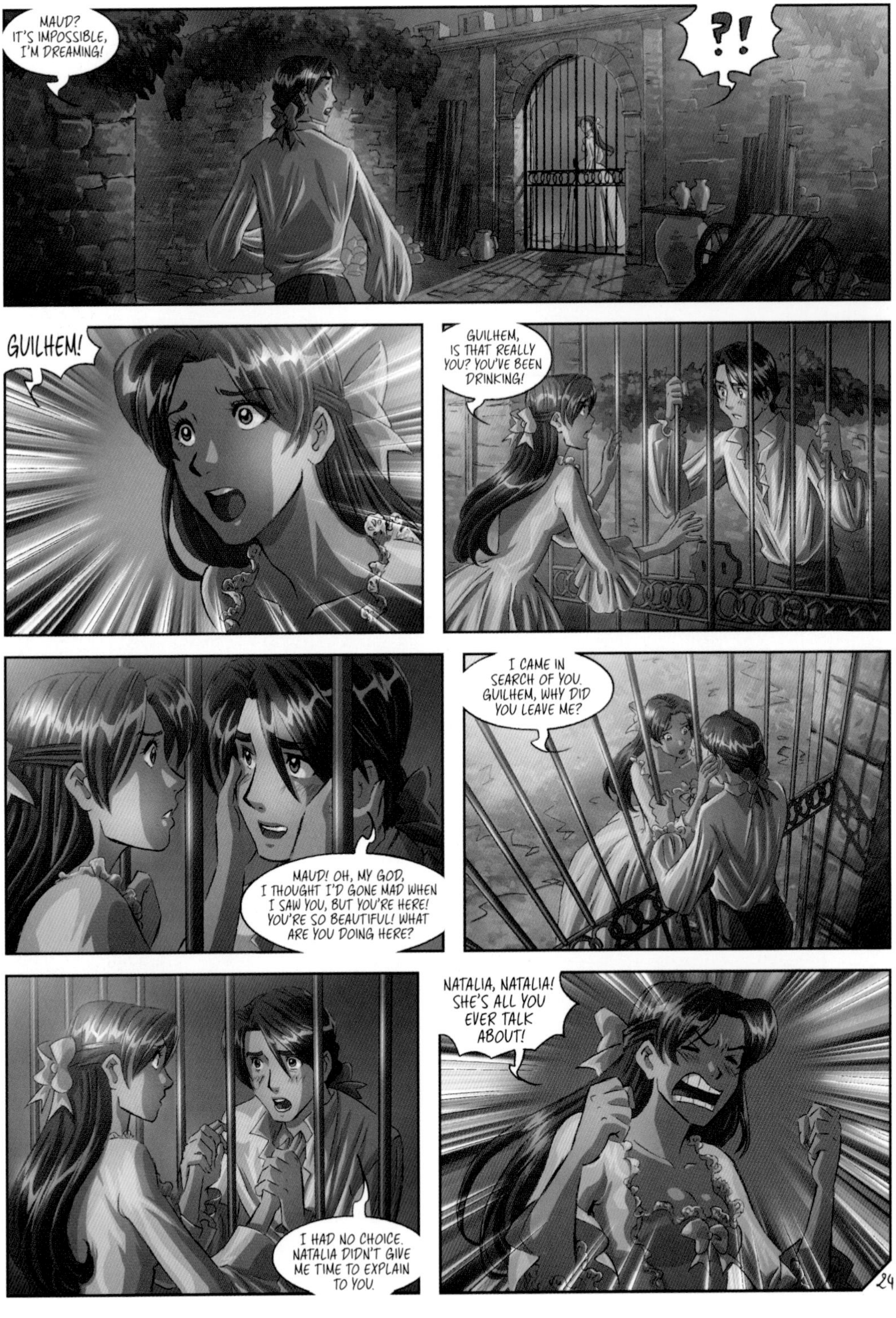
MAUD? IT'S IMPOSSIBLE, I'M DREAMING!
?!
GUILHEM!
GUILHEM, IS THAT REALLY YOU? YOU'VE BEEN DRINKING!
MAUD! OH, MY GOD, I THOUGHT I'D GONE MAD WHEN I SAW YOU, BUT YOU'RE HERE! YOU'RE SO BEAUTIFUL! WHAT ARE YOU DOING HERE?
I CAME IN SEARCH OF YOU. GUILHEM, WHY DID YOU LEAVE ME?
I HAD NO CHOICE. NATALIA DIDN'T GIVE ME TIME TO EXPLAIN TO YOU.
NATALIA, NATALIA! SHE'S ALL YOU EVER TALK ABOUT!
24

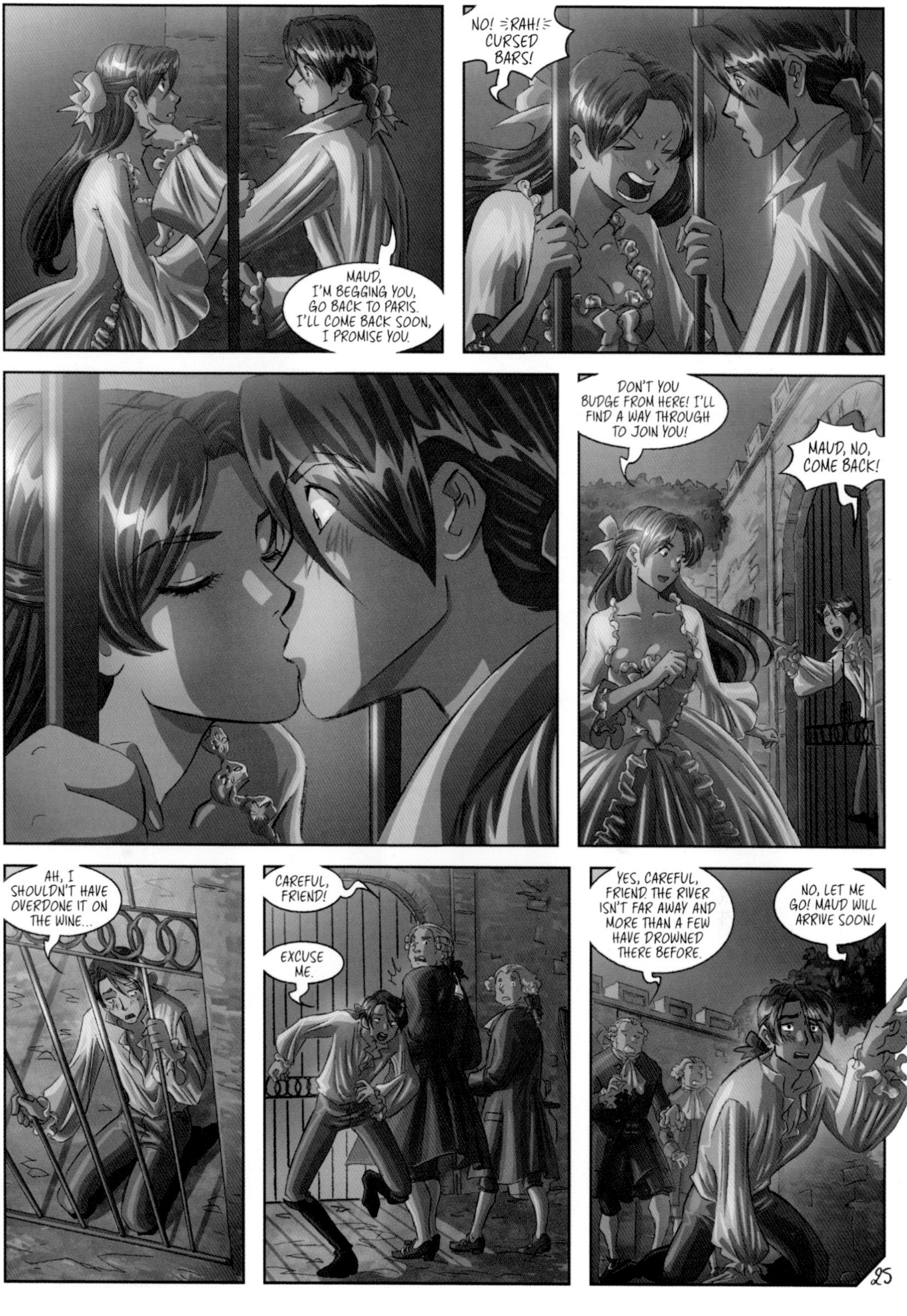
MAUD, I'M BEGGING YOU, GO BACK TO PARIS. I'LL COME BACK SOON, I PROMISE YOU.
NO! RAH! CURSED BARS!
DON'T YOU BUDGE FROM HERE! I'LL FIND A WAY THROUGH TO JOIN YOU!
MAUD, NO, COME BACK!
AH, I SHOULDN'T HAVE OVERDONE IT ON THE WINE...
CAREFUL, FRIEND!
EXCUSE ME.
YES, CAREFUL, FRIEND. THE RIVER ISN'T FAR AWAY AND MORE THAN A FEW HAVE DROWNED THERE BEFORE.
NO, LET ME GO! MAUD WILL ARRIVE SOON!
25

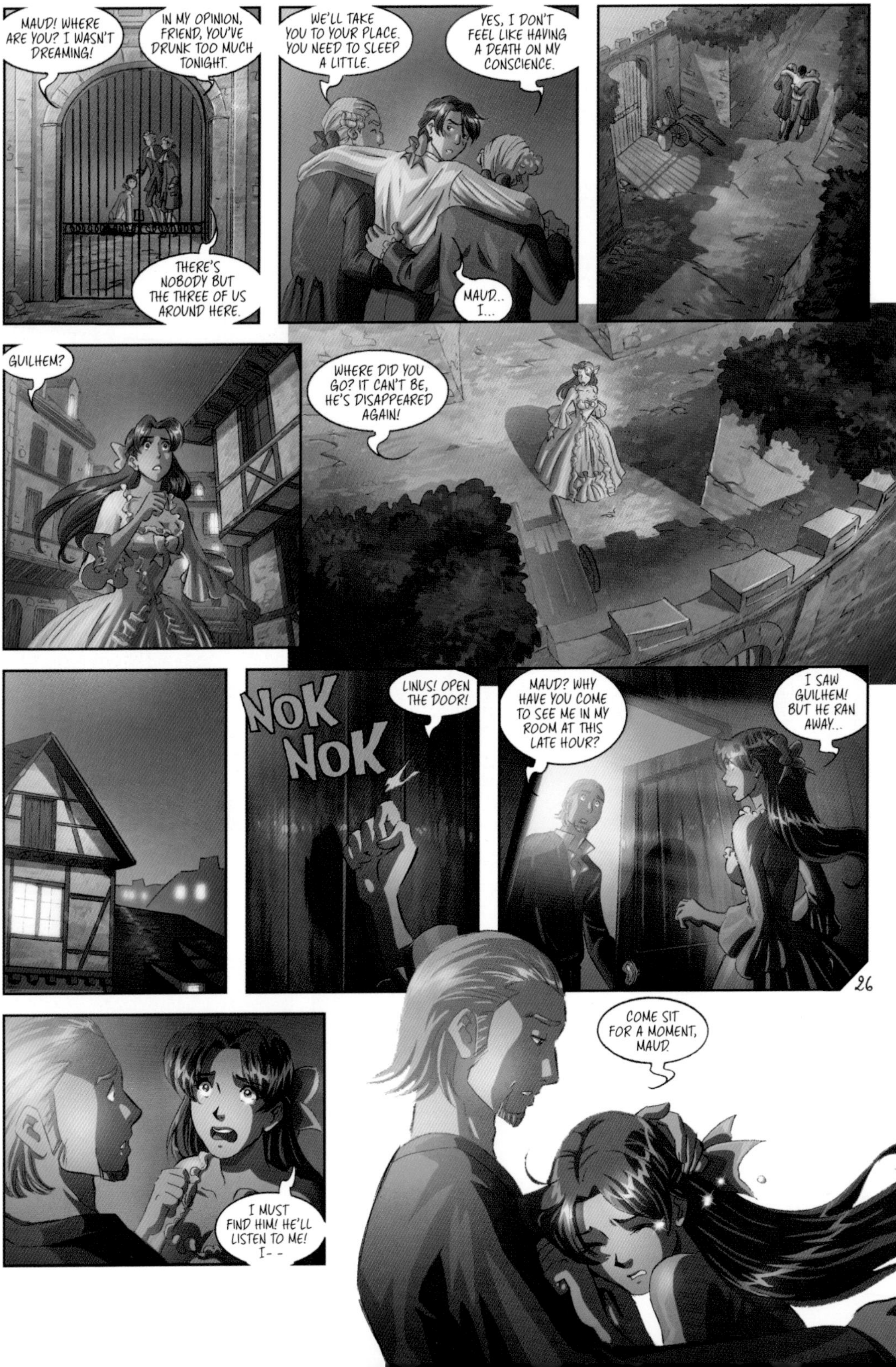
MAUD! WHERE ARE YOU? I WASN'T DREAMING!
IN MY OPINION, FRIEND, YOU'VE DRUNK TOO MUCH TONIGHT.
THERE'S NOBODY BUT THE THREE OF US AROUND HERE.
WE'LL TAKE YOU TO YOUR PLACE. YOU NEED TO SLEEP A LITTLE.
YES, I DON'T FEEL LIKE HAVING A DEATH ON MY CONSCIENCE.
MAUD... I...
GUILHEM?
WHERE DID YOU GO? IT CAN'T BE, HE'S DISAPPEARED AGAIN!
NOK NOK
LINUS! OPEN THE DOOR!
MAUD? WHY HAVE YOU COME TO SEE ME IN MY ROOM AT THIS LATE HOUR?
I SAW GUILHEM! BUT HE RAN AWAY...
I MUST FIND HIM! HE'LL LISTEN TO ME! I- -
COME SIT FOR A MOMENT, MAUD.

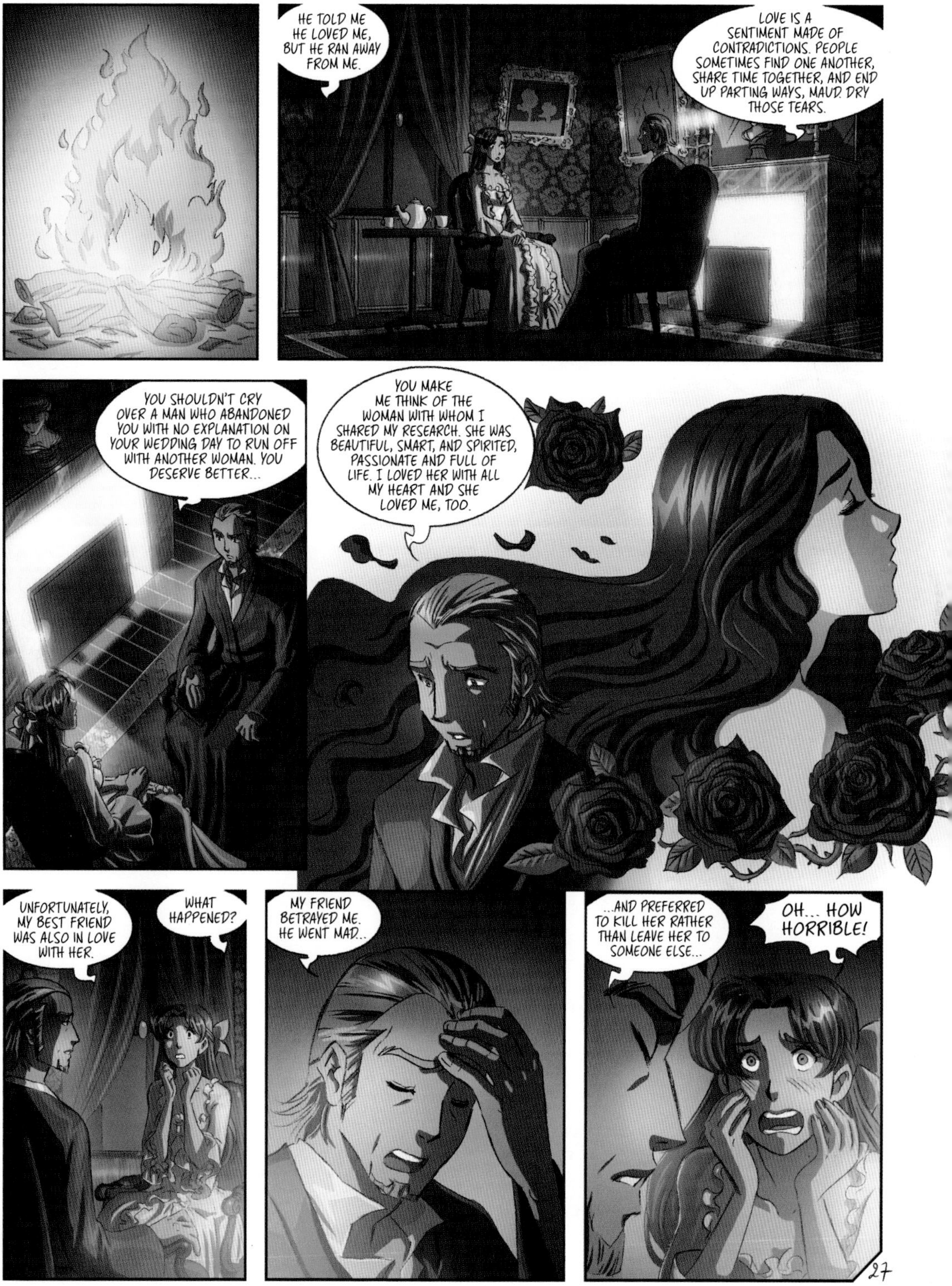
HE TOLD ME HE LOVED ME, BUT HE RAN AWAY FROM ME.
LOVE IS A SENTIMENT MADE OF CONTRADICTIONS. PEOPLE SOMETIMES FIND ONE ANOTHER, SHARE TIME TOGETHER, AND END UP PARTING WAYS, MAUD. DRY THOSE TEARS.
YOU SHOULDN'T CRY OVER A MAN WHO ABANDONED YOU WITH NO EXPLANATION ON YOUR WEDDING DAY TO RUN OFF WITH ANOTHER WOMAN. YOU DESERVE BETTER...
YOU MAKE ME THINK OF THE WOMAN WITH WHOM I SHARED MY RESEARCH. SHE WAS BEAUTIFUL, SMART, AND SPIRITED, PASSIONATE AND FULL OF LIFE. I LOVED HER WITH ALL MY HEART AND SHE LOVED ME, TOO.
UNFORTUNATELY, MY BEST FRIEND WAS ALSO IN LOVE WITH HER.
WHAT HAPPENED?
MY FRIEND BETRAYED ME. HE WENT MAD...
...AND PREFERRED TO KILL HER RATHER THAN LEAVE HER TO SOMEONE ELSE...
OH... HOW HORRIBLE!
27

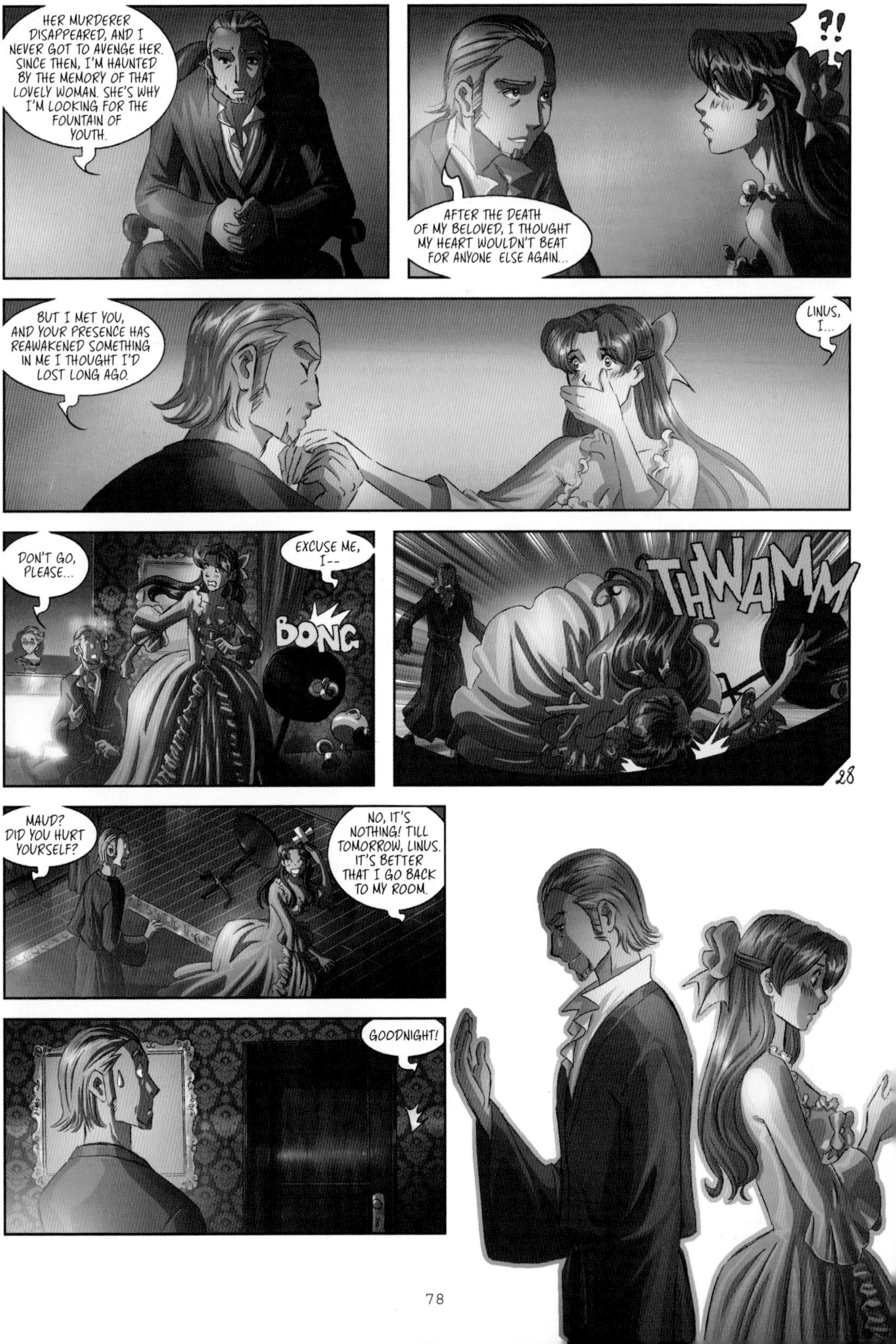
HER MURDERER DISAPPEARED, AND I NEVER GOT TO AVENGE HER. SINCE THEN, I'M HAUNTED BY THE MEMORY OF THAT LOVELY WOMAN. SHE'S WHY I'M LOOKING FOR THE FOUNTAIN OF YOUTH.
?!
AFTER THE DEATH OF MY BELOVED, I THOUGHT MY HEART WOULDN'T BEAT FOR ANYONE ELSE AGAIN...
BUT I MET YOU, AND YOUR PRESENCE HAS REAWAKENED SOMETHING IN ME I THOUGHT I'D LOST LONG AGO.
LINUS, I...
DON'T GO, PLEASE...
EXCUSE ME, I--
BONG
THWAMM
28
MAUD? DID YOU HURT YOURSELF?
NO, IT'S NOTHING! TILL TOMORROW, LINUS. IT'S BETTER THAT I GO BACK TO MY ROOM.
GOODNIGHT!

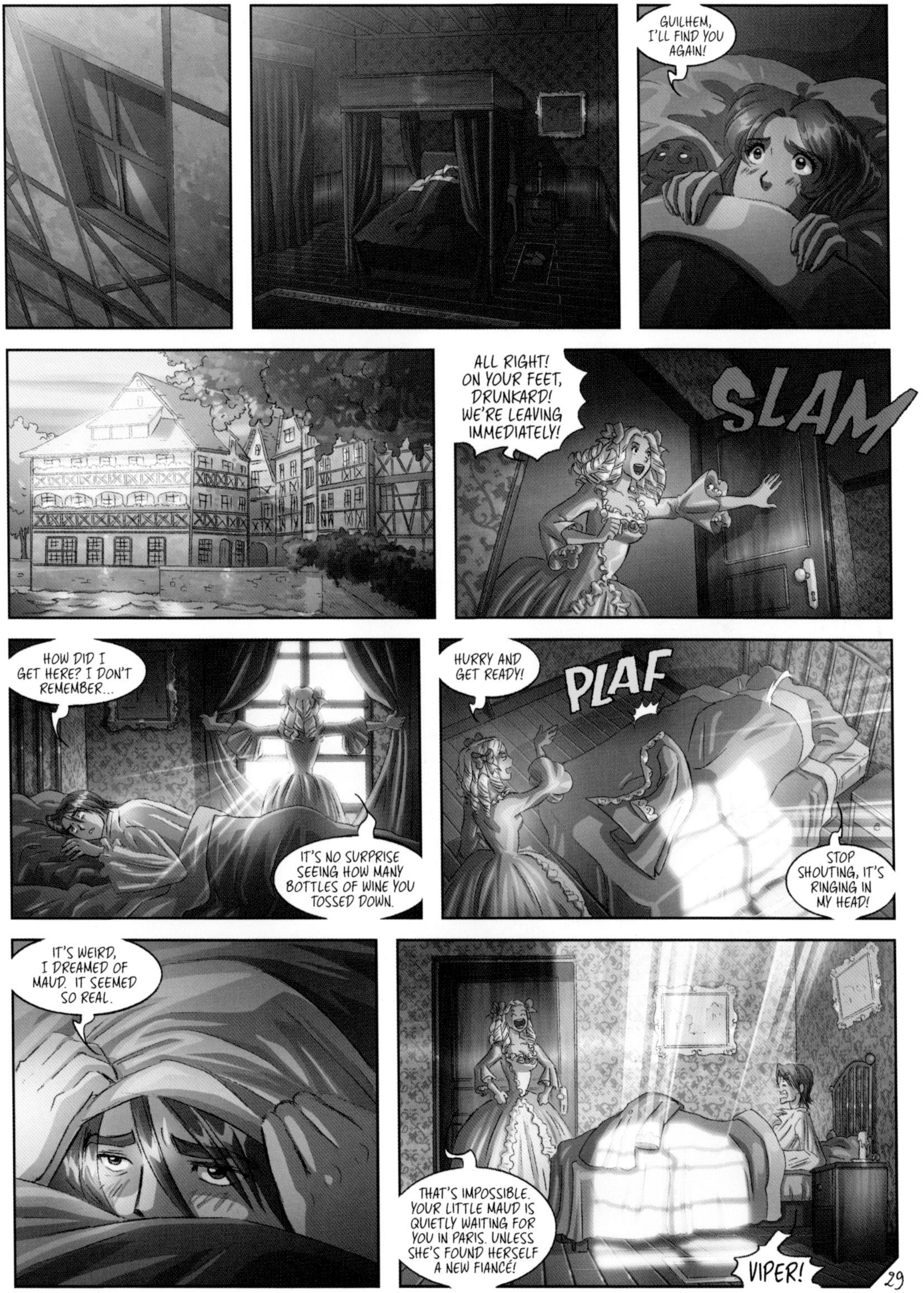
GUILHEM, I'LL FIND YOU AGAIN!
ALL RIGHT! ON YOUR FEET, DRUNKARD! WE'RE LEAVING IMMEDIATELY!
SLAM
HOW DID I GET HERE? I DON'T REMEMBER...
IT'S NO SURPRISE SEEING HOW MANY BOTTLES OF WINE YOU TOSSED DOWN.
HURRY AND GET READY!
PLAF
STOP SHOUTING, IT'S RINGING IN MY HEAD!
IT'S WEIRD, I DREAMED OF MAUD. IT SEEMED SO REAL.
THAT'S IMPOSSIBLE. YOUR LITTLE MAUD IS QUIETLY WAITING FOR YOU IN PARIS. UNLESS SHE'S FOUND HERSELF A NEW FIANCÉ!
VIPER!
29

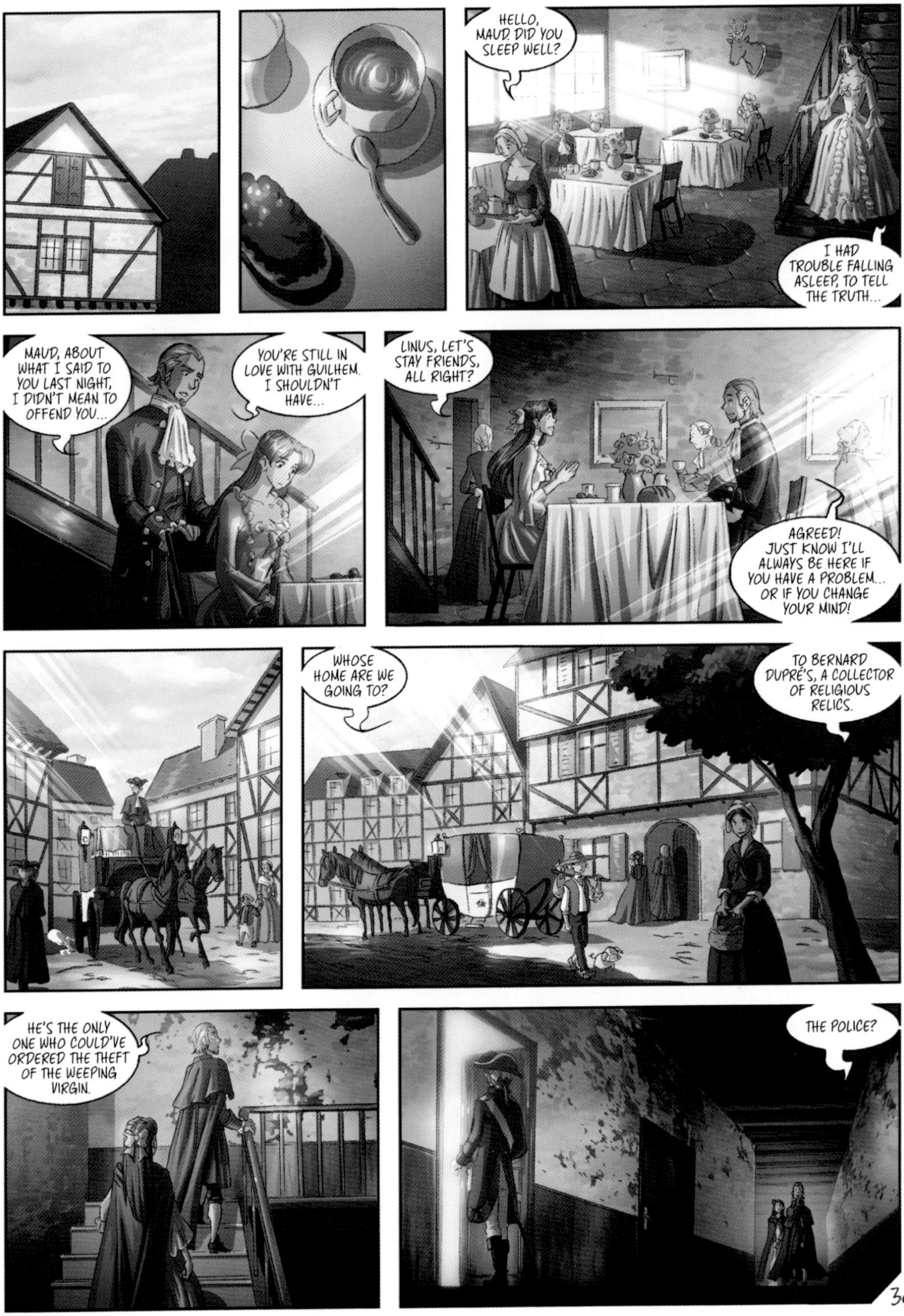
HELLO, MAUD. DID YOU SLEEP WELL?
I HAD TROUBLE FALLING ASLEEP, TO TELL THE TRUTH...
MAUD, ABOUT WHAT I SAID TO YOU LAST NIGHT, I DIDN'T MEAN TO OFFEND YOU...
YOU'RE STILL IN LOVE WITH GUILHEM. I SHOULDN'T HAVE...
LINUS, LET'S STAY FRIENDS, ALL RIGHT?
AGREED! JUST KNOW I'LL ALWAYS BE HERE IF YOU HAVE A PROBLEM... OR IF YOU CHANGE YOUR MIND!
WHOSE HOME ARE WE GOING TO?
TO BERNARD DUPRÉ'S, A COLLECTOR OF RELIGIOUS RELICS.
HE'S THE ONLY ONE WHO COULD'VE ORDERED THE THEFT OF THE WEEPING VIRGIN.
THE POLICE?
30

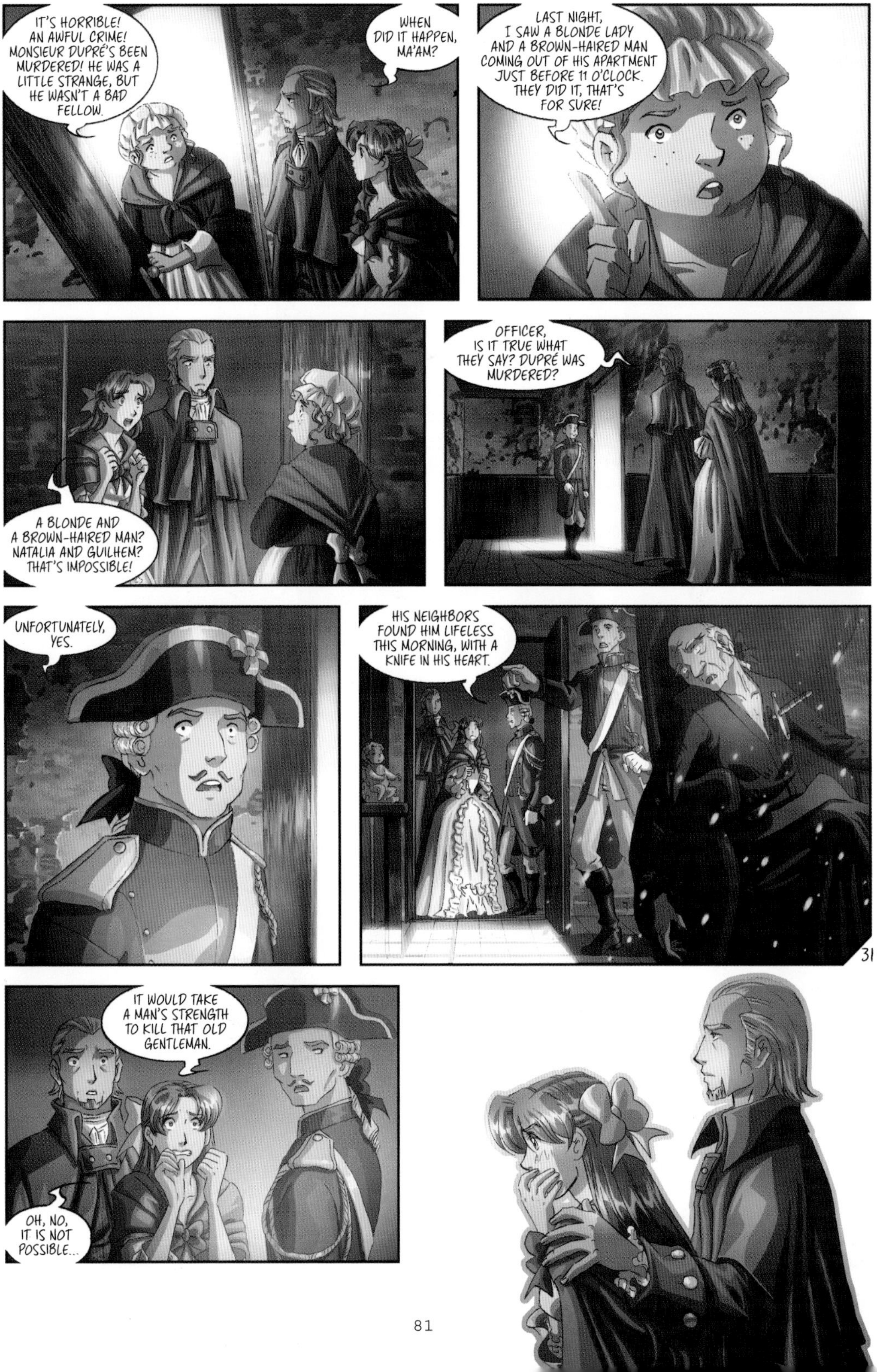
IT'S HORRIBLE! AN AWFUL CRIME! MONSIEUR DUPRÉ'S BEEN MURDERED! HE WAS A LITTLE STRANGE, BUT HE WASN'T A BAD FELLOW.
WHEN DID IT HAPPEN, MA'AM?
LAST NIGHT, I SAW A BLONDE LADY AND A BROWN-HAIRED MAN COMING OUT OF HIS APARTMENT JUST BEFORE 11 O'CLOCK. THEY DID IT, THAT'S FOR SURE!
A BLONDE AND A BROWN-HAIRED MAN? NATALIA AND GUILHEM? THAT'S IMPOSSIBLE!
OFFICER, IS IT TRUE WHAT THEY SAY? DUPRÉ WAS MURDERED?
UNFORTUNATELY, YES.
HIS NEIGHBORS FOUND HIM LIFELESS THIS MORNING, WITH A KNIFE IN HIS HEART.
31
IT WOULD TAKE A MAN'S STRENGTH TO KILL THAT OLD GENTLEMAN.
OH, NO, IT IS NOT POSSIBLE...

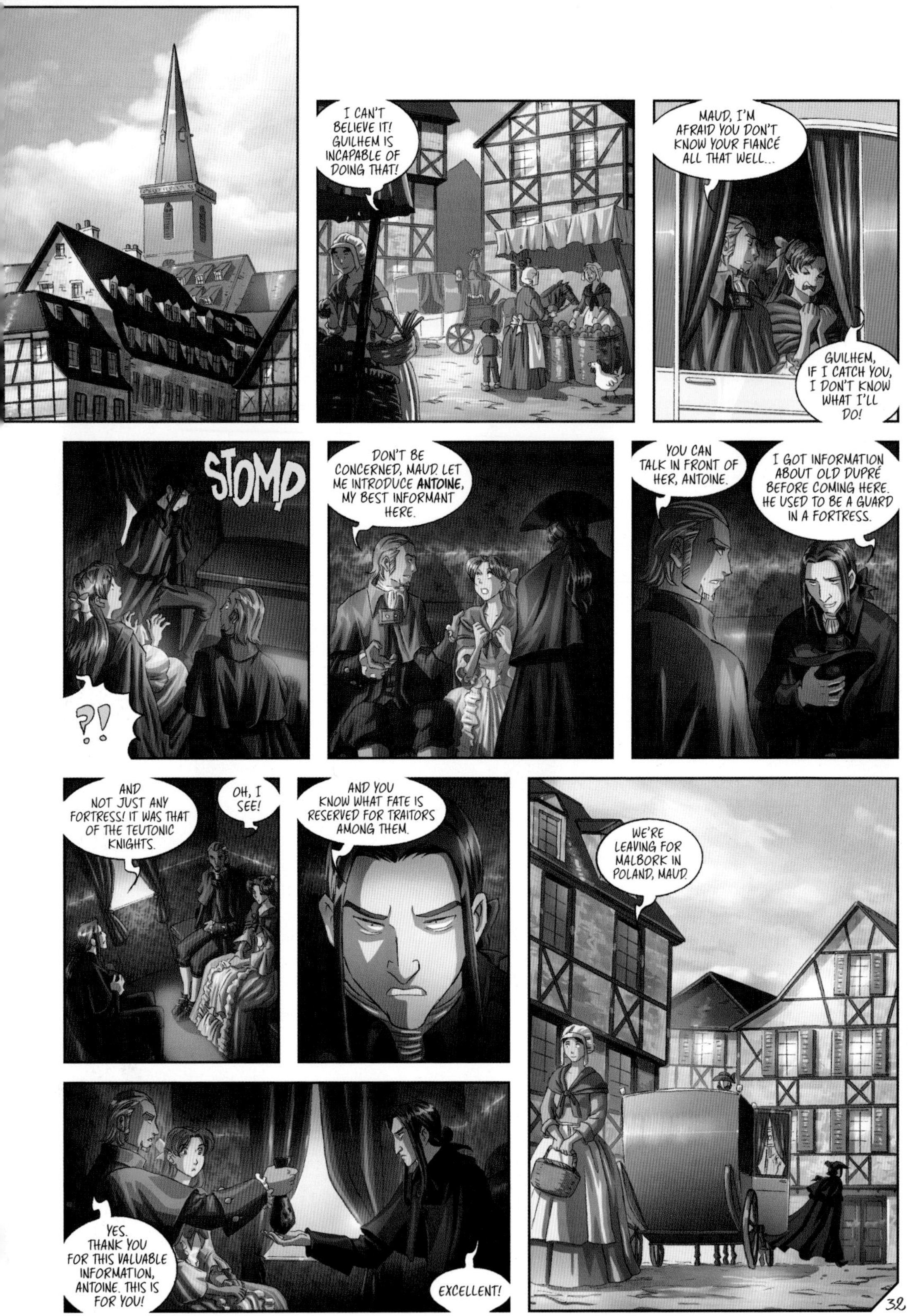
I CAN'T BELIEVE IT! GUILHEM IS INCAPABLE OF DOING THAT!
MAUD, I'M AFRAID YOU DON'T KNOW YOUR FIANCÉ ALL THAT WELL...
GUILHEM, IF I CATCH YOU, I DON'T KNOW WHAT I'LL DO!
STOMP
?!
DON'T BE CONCERNED, MAUD. LET ME INTRODUCE ANTOINE, MY BEST INFORMANT HERE.
YOU CAN TALK IN FRONT OF HER, ANTOINE.
I GOT INFORMATION ABOUT OLD DUPRÉ BEFORE COMING HERE. HE USED TO BE A GUARD IN A FORTRESS.
AND NOT JUST ANY FORTRESS! IT WAS THAT OF THE TEUTONIC KNIGHTS.
OH, I SEE!
AND YOU KNOW WHAT FATE IS RESERVED FOR TRAITORS AMONG THEM.
YES. THANK YOU FOR THIS VALUABLE INFORMATION, ANTOINE. THIS IS FOR YOU!
EXCELLENT!
WE'RE LEAVING FOR MALBORK IN POLAND, MAUD.
32

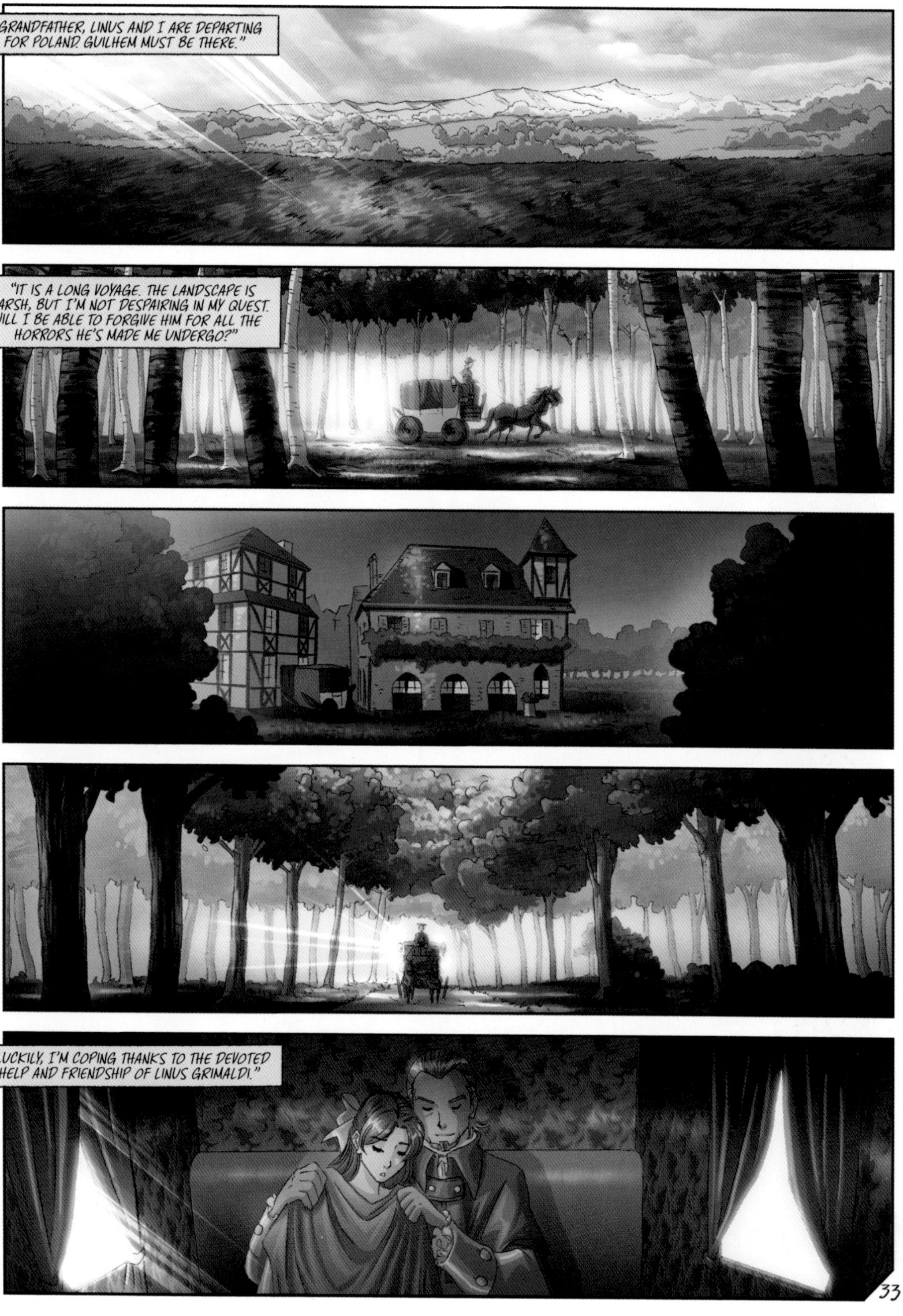
"GRANDFATHER, LINUS AND I ARE DEPARTING FOR POLAND. GUILHEM MUST BE THERE."
"IT IS A LONG VOYAGE. THE LANDSCAPE IS HARSH, BUT I'M NOT DESPAIRING IN MY QUEST. WILL I BE ABLE TO FORGIVE HIM FOR ALL THE HORRORS HE'S MADE ME UNDERGO?"
"LUCKILY, I'M COPING THANKS TO THE DEVOTED HELP AND FRIENDSHIP OF LINUS GRIMALDI."
33

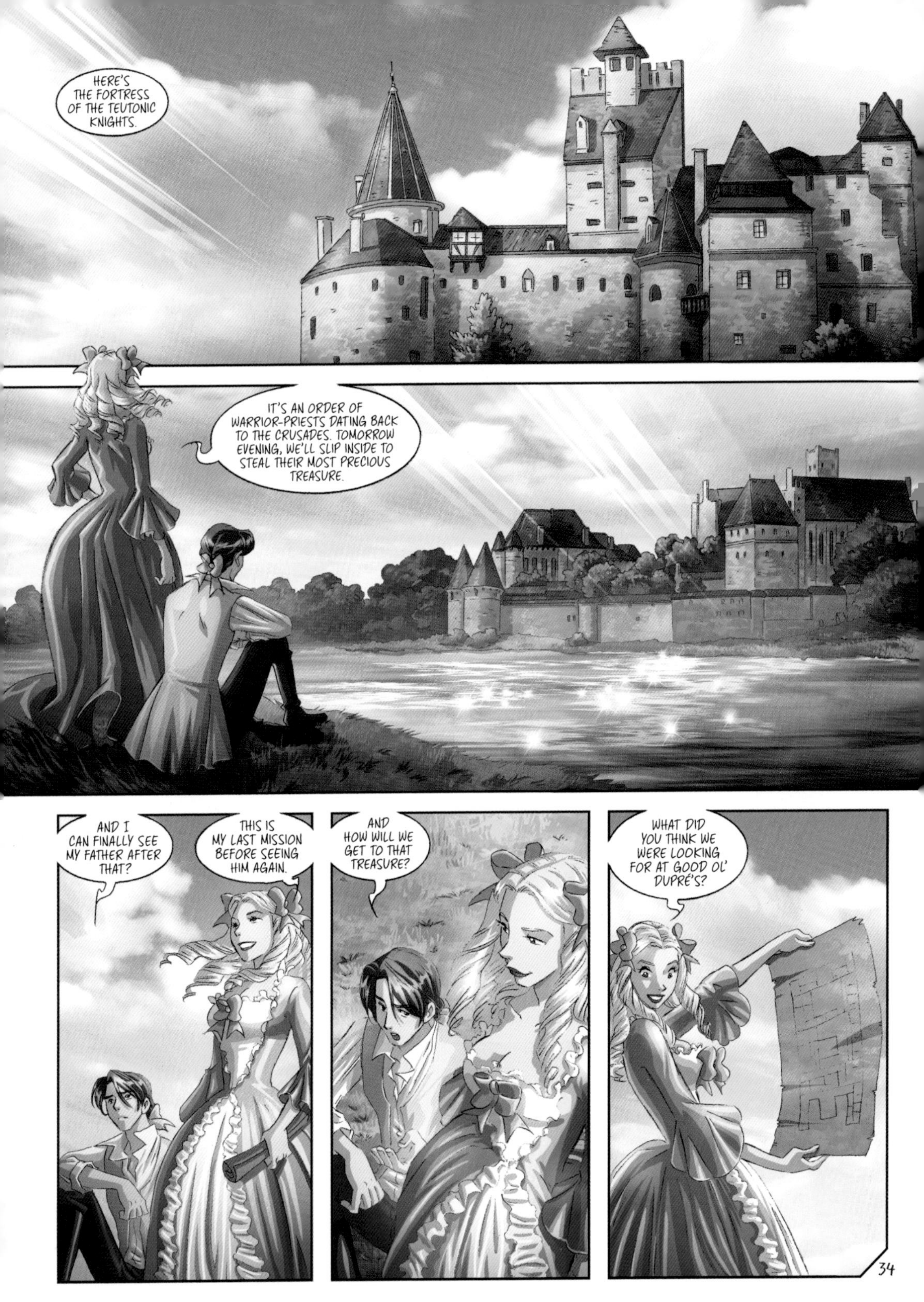
HERE'S THE FORTRESS OF THE TEUTONIC KNIGHTS.
IT'S AN ORDER OF WARRIOR-PRIESTS DATING BACK TO THE CRUSADES. TOMORROW EVENING, WE'LL SLIP INSIDE TO STEAL THEIR MOST PRECIOUS TREASURE.
AND I CAN FINALLY SEE MY FATHER AFTER THAT?
THIS IS MY LAST MISSION BEFORE SEEING HIM AGAIN.
AND HOW WILL WE GET TO THAT TREASURE?
WHAT DID YOU THINK WE WERE LOOKING FOR AT GOOD OL' DUPRÉ'S?
34

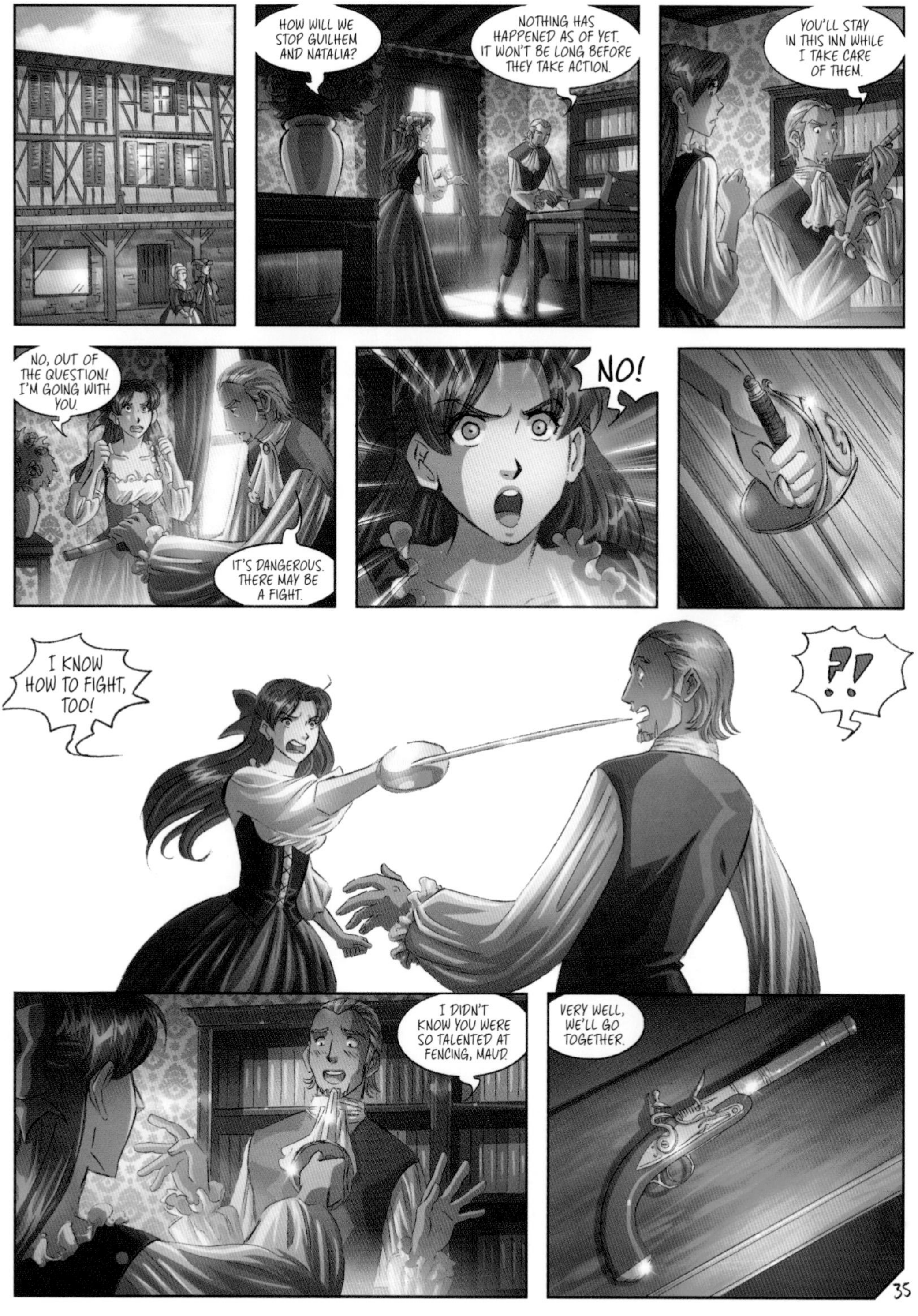
HOW WILL WE STOP GUILHEM AND NATALIA?
NOTHING HAS HAPPENED AS OF YET. IT WON'T BE LONG BEFORE THEY TAKE ACTION.
YOU'LL STAY IN THIS INN WHILE I TAKE CARE OF THEM.
NO, OUT OF THE QUESTION! I'M GOING WITH YOU.
IT'S DANGEROUS. THERE MAY BE A FIGHT.
NO!
I KNOW HOW TO FIGHT, TOO!
?!
I DIDN'T KNOW YOU WERE SO TALENTED AT FENCING, MAUD.
VERY WELL, WE'LL GO TOGETHER.
35

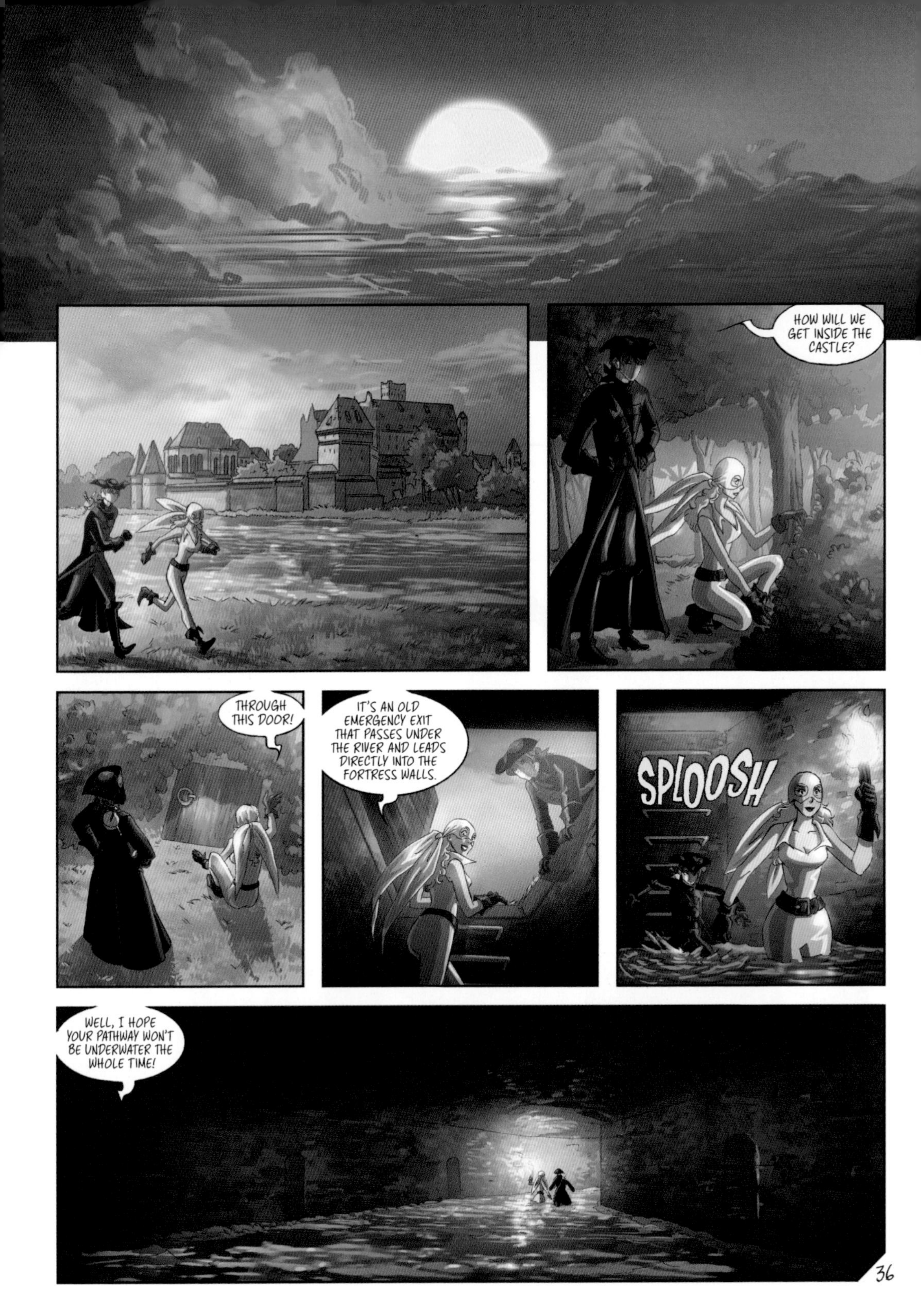
HOW WILL WE GET INSIDE THE CASTLE?
THROUGH THIS DOOR!
IT'S AN OLD EMERGENCY EXIT THAT PASSES UNDER THE RIVER AND LEADS DIRECTLY INTO THE FORTRESS WALLS.
SPLOOSH
WELL, I HOPE YOUR PATHWAY WON'T BE UNDERWATER THE WHOLE TIME!
36

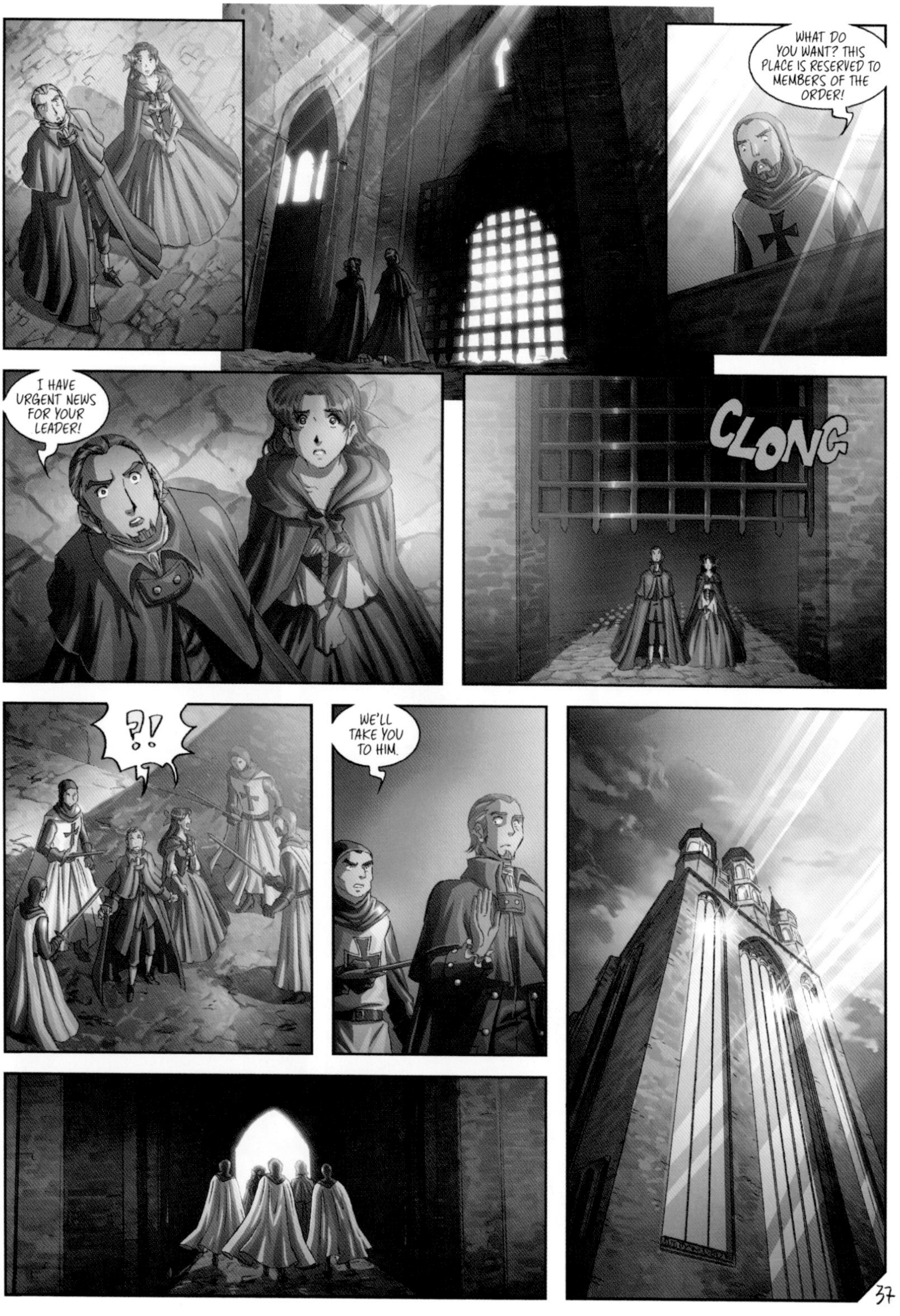
WHAT DO YOU WANT? THIS PLACE IS RESERVED TO MEMBERS OF THE ORDER!
I HAVE URGENT NEWS FOR YOUR LEADER!
CLONG
?!!
WE'LL TAKE YOU TO HIM.
37

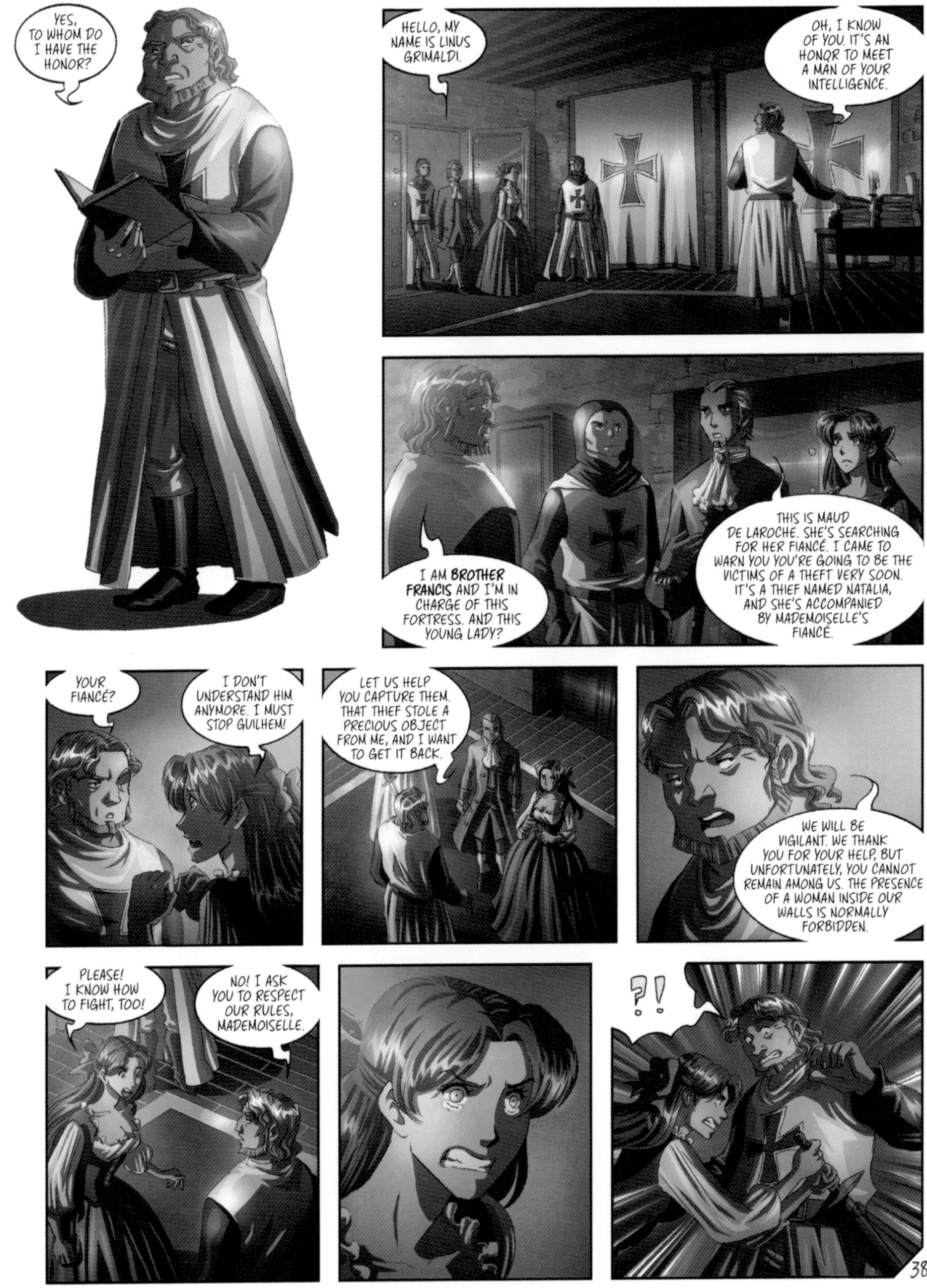
YES, TO WHOM DO I HAVE THE HONOR?
HELLO, MY NAME IS LINUS GRIMALDI.
OH, I KNOW OF YOU. IT'S AN HONOR TO MEET A MAN OF YOUR INTELLIGENCE.
I AM BROTHER FRANCIS AND I'M IN CHARGE OF THIS FORTRESS. AND THIS YOUNG LADY?
THIS IS MAUD DE LAROCHE. SHE'S SEARCHING FOR HER FIANCÉ. I CAME TO WARN YOU YOU'RE GOING TO BE THE VICTIMS OF A THEFT VERY SOON. IT'S A THIEF NAMED NATALIA, AND SHE'S ACCOMPANIED BY MADEMOISELLE'S FIANCÉ.
YOUR FIANCÉ?
I DON'T UNDERSTAND HIM ANYMORE. I MUST STOP GUILHEM!
LET US HELP YOU CAPTURE THEM. THAT THIEF STOLE A PRECIOUS OBJECT FROM ME, AND I WANT TO GET IT BACK.
WE WILL BE VIGILANT. WE THANK YOU FOR YOUR HELP, BUT UNFORTUNATELY, YOU CANNOT REMAIN AMONG US. THE PRESENCE OF A WOMAN INSIDE OUR WALLS IS NORMALLY FORBIDDEN.
PLEASE! I KNOW HOW TO FIGHT, TOO!
NO! I ASK YOU TO RESPECT OUR RULES, MADEMOISELLE.
?!
38

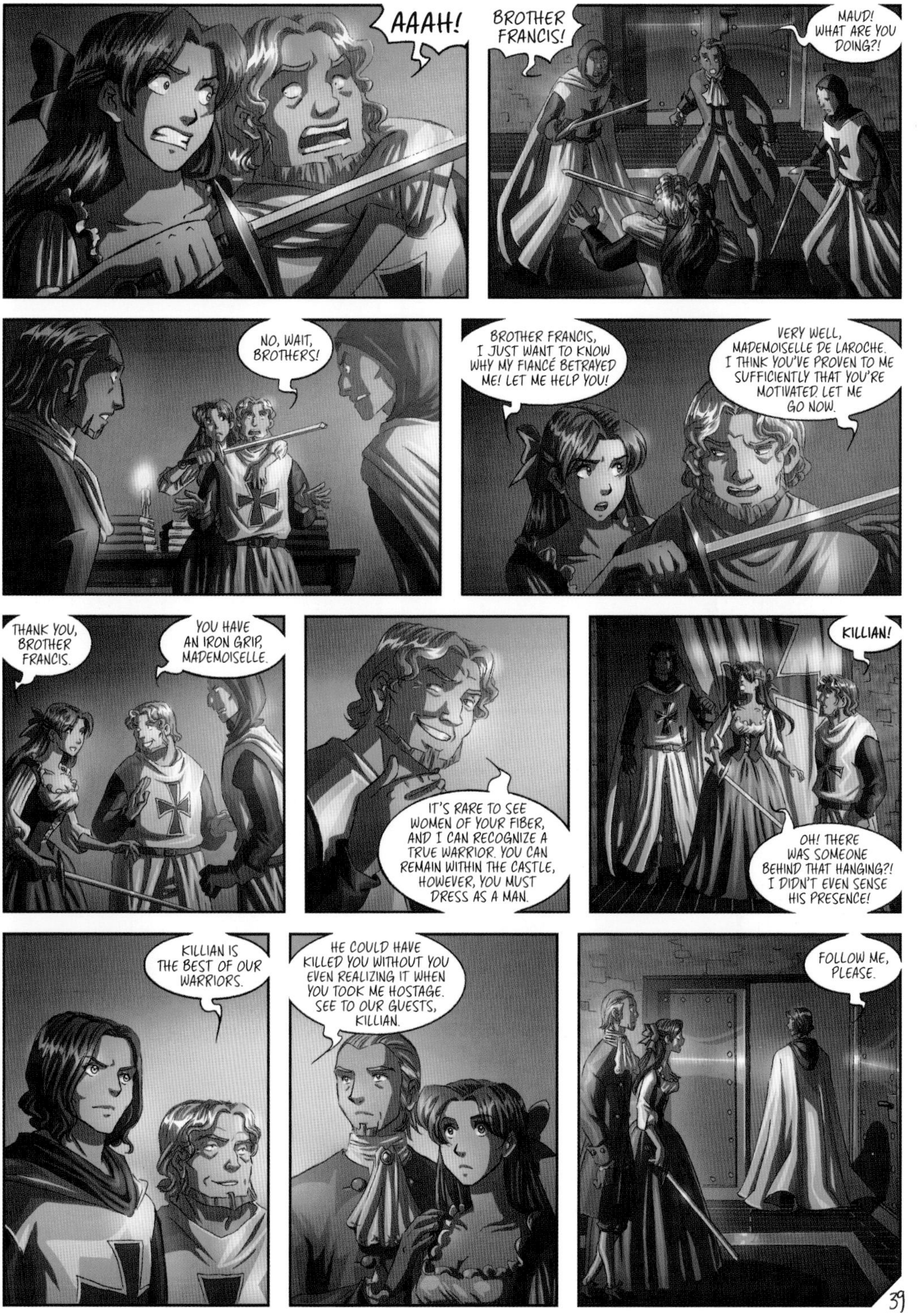
AAAH!
BROTHER FRANCIS!
MAUD! WHAT ARE YOU DOING?!
NO, WAIT, BROTHERS!
BROTHER FRANCIS, I JUST WANT TO KNOW WHY MY FIANCÉ BETRAYED ME! LET ME HELP YOU!
VERY WELL, MADEMOISELLE DE LAROCHE. I THINK YOU'VE PROVEN TO ME SUFFICIENTLY THAT YOU'RE MOTIVATED. LET ME GO NOW.
THANK YOU, BROTHER FRANCIS.
YOU HAVE AN IRON GRIP, MADEMOISELLE.
IT'S RARE TO SEE WOMEN OF YOUR FIBER, AND I CAN RECOGNIZE A TRUE WARRIOR. YOU CAN REMAIN WITHIN THE CASTLE, HOWEVER, YOU MUST DRESS AS A MAN.
KILLIAN!
OH! THERE WAS SOMEONE BEHIND THAT HANGING?! I DIDN'T EVEN SENSE HIS PRESENCE!
KILLIAN IS THE BEST OF OUR WARRIORS.
HE COULD HAVE KILLED YOU WITHOUT YOU EVEN REALIZING IT WHEN YOU TOOK ME HOSTAGE. SEE TO OUR GUESTS, KILLIAN.
FOLLOW ME, PLEASE.
39

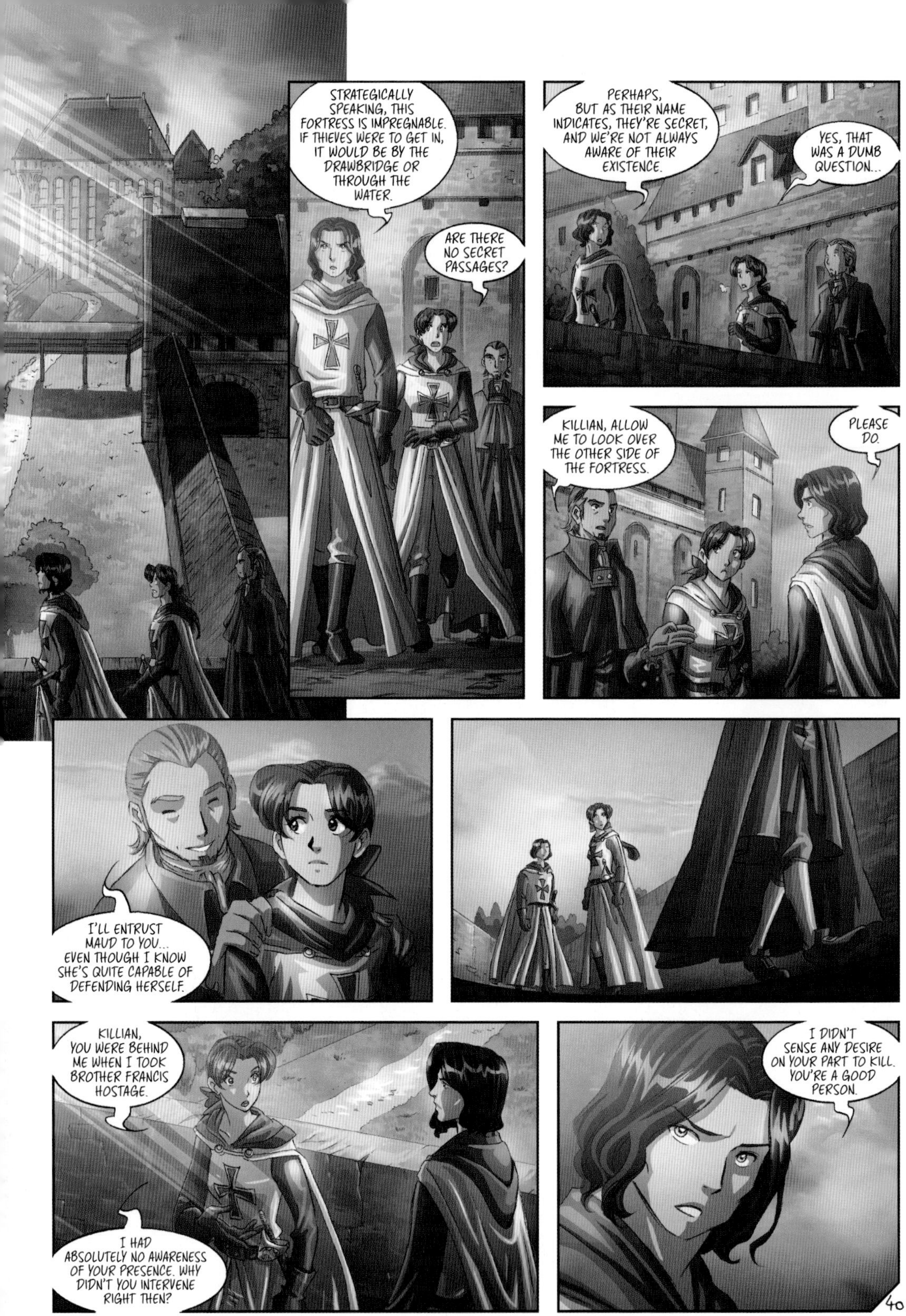

STRATEGICALLY SPEAKING, THIS FORTRESS IS IMPREGNABLE. IF THIEVES WERE TO GET IN, IT WOULD BE BY THE DRAWBRIDGE OR THROUGH THE WATER.
ARE THERE NO SECRET PASSAGES?
PERHAPS, BUT AS THEIR NAME INDICATES, THEY'RE SECRET, AND WE'RE NOT ALWAYS AWARE OF THEIR EXISTENCE.
YES, THAT WAS A DUMB QUESTION...
KILLIAN, ALLOW ME TO LOOK OVER THE OTHER SIDE OF THE FORTRESS.
PLEASE DO.
I'LL ENTRUST MAUD TO YOU... EVEN THOUGH I KNOW SHE'S QUITE CAPABLE OF DEFENDING HERSELF.
KILLIAN, YOU WERE BEHIND ME WHEN I TOOK BROTHER FRANCIS HOSTAGE.
I HAD ABSOLUTELY NO AWARENESS OF YOUR PRESENCE. WHY DIDN'T YOU INTERVENE RIGHT THEN?
I DIDN'T SENSE ANY DESIRE ON YOUR PART TO KILL. YOU'RE A GOOD PERSON.
40

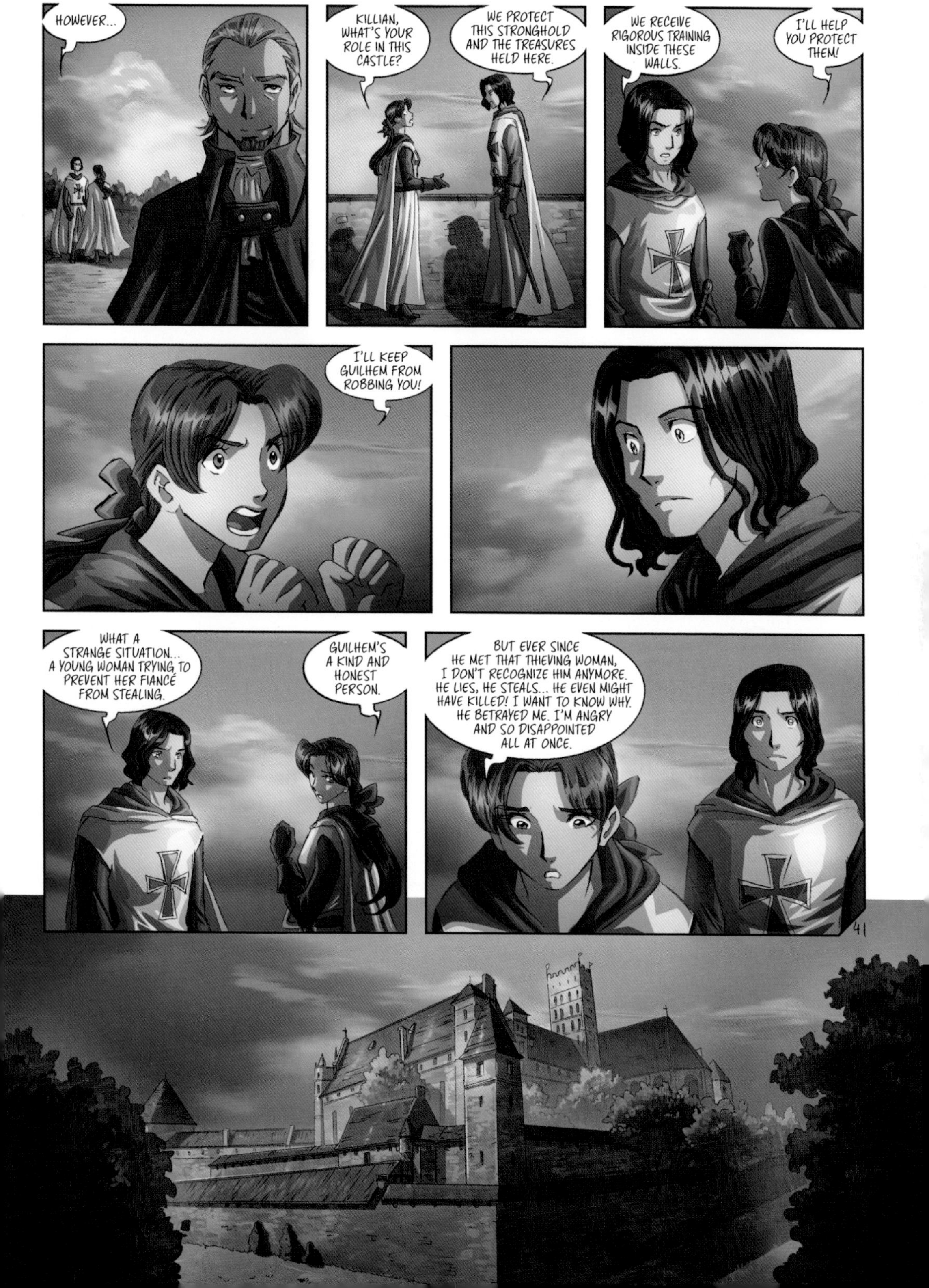
HOWEVER...
KILLIAN, WHAT'S YOUR ROLE IN THIS CASTLE?
WE PROTECT THIS STRONGHOLD AND THE TREASURES HELD HERE.
WE RECEIVE RIGOROUS TRAINING INSIDE THESE WALLS.
I'LL HELP YOU PROTECT THEM!
I'LL KEEP GUILHEM FROM ROBBING YOU!
WHAT A STRANGE SITUATION... A YOUNG WOMAN TRYING TO PREVENT HER FIANCÉ FROM STEALING.
GUILHEM'S A KIND AND HONEST PERSON.
BUT EVER SINCE HE MET THAT THIEVING WOMAN, I DON'T RECOGNIZE HIM ANYMORE. HE LIES, HE STEALS... HE EVEN MIGHT HAVE KILLED! I WANT TO KNOW WHY. HE BETRAYED ME. I'M ANGRY AND SO DISAPPOINTED ALL AT ONCE.

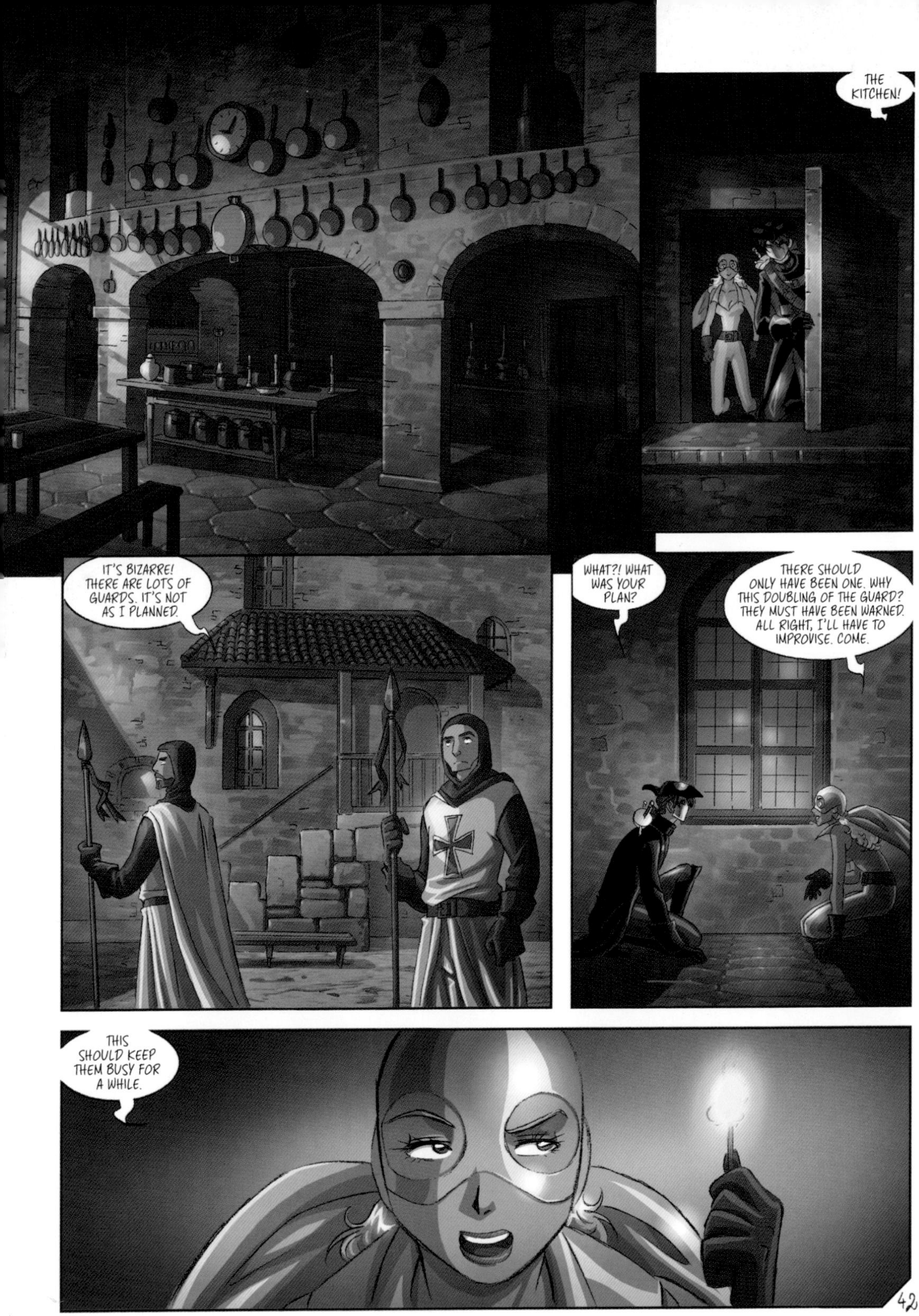
THE KITCHEN!
IT'S BIZARRE! THERE ARE LOTS OF GUARDS. IT'S NOT AS I PLANNED.
WHAT?! WHAT WAS YOUR PLAN?
THERE SHOULD ONLY HAVE BEEN ONE. WHY THIS DOUBLING OF THE GUARD? THEY MUST HAVE BEEN WARNED. ALL RIGHT, I'LL HAVE TO IMPROVISE. COME.
THIS SHOULD KEEP THEM BUSY FOR A WHILE.
42

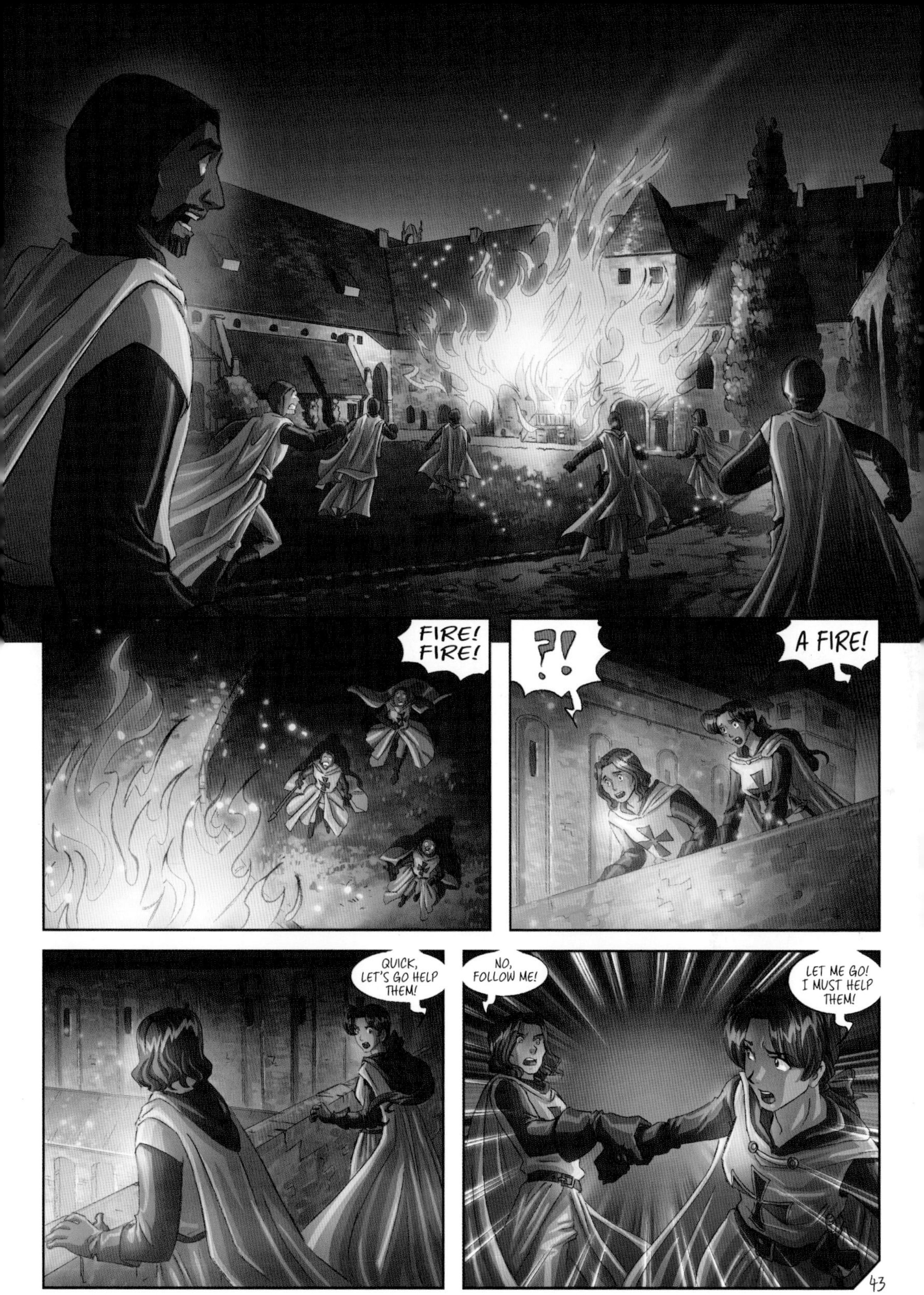
FIRE! FIRE!
?!
A FIRE!
QUICK, LET'S GO HELP THEM!
NO, FOLLOW ME!
LET ME GO! I MUST HELP THEM!
43

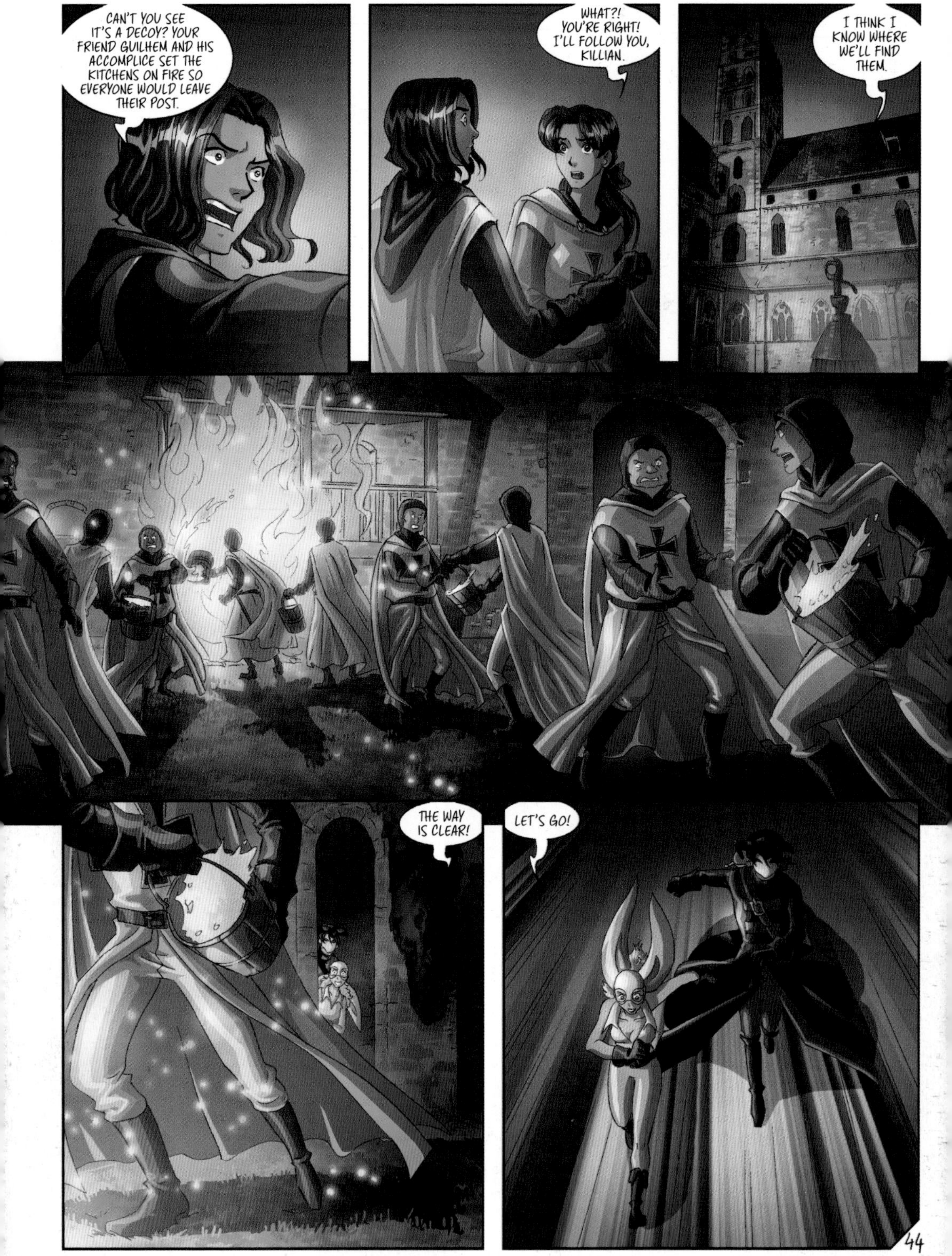
CAN'T YOU SEE IT'S A DECOY? YOUR FRIEND GUILHEM AND HIS ACCOMPLICE SET THE KITCHENS ON FIRE SO EVERYONE WOULD LEAVE THEIR POST.
WHAT?! YOU'RE RIGHT! I'LL FOLLOW YOU, KILLIAN.
I THINK I KNOW WHERE WE'LL FIND THEM.
THE WAY IS CLEAR!
LET'S GO!
44

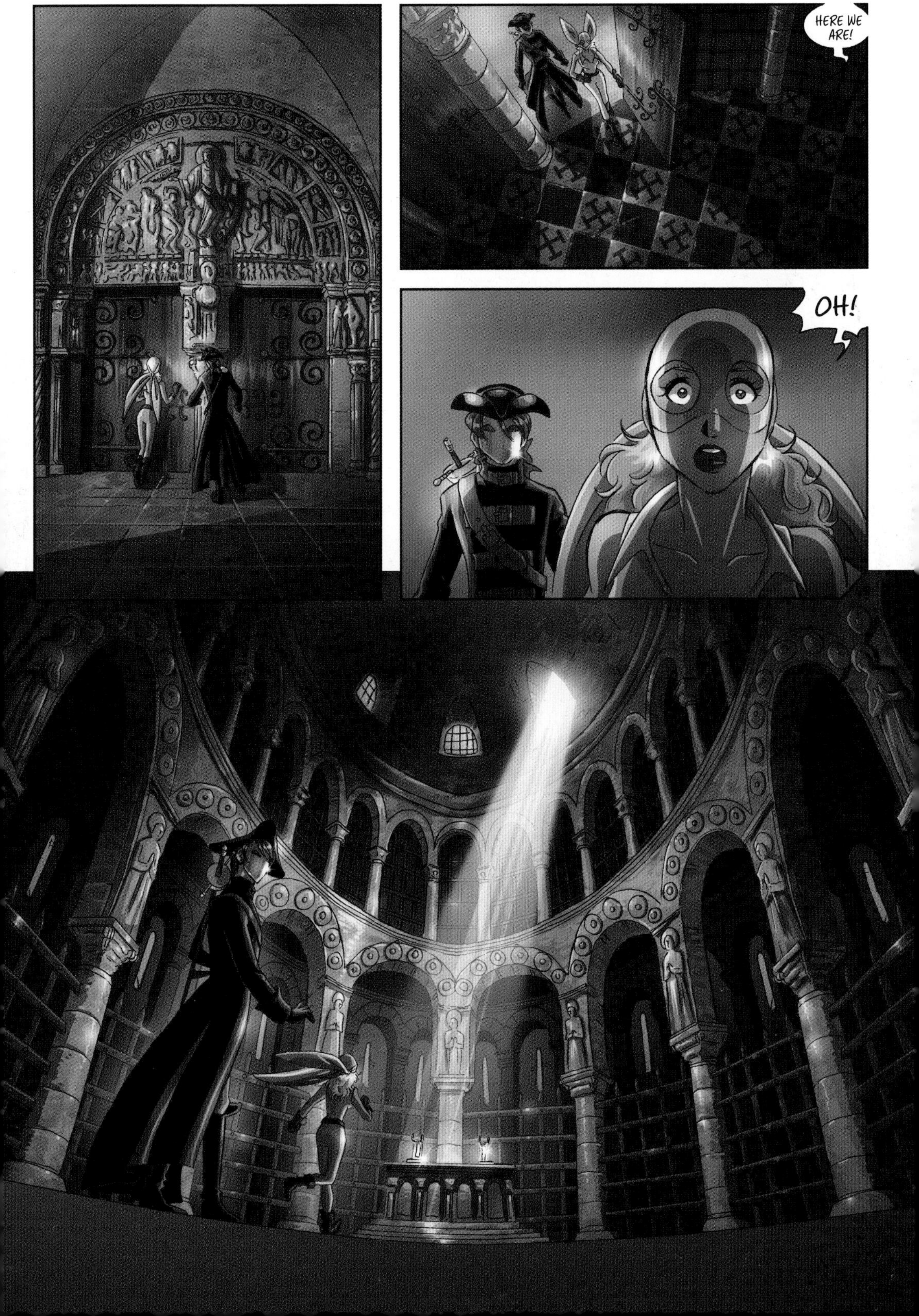
HERE WE ARE!
OH!

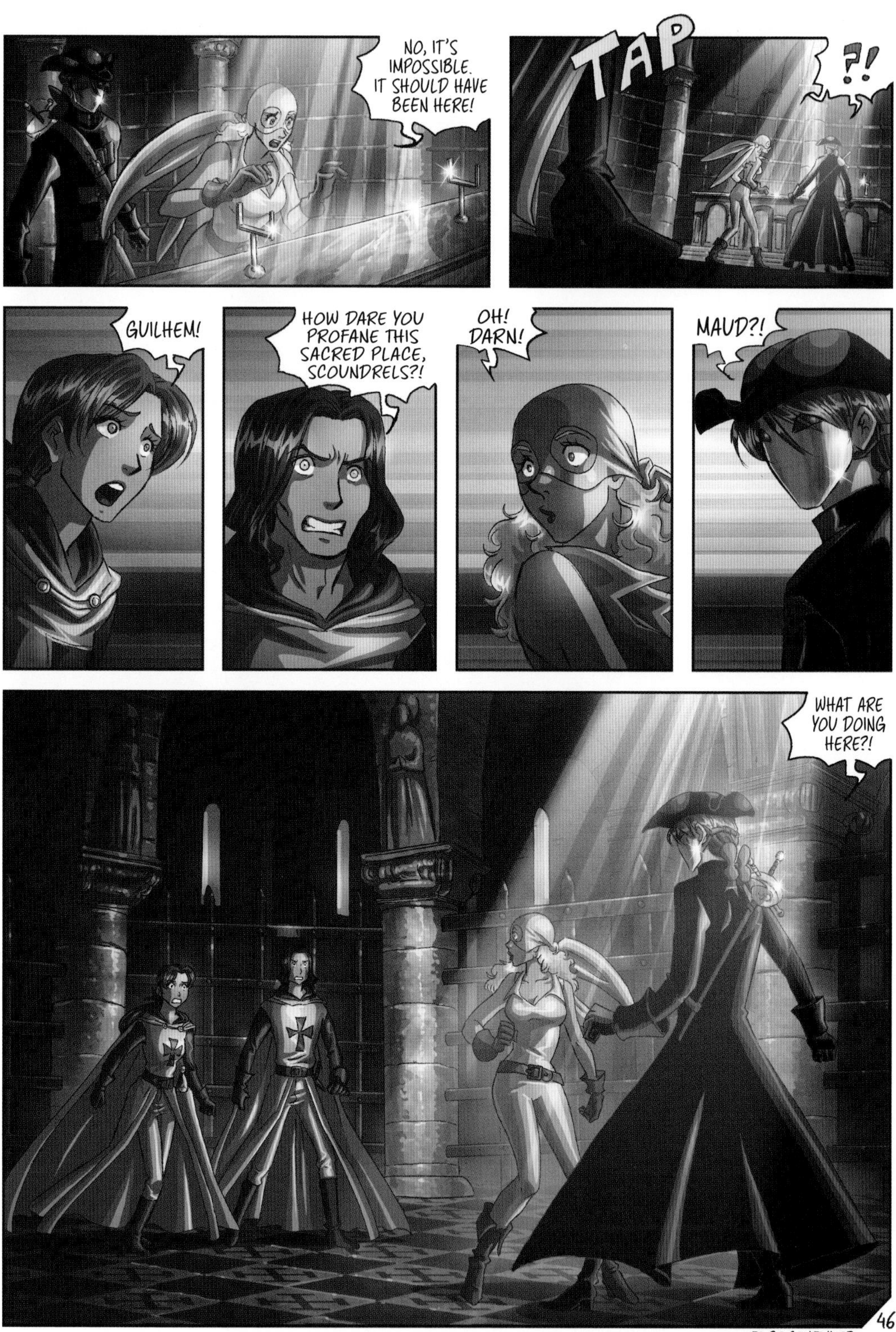
NO, IT'S IMPOSSIBLE. IT SHOULD HAVE BEEN HERE!
TAP
?!
GUILHEM!
HOW DARE YOU PROFANE THIS SACRED PLACE, SCOUNDRELS?!
OH! DARN!
MAUD?!
WHAT ARE YOU DOING HERE?!
46

TO BE CONTINUED...

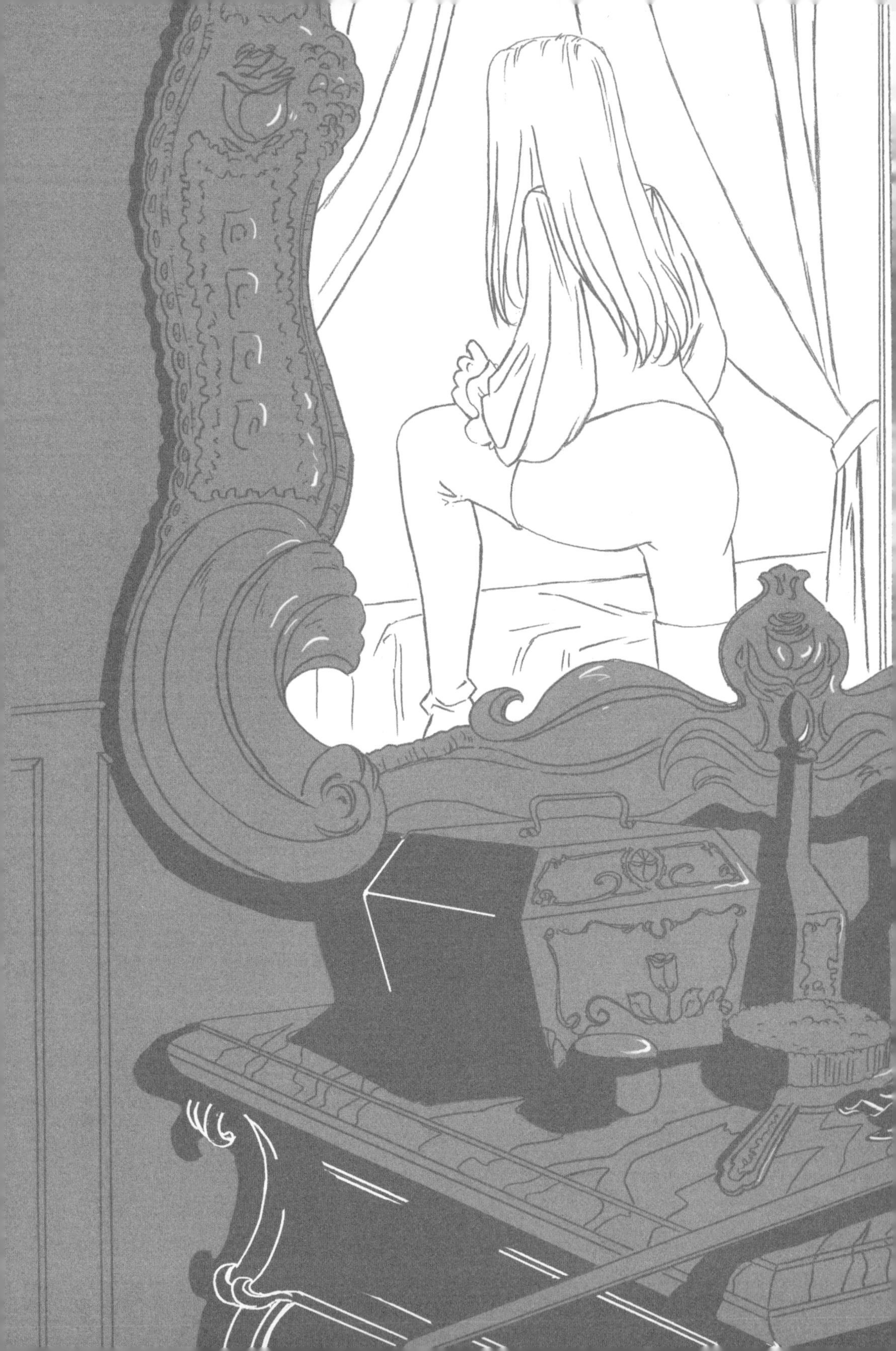